Murder of a
Wedding Belle

**Center Point
Large Print**

Also by Denise Swanson
and available from Center Point Large Print:

Murder of a Royal Pain

**This Large Print Book carries the
Seal of Approval of N.A.V.H.**

Murder of a Wedding Belle

A Scumble River Mystery

Denise Swanson

CENTER POINT PUBLISHING
THORNDIKE, MAINE

This Center Point Large Print edition
is published in the year 2010 by arrangement with
Obsidian, an imprint of New American Library,
a member of Penguin Group (USA) Inc.

The text of this Large Print edition is unabridged.
In other aspects, this book may vary
from the original edition.
Printed in the United States of America
on permanent paper.
Set in 16-point Times New Roman type.

ISBN: 978-1-60285-792-6

Library of Congress Cataloging-in-Publication Data

Swanson, Denise.
  Murder of a wedding belle : a Scumble River mystery / Denise Swanson. -- Center
Point large print ed.
    p. cm.
  ISBN 978-1-60285-792-6 (library binding : alk. paper)
  1. Denison, Skye (Fictitious character)—Fiction. 2. School psychologists—Fiction.
  3. Women psychologists—Fiction. 4. Weddings—Fiction. 5. Large type books.
  I. Title.
  PS3619.W36M893 2010
  813'.6—dc22
                                                                    2010007811

To my good friend Sharon Postil.
Boomerang and I both thank you for
your help and friendship.

CHAPTER 1

Just a Matter of Time

November

Skye Denison twisted her left hand from side to side, admiring the glitter of the diamond engagement ring on her finger. Sunshine streaming through the windshield of her aqua 1957 Bel Air made the two-carat gemstone blaze like a Fourth of July sparkler. Reluctantly, she slid the ring off, tucked it into its Tiffany blue box, and zipped it into the inner pocket of her purse. The last thing she needed was her mother getting the wrong idea.

Wally Boyd, Scumble River police chief and secret heir to a Texas oil fortune, had proposed to Skye a month ago. Although she hadn't said yes, he'd insisted that she hold on to the ring until she decided. It wasn't that she didn't love him; she just didn't trust her judgment where men were concerned. After making some bad choices in the past, she was leery of commitment.

She had to make up her mind about Wally soon, but not today. Today was all about Skye's cousin Riley Erickson. Ten years ago, while Skye had still been away working in the Peace Corps, Riley had left their hometown of Scumble River to attend college in California, and decided to stay there permanently. She had finally returned for a visit, and Skye didn't want to be late for her party.

After checking her lipstick in the rearview mirror, Skye picked up the seven-layer salad—her food assignment for the gathering—and got out of the Chevy, which she'd parked in the alley behind her grandma Cora's house. The Denisons didn't get together as often as her mother's extended Italian clan, the Leofantis, did, and Skye looked forward to catching up with her dad's side of the family.

However, when she put her hand on the knob of the kitchen's screen door, the excited chatter echoing through the aluminum mesh brought her up short. For an instant she wasn't sure she was at the right house. The Denisons came from stoic Swedish farm stock. They never got worked up. Heck, they seldom raised their voices, and they certainly didn't squeal like a gaggle of schoolgirls.

What in the world could cause her unflappable relatives to make sounds like whooping cranes on crack?

Skye pushed open the door and walked into pandemonium. Her great-aunt Dora was crying. *Yikes!* Had someone died? No. A blond beauty with white-gold curls was standing at the heart of the uproar, surrounded by a flock of chirping women who were all fluttering around her like birds at a feeder and patting her as if she were a prize parakeet.

It had been nearly seventeen years since Skye had seen her cousin, and she wouldn't have recognized her in a crowd, but she figured the blonde must be Riley.

No doubt the men were in the living room, probably watching a football game, or whatever sporting event was on TV in late November, but Skye was surprised that there wasn't anyone at the stove cooking. One thing the Denison and Leofanti females had in common was their culinary skills.

Skye spotted her mother on the fringe of the group and joined her. Come August, May would turn sixty, but she looked at least fifteen years younger. With her petite build and the perkiness of the high school cheerleader she'd once been, she was the personification of eternal youth.

Before Skye could speak, May grabbed her arm. "Isn't it thrilling?"

"What?" Skye set down her salad bowl on the kitchen counter before her mom could accidentally knock it out of her hands.

"Riley's getting married right here in Scumble River on June twenty-fifth!" May trilled.

"She's having the ceremony here?" Skye had heard of destination weddings but had never imagined Scumble River as one of those destinations.

"Yes." May beamed. "And she wants you to be her maid of honor."

"Why me?" The question slipped out before Skye could stop it.

"Shh! Do you want Riley to hear you?" May dragged Skye through the dining room into the nearest bedroom and whispered, "She'll think you aren't tickled pink that she asked you."

"Well, technically, she hasn't asked me." Skye stalled for time. May would be unhappy with her decision to refuse Riley's request, but sometime after Skye had hit thirty, being a bridesmaid had lost its appeal.

She'd stood up for several of her sorority sisters right after college, a couple of friends while she'd been in the Peace Corps, and her graduate school roommate the year before she'd moved home. Being in a wedding was a lot of work, not to mention a huge expense, and seven hideous dresses she could never wear again were her limit.

May narrowed her eyes and stared at Skye. "But once she asks you, you are going to say yes, right?"

"My question stands. Why would Riley want me to be her maid of honor?" Skye held firm. "She was only twelve when I left for college, and we haven't seen each other since."

"Blood is blood, no matter how much time has passed," May countered. "She idolized you. She followed you around at family gatherings and begged her mother to hire you as her babysitter."

Skye refused to be swayed. "But we haven't kept in touch. Not to mention I'm not even entirely sure how we're related."

"Your grandma Denison and Riley's grand-mother Dora are sisters. That makes your father and Riley's mother, Anita, first cousins," May explained. "And since both Anita and Riley are only children, close or not, you are Riley's only female relative young enough to be in her wedding."

"How about Riley's father's people?" Skye knew Anita had been married and widowed during a brief time when she had lived out east, but couldn't remember the details.

"Anita lost touch with them after he died and she moved back home."

"Oh." Skye paused, then shook her head. "Anyway, I just don't have the money."

"That's the best part. Riley's fiancé is filthy rich. Nick is some big developer in California. He drives a Maserati."

"Owning an expensive car doesn't impress me." Skye attempted to distract her mother. "It doesn't take any special talent to make a car payment each month."

"He collects art, too," May gushed, ignoring Skye's comment. "It's a shame he couldn't come with her so the family could meet him, but he's paying for everything. They've even hired a wedding planner from Beverly Hills who's going to be in Scumble River for the entire month before the wedding."

"That's wonderful." Skye understood her

mother's awe. May had never had a lot of money, so being able to spend it on frivolous nonessentials seemed like a fairy tale to her. "But I'm sorry. The answer's still no."

"I wish you'd reconsider, Skye," an elderly voice quavered from the bed.

Skye whirled around. She had been so intent on her conversation with May, she hadn't realized that someone else was in the room.

Cora Denison, Skye's grandmother, swung her legs over the side of the mattress and struggled to stand. At eighty-five, she had buried a husband, two stillborn babies, and a teenage grandson. Up until Halloween, she'd made a batch of her famous Parker House rolls nearly every Sunday, but she hadn't been feeling well for the past few weeks.

Skye rushed to Cora's side and helped her to her feet, then handed her the cane that had been leaning against the wall. Skye's heart sank. Having lost both her grandfathers and Grandma Leofanti, she wasn't ready for her last remaining grand-parent to die, but it was clear that Cora was failing.

Once she was steady, Cora said, "I'd really like you to be in Riley's wedding."

Skye opened her mouth to explain why she couldn't, but a movement near the door drew her attention. Her father, Jed, was standing on the threshold, his faded brown eyes pleading with Skye to agree to her grandmother's request.

What could she do? Skye knew a lot of people

14

thought she needed to grow a spine where her family was concerned, but there was no way she could disappoint her grandmother or her father, both of whom rarely asked her for anything.

She forced a smile to her lips. "If *you* want me to, Grandma, I'd be happy to be Riley's maid of honor."

As she gave Cora a hug, Skye mentally shrugged. How bad could it be? All she'd have to do was buy a few gifts, throw a bridal shower, and attend the rehearsal dinner, the ceremony, and the reception. The wedding planner would do the rest.

Suddenly a shiver ran down Skye's spine. She wasn't sure whether it was brought on by the thought of an eighth ghastly bridesmaid's dress hanging in her closet or the idea of a swarm of strangers descending on Scumble River. Considering her experiences, she had a theory that mixing a horde of out-of-towners with a crowd of Scumble Riverites nearly always produced a lethal concoction. She sure hoped this wedding didn't turn out to be the event that proved her hypothesis correct.

CHAPTER 2

The Belle of the Ball

May

Skye frowned as she peered through the peep-hole of her front door. What was a fashionista clutching a Chanel umbrella doing on her porch? What possible reason could a woman who looked like this have for showing up at an isolated old house along a barely paved farm road in Illinois on a rainy Saturday afternoon?

Her visitor wore Couture Couture tuxedo-style pants, a silk blouse with a ruffled bib, and a blond mink shrug. Skye had seen the exact same outfit in *Elle* and knew it cost more than a year's tuition at the local community college. The woman's blue-black hair was held back at the temples with Swarovski crystal–bow barrettes that emphasized a dramatic widow's peak. Her bright red lips pursed as she rang the bell a second time.

Bingo, Skye's black cat, was sitting by her feet, and she whispered to him, "What do you think she wants?"

He twitched his tail and meowed sharply, perhaps trying to remind Skye of stranger danger—a lesson most children had learned by age six, but one Skye often ignored.

"I'm sure there's a perfectly logical reason why a woman dressed for lunch at Spago has shown up at my house." Another *ding-dong* made Skye reach for the knob. "She probably has car trouble and needs to use the telephone."

Bingo's ears flattened, and he seemed to shake his head.

"A lot of cell phones don't work around here," Skye informed him. "I can't just let her stand out there in the rain." Keeping the chain on, she opened the door a few inches—she was ready to help someone in need, but she wasn't totally naive. "Yes?"

"I'm Belle Canfield."

Skye was taken aback by the woman's high-pitched voice. She'd been expecting a throaty purr. "Nice to meet you."

Belle looked Skye up and down, a faint sneer on her perfectly made-up face. "Are you Skye Denison?"

"Yes," Skye admitted, wishing she had on something other than ratty sweatpants and a faded orange Illini T-shirt. "Can I help you?"

"Well, duh. How about we start with you letting me come inside?"

"And why should I do that?" If her visitor was going to be snarky, so was Skye.

"Because we have an appointment." Belle's tone conveyed that she was stating the obvious. "You don't think I drove down this rutted path

17

you people call a street for the fun of it, do you?"

"We have an appointment?" Skye tucked an escaped chestnut curl back into her ponytail. Surely she'd have remembered agreeing to meet with *this* woman. "For what?"

"To go over details for Riley's wedding." Belle handed Skye a candy-apple red business card. Printed under her name were the words *Bridal Consultant*. "You're my local liaison."

"No, I'm the maid of honor."

"Yes, but you're also acting as my assistant." When Skye shook her head, Belle enunciated slowly, as if she thought Skye might be a little dim, "You know, my helper."

"You've been misinformed." A sharp wind dashed a sheet of rain into Skye's face. "But I guess you'd better come inside so we can straighten this out." She unchained the door and swung it open.

"Finally," Belle muttered loud enough for Skye to hear. The wedding planner closed her umbrella, leaned it against the side of the house, then stepped over the threshold, her Alexander McQueen ankle boots clicking on the hardwood floor. Belle's gaze swept the foyer from the freshly painted mocha walls to the curving staircase. A slight smile on her lips, she said, "This is so sick. That spot would really rock it for a picture."

Sick? Was that the new word for *hot?* "Not really." Skye pointed to her left. "Let's sit in here

18

while we figure this out." She needed to get the woman seated before she insisted on a tour of the house. Only the foyer, parlor, and dining room were fully remodeled. Skye had run out of money before completing all the needed renovations, and she didn't want to see Belle's look of contempt when she saw the rest of the place.

After they were settled, Belle asked, "Seriously, you're telling me that no one talked to you about assisting me?"

"Yes. I'm fairly sure I would have remembered that conversation."

Bingo, who had followed them in, began sniffing the woman's legs. Belle moved her feet. "I'm allergic to cats."

"Would you like a Benadryl?" Skye fought the impulse to put Bingo in another room. She didn't see any indication of red eyes or a runny nose, but if the bridal consultant was truly allergic, maybe she wouldn't stick around long.

"Let's just get this over with." Belle took a legal pad from her briefcase. "Next time we can meet somewhere else."

"I told you"—Skye barely held on to her temper—"there won't be a next time." Clearly the woman was used to ignoring whatever she didn't want to hear.

Belle's squeaky voice was petulant. "Do you know who I am?"

"Riley's wedding planner." Skye raised an eye-

19

brow. "Unless you just gave me a fake business card."

"Not just *a* wedding planner." Belle tossed her head. "*The* wedding planner to the stars."

"Sorry, never heard of you." Skye watched the occasional episode of *Access Hollywood* and read the tabloids while waiting in line at the grocery store, but the name Belle Canfield didn't sound familiar. "Whose weddings did you do?"

"I don't have to prove myself to you." A tiny crease appeared between Belle's eyes. "I've worked on plenty of celebrity weddings." Under her breath she muttered, "This is so not fair. I'm way prettier than Paris Hilton, and my family's way richer, but no matter how much I bust my ass, that ditzy nut job still gets all the media attention."

"Well." Skye struggled to keep her expression neutral. Belle had seemed so confident until now, but her insecurity was starting to show. "I've still never heard of you." Why would anyone want to be like Paris Hilton, someone who was famous only for being famous?

"My father is Mickey Canfield." When Skye remained unimpressed, Belle added, "Of the Canfield Corporation."

"Okaaay." Skye drew out the word.

Belle snapped, "Surely, even here in the sticks, you've heard of Canfield Hotels and Resorts." She shot Skye a scornful look and said, "Now can we get to work?"

"I really don't care who your daddy is." Skye narrowed her emerald green eyes. How shallow was this woman to think having a famous father would get her what she wanted? "I'm not the person Riley arranged to assist you, so we won't be getting to work." With her ebony hair, porcelain skin, and heart-shaped face, Belle may have looked like Snow White, but Skye wasn't giving in to a spoiled princess who couldn't take no for an answer.

"Yes, you are," Belle insisted. "Riley promised me her cousin, Skye Denison, would help me with the local parts of her wedding."

"Riley said she talked to me about this?" Skye felt as if she were in some alternate universe. "And I agreed?"

"Her exact words were . . ." Belle held up a device the size of a thumb, and Skye heard Riley's voice say, "Mom talked to Grandma . . ."

Wow. Skye stared, fascinated by the tiny machine. *Heaven knows what kind of trouble I'd get into with that gadget. I can barely figure out my cell phone.* Although she admired technology, she also feared it.

Focusing, Skye listened to her cousin say, "And Grandma talked to Great-Aunt Cora, and Great-Aunt Cora said Skye will help you with things in Scumble River."

"Damn!" Skye was getting better at saying no to her mom, but how could she refuse her sick grandmother? "Look, I'm a school psychologist and classes don't get out for another two weeks, so I can't do much until then," she explained, hoping Belle would demand that Riley find someone who was available immediately.

"I'm guessing you aren't married"—Belle flicked a derisive glance at Skye's curvy frame and disheveled appearance—"or you'd understand the importance of this event."

"No. I'm single." Skye refused to be intimidated by the gorgeous wedding planner. No way could her incredible amethyst eyes be real. The color had to come from contact lenses. "How about you?"

"Why would I get married? Unlike ordinary women, I can have the whole box of chocolates. Men find me irresistible, so why should I tie myself down to a buttercream when I can hook up with a different flavor every night? I only sleep alone when I want to."

Skye decided that if it was pointed out to her, Belle would just ignore the contradiction of a wedding planner who scorned romantic commitments, so instead she repeated her earlier objection. "Nevertheless, I have a contract with the school district, so I'm not free for the next fourteen days."

"I told Riley and Nick that I would only agree to put on an event of this size, two thousand miles away from my usual vendors, if I had a local person to assist me." Belle pulled a cell phone from her purse. She pressed a single button, waited a couple of seconds, then said, "Riley, it's Belle. No one told your cousin about helping me, and she says she's too busy. If she won't help, we'll have to cancel everything here, postpone the wedding, and move it all back to California."

Skye cringed. Grandma Cora would be so disappointed. She'd explained to Skye how important it was that Riley get married in Scumble River, since neither she nor her sister Dora was strong enough to travel to the West Coast. Tapping the wedding planner on the arm, Skye asked, "How about Anita? I bet she'd be thrilled to be involved."

"No!" Belle held the tiny phone to her chest. "I do not have any contact with mothers of the bride. Not after The Incident."

"I won't ask what happened." Skye had had her own episode with a crazy mother not too long ago, and the school lawyer was still hashing it out with that woman's attorney.

Belle put the phone back up to her ear and listened, then handed the device to Skye. "Your cousin wants to talk to you."

Reluctantly, Skye took the phone. "Hi, Riley. It's Skye."

"Skye, I'm so sorry no one asked you, but I thought Grandma took care of it. Please, please, don't say no."

"The problem is I'm tied up during business hours while school is still in session," Skye clarified.

"Belle has me over a barrel. It's only a month before the wedding, so it's too late to rearrange everything. And Grandma would be so upset if the wedding wasn't in Scumble River." Riley's voice took on a cajoling tone. "I know. Give Belle a couple of hours a day until school ends. Then when you're free, you can act as Belle's assistant full-time. We'll pay you the same salary you'd get on your regular job."

"Well, I do usually work as a lifeguard at the recreation club during the summer, but it's been such a cool spring, the board decided not to open the beach until the weather gets warmer."

"See, this will be perfect." Riley giggled. "Nick's got scads of money, and as long as I do a few little icky things he likes—thank God I'm double-jointed—he's willing to spend it on me. Besides, Mom said you're still trying to fix up that money pit you got stuck with."

"That's true." Skye had inherited the old house from Alma Griggs nearly two years ago. "The upstairs has barely been touched."

"So you'll help Belle?"

Could she handle working for a self-important socialite? It couldn't be any worse than dealing with some of the teen queens at the high school. Wait a minute. That's what she'd thought when she agreed to be Riley's maid of honor last November, and now look what had happened.

"Pretty please with sugar on top?" Riley pleaded.

Skye gave in. "Okay. I'll help her." She'd probably only have to make a few phone calls, address some envelopes, and keep Anita out of the way. Surely Belle wouldn't assign her any task that could ruin the wedding.

CHAPTER 3

The Countdown Begins

June

Skye cringed as the shrill blare of a whistle pierced the silence. It was late Saturday morning, a week before Riley's wedding, and that strident trill could mean only one thing. Belle was about to pounce on her with another list of jobs that had to be completed yesterday.

When it came to getting what she wanted, the wedding planner was willing to go as far as she had to, and if she had to throw someone under a bus, she made sure it was a double-decker Greyhound.

Belle was relentless, terrorizing everyone in her path. It was a good thing that Skye had worked in public education for five years. After her daily dealings with bureaucratic principals and egomaniacal superintendents, a dictatorial bridal consultant didn't faze her. She just kept her mouth shut, her head down, and avoided eye contact.

When Skye heard a second whistle blast, she reluctantly stopped what she had been doing and inspected her work space—a cabin at the Up A Lazy River Motor Court. If everything wasn't just the way Belle wanted it, there would be hell to pay.

Since her arrival three weeks ago, Belle had been living in one of the cottages and using the two adjoining ones as storage. But as of today, the remaining nine rooms were reserved for the bridal party and vendors.

Skye was presently in number five, the cabin housing the reception materials. One of her many duties as Belle's assistant was to accept, verify, and inventory the daily deliveries of supplies. When she'd heard the first whistle, she'd been inspecting five hundred crystal champagne flutes engraved with the bride and groom's initials that had arrived a few hours before via FedEx.

Each couple would receive two glasses, a bottle of Veuve Clicquot Rosé, and a box of Godiva chocolates, all arranged in a pearl white wicker basket swathed in pink tulle and tied with gold ribbons. Single guests would receive a smaller version with only one flute. The welcome baskets were meant to convey the wedding's colors and theme: Pink Fantasy Fairy Tale.

The whistle screeched again, this time much closer, and Skye got up from the floor, dusted off the seat of her jeans, and braced herself.

A few seconds later, the door slammed open

and Belle entered the room. Skye estimated that her outfit—a bright fuchsia Juicy Couture cashmere hoodie and sweatpants—cost more than six hundred dollars, and that was without adding the Louboutin moiré espadrilles. Unless bridal consultants made a lot more money than Skye thought they did, Daddy Canfield must be paying for her wardrobe.

"Why, GiGi, why?" Belle's attention was focused on the cell phone she held clamped to her ear. "I've said I was sorry. You've got to make him give me another chance."

Who is she talking about? Skye studied the wedding planner, surprised to see that Belle had a weak spot, but there was definitely a hint of desperation in her tone and a suggestion of vulnerability on her face.

Embarrassed at overhearing an obviously personal conversation, Skye turned toward the dresser and adjusted her headband as she tried to tune out Belle's voice.

"I bet you don't have your hair colored around here." Belle grabbed one of Skye's curls, making her jump. "This shade of chestnut is hard to get right."

"No, I don't." Skye faced her. "It's natural." She knew Belle wouldn't believe her. The wedding planner was so artificial that anything real was beyond her comprehension. She had bragged about all the "work" she'd had done—everything

27

from a boob job to eyeliner tattoos. It was hard to believe that a twenty-eight-year-old had really needed all that plastic surgery, but Skye had to admit, the woman was stunning.

Belle shrugged. "I have either Sally Hershberger or Christophe do me. They come right to my place, the one in Malibu." She giggled. "I'm a little bit into myself, but that's not bad or anything."

"Wow." Skye assumed an impressed expression, the one she had perfected in the twenty-one days she'd worked for Belle and listened to her name-drop and boast about her celebrity friends. "I'd love to have a hairdresser who made house calls. My bro—"

"Iris is back." Belle cut Skye off, plainly uninterested in any topic that wasn't about her. The floral designer, Iris Yee, who had flown in from California the day before, had been in Chicago all morning picking up rental equipment and purchasing supplies. "I was going to send you to help her unload, but I made a teeny suggestion regarding her centerpiece designs and she called me bossy, so now I'm not sure I will." The wedding planner's squeaky voice reached a glass-shattering pitch. "I told her I am not bossy; I just know what everybody should be doing."

Skye said in a neutral tone, "Then should I go help her or not?"

"Obviously." Belle swished her ponytail. "I just like keeping Iris off balance. She's totally a creative genius, but she's so insecure about her work, it's easy to rattle her, which keeps her prices down." Before Skye could leave, Belle handed her a manila envelope. "Not so fast. Here's the list of people who have not returned their response cards. Call them tonight and find out if they're attending. The caterer needs the final, final count tomorrow before ten a.m. Since you insist on going to church on Sunday, you can drop it off on your way."

"But the attendants' party is tonight," Skye protested. She'd been surprised to learn that the matron of honor and the other two bridesmaids, as well as the best man and three groomsmen, were coming to Scumble River and staying for the entire week before the wedding. However, Riley and Belle had assured Skye that they'd all be busy the full seven days.

"You'll have to make the calls before you go, or take your cell and do it from the restaurant." Belle twitched her shoulder. "I can't do every-thing. I'm meeting with the linen consultant in a few minutes to make sure all the tablecloths, napkins, et cetera are in order, and after that, the photographer and the DJ are driving in from Chicago to firm up the picture and song lists. Then I have to go to the country club to work with the lighting and tent guy. I suppose you think I should do your job, too."

"Fine." *One more week.* Skye silently chanted her new mantra. "I'll make the calls." One more week and the wedding would be over and Belle would be on her way back to California. Best of all, Skye would have made enough money to renovate the master bathroom. Heck, the way the hours were piling up, maybe she could have some landscaping done, too.

"Then why are you still standing here?" Belle poked Skye in the shoulder. "Are you hoping Iris will finish without you?"

Skye ground her teeth but managed to walk out the door without slapping the obnoxious woman. Outside, she swept her gaze over the parking lot, searching for the floral designer.

Iris was staying in cottage two, but Skye spotted the tiny woman by the refrigerated storage unit that had been installed in front of number three, the cabin that was being used to assemble her creations.

Iris paused when Skye greeted her, blowing a strand of short dark hair out of her eyes and adjusting her horn-rimmed glasses, but once she gave Skye instructions, they worked in silence.

While Skye helped Iris unload and put away her purchases, she saw signs that the bridesmaids and groomsmen had checked into their cabins. She wondered what they'd be like. Would they resemble Belle, whose continual bragging about her designer clothes, Jaguar convertible, and personal chef precluded any other conversation? Or would they be more similar to Riley, who claimed she wasn't spoiled, just well taken care of?

When the supplies were unloaded, Skye returned to examining the champagne flutes but continued to think about her fellow attendants. She hoped that despite living in Beverly Hills and Laguna Beach, they would be down-to-earth and easy to get along with.

Skye spent the rest of the afternoon assembling the baskets, and when she arrived home at five, she hurriedly changed into her party outfit, then started making phone calls. Half a dozen names remained on her list when the doorbell rang at six o'clock. After slipping on her new red high heels, she ran down the stairs.

When she opened the front door, Wally gathered her into his arms and kissed her. He was a ruggedly handsome man who had turned forty-two in March. The silver in his black hair and the slight lines around his mouth made him even more attractive to Skye. Although they'd been dating for less than two years, Skye had had a crush on him since she was a teenager and he was a twenty-two-year-old rookie on the Scumble River police force.

Moving farther into the foyer, Wally held her a few inches away and examined her left hand. "Damn! I thought maybe you'd be wearing my diamond." He shook his head in disappointment. "You know, I'm getting mighty tired of waiting for your answer."

Skye hung her head. "Sorry. I just haven't had time to think." She loved him. What was holding her back? Was she afraid of commitment, of his family's wealth? Or maybe she just wasn't sure she wanted to be married at all. "I promise as soon as Riley's wedding is over, I'll give you my answer." It had been more than six months since he'd proposed, and she knew it was unfair to make him wait so long, but she just couldn't seem to make up her mind.

Wally put a knuckle under her chin and tilted up her face; his smoldering brown eyes stared into her apprehensive green ones. "A week from tomorrow?"

"Next Sunday." Skye swallowed hard and vowed, "I promise."

The attendants' party was being held at Harry's, a new restaurant in the neighboring town of Laurel. Skye was impressed with the building's sleek design and wondered whether a rural community like Laurel, albeit the county seat, could support such an elegant and expensive place.

Riley and her fiancé, Nick Jordan, greeted Skye and Wally just inside the door of the restaurant's private dining room. Skye noticed that although Nick had his arm possessively around Riley's waist, and Riley appeared to be clinging to him, her expression when Nick wasn't looking was less than loving. Skye raised an eyebrow at Wally, who nodded imperceptibly, acknowledging that he'd also observed Riley's behavior.

This was the first time Skye had met Nick. In fact, no one from Scumble River had seen the groom before today. Even the photograph accompanying the engagement announcement in the *Scumble River Star* had been of only Riley. Looking at Nick, Skye wondered whether the omission had been deliberate. Riley and her husband-to-be reminded Skye of Beauty and the Beast.

May had mentioned something about the difference in age, but Skye had assumed her mother meant a few years, not close to twenty. Nick was at least forty-five, balding, and several inches shorter than his five-foot-ten-inch fiancée.

Skye had pictured Nick as a stallion, but in reality he was more like a miniature pony—a very expensive one, since everything from his diamond-studded gold Submariner Rolex watch to his Clive Christian cologne reeked of wealth and power. It was as if he wore an invisible badge with *veni, VIP, vici*—I came, I'm a very important person, I conquered—written on it.

As they walked toward the bar, she wasn't surprised to see that only two other people had already arrived. She and Wally were fifteen minutes early, which was on time by Scumble River standards but was gauchely premature for city folks.

Leading Wally over to where the couple was sitting sipping martinis, Skye said, "Hi, I'm Skye

Denison, Riley's maid of honor, and this is my boyfriend, Wally Boyd."

The woman held out her hand. "I'm Paige Hathaway, matron of honor."

Paige wore a jade green formfitting designer minidress with zippers running up both sleeves and a pair of ultrachic matching lace gloves. In comparison, Skye felt dowdy in her simple red and black sheath, her only accessory being dangling onyx earrings.

The matron of honor flipped a strand of waist-length copper red hair behind her shoulder and said, "This is my husband, Zach. He's the best man."

Zach was an inch or two taller than Nick and had slightly more hair, but he was similar in age and appearance. He, too, was overly tanned and radiated an aura of success and new money—the garish gold chain resting on his hairy chest could pay most people's salary for a year, not to mention that his fingernails were more nicely manicured than Skye's.

Skye and Wally shook hands with Paige and Zach, then sat and placed their order.

"You're Riley's cousin, right?" Paige asked.

"Yes." Skye nodded. "I was a little surprised that she wanted to have her wedding in her hometown."

"Really?" Paige's smile was sardonic. "Can't you guess why?"

"Well . . ." Skye bit her lip. "I'm sure family was a big consideration. Despite having moved away, she's close to her mother and grandmother."

"And?" Paige prompted.

"And, I suspect, a part of her is still a small-town girl who wants everyone from her past to see how far she's come. The wedding will certainly create a splash Scumble Riverites will never forget."

"True. She definitely likes to be the best." Paige's expression was indecipherable. "But you're missing the most important point. Why do you think she wanted *you* to be her maid of honor?"

"I'm her cousin?"

"Guess again," Paige ordered, then didn't give Skye a chance to respond. "You were also her idol."

Skye's heart sank. "Oh." Being put on a pedestal was never good. It only meant there was a long way to fall.

"When we first met, all she could talk about was how you had gotten away from Scumble River and were living in foreign countries and 'showing' everyone. She was really disappointed when you moved back home. This is her opportunity to surpass her hero."

"I see." Skye decided it was time to change the subject. "How long have you and Riley been friends?"

"We met freshman year at Cal State and roomed

together until Zach and I got married this past December." Paige's green eyes had a faraway look in them. "Riley and I sure had a good time together in college. They called us the Fire and Ice twins."

Zach added, "Nick and I do a lot of business together, and after I started dating Paige, she and I introduced Riley to Nick."

"It's always fun when friends marry friends." Skye smiled at the couple. "So you're newlyweds. Riley probably mentioned that I'm helping out the wedding planner. I'm surprised by the amount of time and money involved. Did you two opt for a big wedding, too?"

"Oh, yeah." Zach made a face.

"I hope you don't think this is a rude question," Skye said hesitantly, "but I'm really curious. Since it seems Riley's wedding is so expensive, even at Midwest prices, how much does it cost to get married in California?"

"I don't know." Zach tone was mocking. "I'm still paying."

"Good thing you can afford it." Paige punched him lightly in the arm. "Otherwise, I wouldn't have said 'I do.'" She arched a brow at Skye. "Money may not buy happiness, but it's sure more comfortable crying in a Rolls-Royce than a Volkswagen."

The bartender served their drinks, saving Skye from coming up with a response. After Wally took a swig of his beer, he said, "Nick is paying, too. Around here, the bride's family usually takes care of the wedding. Is it common practice on the West Coast for the groom to foot the bill?"

"No." Zach shrugged. "But in the type of businesses Nick and I are in, it's important to make the right impression, so I figured if I paid, nobody but me would be griping about the tab. Plus, I wanted to get married in L.A., not in Paige's hometown."

"That seems fair," Skye said. "I guess Nick didn't care about the location. Of course, he is flying two hundred of his closest friends into Chicago and hiring a fleet of limo-buses to bring them to Scumble River the day of the wedding." Skye took a sip of her mojito. "Where are you from, Paige?"

"A little town in Florida, north of Tampa. My dad's a rancher."

"Mine, too." Wally grinned. "But in west Texas."

Skye held her breath. Wally hardly ever mentioned his father. Would he admit that besides owning a ranch in El Paso, Carson Boyd was also the head of a multimillion-dollar corporation?

When Wally didn't go on, Skye wasn't sure whether she was relieved or disappointed. Part of her—the superficial and competitive part—wanted Riley's friends to know that her boyfriend was rich, too. She hadn't missed Zach's quick assessment and dismissal of her off-the-rack dress and nondesigner shoes.

But another part—the one that worried that

Wally would get tired of her and leave her, the part that wondered whether marrying him was a good idea—was glad he'd kept quiet about his wealthy background. Talking about it might mean he was considering resigning as chief of police and taking over CB International as his father wanted him to do.

"Sorry." Skye realized she'd been lost in thought when she noticed they were all waiting for her to answer a question. "What did you say?"

Wally put his arm around her. "Just that your dad is a farmer, so all three of us come from rural backgrounds."

"How about you, Zach?" Skye asked.

"Me, too." Zach's hazel eyes were hooded. "My family owns a vineyard in Napa Valley."

"I'm glad to hear you two are used to small-town life," Skye said. "I was wondering what you all would do with yourself for a week in Scumble River. I was afraid you'd be bored out of your minds."

"I'm looking forward to a little downtime." Paige laid her head on her husband's shoulder. "Zach's business is so hectic, we hardly ever get to spend time with just each other."

"The real estate bubble is going to burst someday, so, as my grandfather used to say, I've got to make hay while the sun shines," Zach said.

"Mine used to say that, too." Skye raised her glass. "Here's to a sunny 2005."

Riley walked up as they finished the toast and pulled Skye away. "I want you to meet the rest of the wedding party." Once they were out of earshot of the bar, she wrinkled her nose at Skye. "I thought your mother said you were going to lose some weight before the wedding."

Skye opened her mouth to make a scathing reply but decided humor would annoy her cousin more. "Sorry, but every time I say the word *diet,* I have to eat a piece of chocolate to get the awful taste out of my mouth."

"Well." Two red circles formed on Riley's cheeks, and she huffed, "Your dress better fit." Not waiting for Skye to answer, Riley led her to another couple and said, "This is my cousin, Skye Denison. Skye, this is Nick's daughter, Hallie, and his son, Hale. They're twins."

"Good to meet you." Skye examined the two young people, who looked remarkably alike. Both were about five-six and slender, with baby-fine brown hair and doelike brown eyes. But while Hallie wore little makeup and no jewelry, her twin had multiple piercings and a scraggily beard and mustache.

"Nice to meet you, ma'am," the twins said in unison.

"It's great you're able to spend the week with us here in Scumble River. Are you in college?" She guessed they were nineteen or twenty.

"Yes, ma'am," they both replied.

Skye wondered whether one could speak without the other. Their unity was a little creepy.

Before Skye could ask anything more, two men and a woman joined them, and Riley said, "This is one of my business partners, Tabitha Urick. Tab, this is my cousin, Skye."

"It's a pleasure to meet you." Skye held out her hand.

The striking ebony-skinned woman smiled and shook it. "Good to meet you, too. Riley's talked about you a lot." Her voice had a slight island lilt. "You are like us, leaving your home to seek your destiny. But you returned. Riley and I are still among the Lotus Eaters."

Skye couldn't tell whether Tabitha thought that was a good or bad thing. "I was gone for twelve years, but it's been nice to be back." *Most of the time,* Skye added silently. "You two own an interior design firm, right?" She remembered her grandmother mentioning Riley's business.

"Yes." Tabitha added, "Paige is our partner as well."

Riley gestured to the two men standing nearby. "And this is Gus Zeitler and Liam Murphy, golfing buddies of Nick's." After Skye and the men exchanged greetings, Riley continued, "Gus is in construction, and Liam is our attorney."

Liam, a tall, ascetic-looking man, frowned. "That reminds me, did you get your marriage license yesterday?"

"Yes." Riley nodded. "We flew into O'Hare yesterday morning and swung by the Stanley County courthouse on our way to Scumble River."

"Good." The lawyer took a BlackBerry out of his pocket and made an entry. "Then all that's left is for us to get together tomorrow so we can finish the prenup."

"I don't know when we'll have time," Riley said. "We're having brunch in Oakbrook tomorrow, then shopping for my wedding jewelry. I doubt we'll be back much before six. Maybe we could wait until we get back from our honeymoon."

"I'll put you down for seven." Liam's expression was unbending. "Excuse me. I need to check my messages."

Skye wondered whether she and Wally would need a prenuptial agreement. If she agreed to marry him, that is.

When Riley went off to tell Nick about their appointment with the lawyer, Gus shook his head. "Poor Liam. He's such a workaholic; leaving his office for a week is killing him."

"Then why did he agree to do it?" Skye asked. "He could have waited and come on Friday."

"Nicky is his biggest client." Gus wiggled bushy eyebrows. He was a beefy man who clearly hadn't started out his working life behind a desk. "Riley wanted everyone here for the week, and Nick wants what Riley wants."

"And you?" Skye couldn't resist asking.

"Let's just say keeping Nicky happy is beneficial to my bottom line, too."

"He must really love her," Skye said, silently wondering why a powerful man like Nick would put up with Riley's narcissistic behavior. He was rich enough to find a less demanding wife. "She certainly seems to have him wrapped around her finger."

"Women as gorgeous as your cousin are always demanding." Gus shrugged. "And Nicky is drawn to beauty. Good thing he enjoys pampering his wives." Gus held up his empty glass. "I need another drink. Can I get you anything from the bar?"

"No, thanks." She had fifteen minutes before dinner. If she was lucky, that gave her just enough time to finish off those phone calls for Belle. The last thing she wanted on a Sunday morning was a ticked-off wedding planner. "See you later."

After she let Wally know what she was doing, she looked for a quiet place where she could sit down. An alcove near the restrooms was screened off by a trifold divider and contained a small conversational furniture grouping. Skye eased into a cushioned chair and kicked off her high heels.

As she dialed the first number, she heard a woman on the other side of the partition screech, "How could you?"

"Dammit!" an infuriated male voice exploded. "I said I was sorry."

"But all that money—"

Not wanting to eavesdrop, Skye cleared her throat and said loudly into her cell phone, "Hi. I'm calling to see if you're planning to attend the Erickson-Jordan wedding next Saturday." As soon as Skye spoke, all went quiet behind the partition, and when she finished making her calls and walked back into the main part of the restaurant, there was no one near where she'd been sitting.

Wally was waiting for her by the entrance to the private dining room, and as he led her to their table, Skye wondered whom she'd overheard and hoped that whatever the couple was arguing about wouldn't interfere with Riley's wedding.

CHAPTER 4

If the Shoe Fits

When Skye pulled into the Up A Lazy River Motor Court a few minutes past eight o'clock Sunday morning, the only movement was the red neon NO VACANCY sign blinking steadily on and off. The front windows of the dozen cabins that formed a horseshoe around the motel's office had their curtains tightly drawn, suggesting the occupants were still snug in their beds.

Which wasn't surprising. Last night, no one had left the restaurant until well after midnight, and most of the group had been drinking steadily for five hours straight. Skye had been concerned that everyone had to drive forty-five miles on unfamiliar country roads to get back to the motor court, but she could think of no way to stop them —it wasn't as if either Laurel or Scumble River had a taxi service—so it was a relief to see the cars intact and parked safely in front of the cottages.

Truth be told, Skye had been a little tipsy herself. She normally stopped after one cocktail, but she had had several mojitos, not to mention a couple of glasses of champagne, and now with the sun glaring into her eyes and her temples pounding, she regretted every lime-flavored swallow and bubbly sip.

In fact, it was a good thing that Bingo had demanded his breakfast, meowing loudly over and over again until Skye finally gave in and emerged from under the covers, or she'd still be sleeping. As it was, she had already missed the first Mass and would have to attend the nine-o'clock one instead. The second service was the one most families chose, and while she loved children, today she was not in the mood for screaming infants and restless toddlers.

Skye waited for a wave of nausea to pass before easing open the door of the Bel Air, careful not to ding the bloodred Porsche in the space next to hers. Belle was leasing the expensive car for the month she was in Scumble River, but she acted as if it were her own, and a dent would send her into a hissy fit to rival Joan Crawford's wire-hanger temper tantrum.

Once she was able to wiggle out of the Chevy, Skye walked gingerly to the door of number six. Mindful of her throbbing head, she tapped softly and waited. When several minutes ticked by with no answer, she forced herself to knock harder. Still no response.

After two more attempts, Skye pounded on the wood and called, "Belle, it's Skye." Nothing. Wincing, she plugged her ears and yelled, "Open up!"

Silence. Where the heck was Belle? Skye glanced around. The motor court had a blank feeling, like a stage just before the play begins. She shivered. Something wasn't right. A moment later, she shook her head. Maybe her ex-boyfriend had had a point. Maybe she did have too much imagination for her own good.

There were only a few places Belle could possibly be—two of which were the adjoining storage and work-space cabins. Cabin five showed no sign of Belle, but when Skye crossed the grass to number four, she saw that the door was ajar.

She stepped over the threshold, then stopped. The interior was pitch-black and silent. Her pulse accelerated. This couldn't be good. Had someone broken in and stolen the wedding supplies? For starters, the Jay Strongwater butterfly clips that would be attached to the fifty-plus center-pieces were worth nearly ten thousand dollars.

Ready to run if the thief was still there, Skye flicked on the light switch. The cabin was empty. She took a quick look around the bedroom and attached bathroom. Everything seemed in order, and there was no sign of either Belle or a burglar.

Great. Now she had two reasons to find Belle —to give her the list and to find out why the storage cabin door wasn't locked. *Shoot.* If she didn't locate Belle soon, Skye'd be late for church.

Father Burns, though charitable about most of his flock's shortcomings, did not tolerate tardiness. He was apt to make an example of anyone who dared come in after the processional, and considering her hangover, Skye already felt like enough of a sinner.

Still, she couldn't just leave. Belle would have a meltdown if she didn't have the RSVPs in time to make the caterer's deadline, and if there *had* been a burglary, it needed to be reported. Skye chewed her lip. Should she slip the list and a note about the unlocked cabin under Belle's door? No. What if she missed it?

Hmm. Maybe Belle was working with the floral designer. Neither had been at the party, and they might be early risers. Skye hurried over to the cabin that Iris was using as a work space and knocked on the door.

When there was no answer, Skye scratched her

head. Now what? Could Belle be at breakfast? Her car wasn't gone, but she could have hitched a ride with someone.

Terrific. She looked around, her gaze falling on the motor court's office.

Uncle Charlie! Her godfather, Charlie Patukas, could give Belle the list when she got back. He owned the motor court and his bungalow was attached to the office, so he could keep an eye out for her return.

Skye headed toward the parking lot. As she edged past the floral cooling unit situated on the asphalt in front of cabin three, she noticed that the motor was running. That was odd. The flowers weren't due to be delivered until Wednesday. Why would Iris have started up the refrigerator?

Skye circled around to the front of the unit, then stopped. When she had learned that the refrigerator would be holding fifty thousand dollars' worth of expensive blooms, she'd made sure its door was equipped with a heavy-duty lock. And while the key was still in the dead bolt just as she'd left it—Iris had insisted the key remain there rather than risk misplacing the tiny piece of steel—it was now sideways, indicating that the mechanism was engaged.

The hair on the nape of Skye's neck stood up. Something was definitely wrong. Her heart raced. She quickly turned the key and swung open the heavy door. A gust of icy air billowed out, and she shuddered. Someone had cranked the temperature way, way down.

Shivering, Skye looked inside the eight-by-eight metal box. Shelves from floor to ceiling formed two narrow aisles from front to back and a third along the rear wall.

The sound of her breathing echoed loudly in the eerie silence. At first the unit appeared empty, but then, as her eyes adjusted to the darkness, she noticed a cobalt satin high-heel shoe peeking from beneath the bottom shelf to the right of the entrance.

Oh-oh. Skye darted forward, picked up the stiletto, and quickly exited. Out in the sunlight, the crystal brooch on the vamp winked up at her, but it was the Manolo Blahnik label on the insole that caught her attention. *Crap!* No woman willingly abandoned a shoe from a pair that cost close to a thousand dollars. This story would not have a happy ending.

Should she close the door and get help? But what would she say—that she was afraid the wicked stepmother had done something to Cinderella? Before she could talk herself out of it, she walked inside and pulled the chain attached to the bulb bolted overhead.

Moving left, Skye peered down that aisle. Seeing nothing but bare shelves, she took a relieved breath. One down, one to go. Next she stepped to the right and examined the space. *Eek!* A spill of blue silk oozed from behind the far end of the shelving.

Skye forced herself to walk toward the fabric and turn the corner. Lying on the cold steel floor was Belle, and she wasn't moving. Without thinking, Skye whirled around and ran for the door.

CHAPTER 5

Reality Check

Skye stopped in midsprint, her first-responder training kicking in and overcoming her fears. She turned back. Even if there was only a small chance that Belle was still alive, Skye had to get her out of the refrigerator and start CPR.

After rolling Belle over, Skye worked her hands underneath her arms, clasped them around her upper chest, and with a mighty heave tugged Belle into a sitting position. Grunting, Skye moved her into the side aisle but had to rest before going any farther. For someone who claimed to wear a size double zero, Belle felt heavier than a sumo wrestler.

Taking a deep breath, Skye grabbed Belle again, then froze as a high-pitched scream echoed off the metal walls. Skye's head popped up like the clown's in a jack-in-the-box. Iris stood in the doorway, her mouth forming a perfect circle and her hands clutching her cheeks.

"Iris, thank God. Help me get her outside," Skye commanded.

The floral designer didn't budge. Her beautiful almond-shaped eyes were huge and her complexion was as white as zinc oxide. It looked as if she was going into shock.

"Iris. Please." Skye tried to calm her. "This could be a matter of life or death."

Iris nodded but sank to the ground, whimpering.

Giving up, Skye turned her attention back to Belle. Laying her down, Skye felt for a pulse in the woman's throat and wrist. Nothing. She leaned forward to check for breathing but looked up as she heard a familiar voice.

Uncle Charlie was rushing toward her, an apoplectic expression on his flushed face. He was a big man, six feet and more than three hundred pounds, but he could move quickly when the situation warranted it. As he reached the floral refrigerator, he bellowed, "What the hell's going on here? Don't tell me you found another body."

"I hope not." Skye said a fevered prayer under her breath. "Help me get her outside."

Charlie and Skye carried Belle out to the warm pavement. Skye checked again for a pulse or breathing but found none. As she started CPR she ordered, "Call the paramedics, then Wally."

"Wally!" Charlie thundered. "Wasn't this an accident?"

Skye shook her head but didn't stop what she was doing.

Charlie groaned, then lumbered off toward the motel office.

Skye continued CPR until the EMTs arrived and pushed her aside. Stationing herself in front of the refrigerator, determined not to let anyone taint the crime scene, she waited for the police. Unfortunately, the commotion drew the bridal party from their cabins.

Liam Murphy was the first to arrive. "What's happened?" He was dressed in a jogging suit and continued to run in place as he spoke.

Skye crossed her arms and maintained her position. "Please return to your cabin. Once the police arrive, they'll speak to you."

"The police! What's happened?"

Skye kept her expression neutral. "The police will explain everything."

"Who put you in charge?" Liam challenged.

"I did." Skye met his stare. "I'm the psychological consultant to the Scumble River Police Department."

Before Liam could respond, Zach and Paige Hathaway, Tabitha Urick, and Gus Zeitler joined them, each wearing some form of nightclothes. The only guests missing were Hale and Hallie Jordan. As Skye tried to decide what, if anything, their absence meant, a police car skidded into the parking lot.

Wally exited from the cruiser, followed closely by a uniformed young woman. A few weeks ago, Wally had hired two additional officers, bringing his staff to six full-timers and two part-timers, but Skye had been so busy with the wedding, she hadn't met the new hires yet and couldn't remember their names.

Wally introduced them. "Skye, this is Officer Martinez. Martinez, this is our psych consultant, Ms. Denison."

"Call me Skye." She noted that the female officer's dark brown hair was drawn tightly back and fastened in a bun at the nape of her neck and her face was bare of makeup. Was the young woman trying to be one of the guys? Being the first female officer on the Scumble River PD couldn't be easy.

"I'm Zelda." Officer Martinez held out a hand with professionally manicured bright red fingernails.

"Nice to meet you." Skye shook the young woman's hand, glad to see Zelda wasn't afraid to let her feminine side show after all.

After ordering everyone back to their rooms, Wally instructed Officer Martinez to see that the guests stayed inside their cabins, then conferred with the paramedics, who shook their heads and packed up their gear.

As the EMTs returned to their ambulance and drove away, Wally took out his cell and called for additional officers to seal off the parking lot. Next he requested the county crime-scene techs and the coroner. When Skye heard the latter, a wave of dizziness overwhelmed her and she sank to the curb. She'd been running on adrenaline, but now, realizing that Belle was really, truly dead, she thought she might throw up.

Wally sat next to her, putting his arm around her. "Sweetheart." He cupped her face, cradling her cheek in his calloused hand. "Are you all right?"

Skye shook her head. "I know it's not as if I've never discovered a dead body before. In fact, I'm beginning to think I might be a magnet for them. But I feel worse each time."

"I wouldn't expect anything else." Wally radiated a strength that drew Skye like a hummingbird to sugar water. "If you didn't feel that way, you wouldn't be the woman I love."

Skye gave him a quick kiss, then resolutely pulled herself together. "Should I tell you what happened?"

Wally gave her hand a squeeze. "Start with why you think this wasn't an accident."

Skye explained about the refrigeration unit being locked from the outside, then told him about her search for Belle, concluding with, "And the door to cabin four was half-open, which is unusual considering there's tens of thousands of dollars' worth of goods being stored inside."

"So you're thinking maybe whatever happened

to Belle started while she was working inside number four." Wally had removed his arm from around her to take notes.

"It makes sense." Skye gestured over her shoulder with her thumb. "Since it's right there."

"I'll take a look while we wait for the crime techs and the coroner. Why don't you check and see if Martinez is doing okay."

"How's she working out?"

"So far, so good." Wally took Skye's hands to help her stand. "But she's only been here a little over a week, and this is her first job after college."

Skye nodded. Like small-town schools, small-town police departments often hired new graduates because they couldn't afford more experienced officers.

As Wally walked over to number four, Skye approached Officer Martinez, who had taken up a position in the center of the parking lot where she could see all the cabins. "Hi. Everyone behaving?"

"More or less. They complained about having to stay in their rooms. It seems several have hangovers and are in desperate need of caffeine."

"Mmm. We may be able to use that to our advantage when we question them." Skye shook her head. "Who knew that Uncle Charlie's refusal to provide coffeepots in the rooms would turn out to our advantage?"

"I don't know," Zelda deadpanned. "Withholding caffeine might be considered torture."

Skye lips twitched. It appeared that Zelda had quickly learned that cops, like mental health workers, often used humor to cope with the grim reality of their jobs. "Guess there's not much we can do until the forensic team shows up."

Zelda adjusted her sunglasses. "I checked out the rooms, and I know they don't have back doors, but do you think any of them are desperate enough to try and climb out the bathroom window?"

"Those windows are pretty small," Skye pointed out. "But how about I do a roll call to make sure everyone is still where they're supposed to be?"

"Sounds like a plan." Zelda nodded. "Just yell if you need me."

Skye started with Zack and Paige in cabin one, then worked her way around the circle. Zelda had been right about the group being unhappy with their confinement, but Skye soothed them with promises of coffee after they'd answered a few questions for the police.

No one answered the door to number ten. Frowning, she checked her list. Hallie Jordan was supposed to be occupying that cabin. She remembered that Hallie and her brother were the only guests who hadn't shown up when the ambulance arrived.

Hale was assigned to number eleven, so Skye moved on to that cottage. When there was no response to her knock there either, she decided she'd better let Wally know that the twins were AWOL.

She found him conferring with Simon Reid next to the cooling unit. Besides being the county coroner, Simon owned the local funeral home and the town bowling alley—which his mother, Bunny, managed. He was also Skye's ex-boyfriend.

They had dated on and off for nearly three years, until Skye caught Simon cheating on her. Actually, he really wasn't, but he'd been too stubborn to explain. Shortly afterward, Wally and Skye became an item. To say that the three of them working together presented an awkward situation was an understatement.

As Skye approached them, both men turned toward her, and as soon as she was near enough, Wally put his arm around her shoulders and said, "Everything okay?"

At the same instant, Simon took her free hand and asked, "Are you all right? Anything I can do?" In appearance, Simon was the antithesis of Wally, tall and lean with stylishly cut auburn hair and golden hazel eyes.

"She's fine," Wally said, stepping back and bringing Skye with him, which caused her hand to slip from Simon's. "I've got it covered."

The two men glowered at each other, and Skye quickly said to Wally, "Two members of the wedding party are not in their cabins."

"Were they here earlier?" Wally whipped out a pad of paper and a pen.

"No. I haven't seen them today. I hope they just

56

went for an early breakfast or to church." Skye wasn't sure that they were religious, but it was Sunday morning, and there weren't many other places they could be.

"Names."

"Hallie and Hale Jordan. They're twins. The groom is their father."

Simon interjected, "They're children?"

"No. College age." Skye turned to him. "Nick is quite a bit older than my cousin."

"Oh." Simon raised a brow and looked between Skye and Wally. "Dating older men must run in the family."

Wally's expression hardened, but he didn't comment. Instead he reached for his cell. "Thea, call in Sergeant Quirk. I need him to locate Hallie and Hale Jordan. Tell him to start with the restaurants in the area, then try the churches." He told the dispatcher to hold on and asked Skye, "Do you know what religion they are?"

"Not a clue." She shook her head. "I know Riley can't get married in the Catholic Church since Nick is divorced."

"Just like Chief Boyd," Simon murmured. "Something else you and your cousin have in common."

It was Skye's turn to glare at Simon. What was he doing? He almost sounded jealous. After the last case they'd worked on together when Wally was out of town, Skye thought she and Simon had made their peace and that they were on the road to becoming friends. In fact, for the last eight months, they'd fallen into the habit of having coffee together on Sunday mornings after Mass. So why was he acting like such a jerk now?

At the thought of those get-togethers, guilt nibbled at Skye's conscience. When she'd mentioned them to Wally, he'd been unhappy, but she'd insisted that she and Simon were friends and there was no harm in her talking to him. Had she misinterpreted Simon's intentions?

Before she could think about it, Wally clicked off his cell and said to Skye, "Reid processed the body and Xavier is taking it to the hospital in Laurel for the medical examiner to perform the autopsy."

Skye nodded. Xavier Ryan was Simon's assistant. She asked Simon, "Do you have a cause of death?"

"My best guess is she died of suffocation. There's a suspicious bruise on her temple, some abrasions on her face, and it looks as if she was hit on the head before being stuffed into the floral refrigerator, which is airtight."

"How about a time of death?"

"No." Simon shook his head. "I wasn't able to determine TOD because the body was refrigerated. But according to FEMA, a unit this size has enough air for about five hours, so she was probably locked in here no later than three a.m."

Simon tapped his chin. "Nothing suggests she tried to get out of the unit, so she *was* probably unconscious the whole time."

"I sure hope so." Skye shuddered. "I pray she didn't know she was dying."

The three of them were silent for a moment; then Simon said, "I've got to get going." As he walked away, he added over his shoulder, "I'll let you know when I get the autopsy results."

Wally turned to Skye. "A couple of boxes were knocked over in cabin four, but the room doesn't appear to have been searched. I checked out the victim's cottage, and her door was unlocked, but there's no sign of a struggle.

"So whatever happened probably started in number four."

"That's my working theory." Wally shoved a hand through his hair. "The county crime-scene techs got here about the same time Reid did, and after they finish with the floral refrigerator, they'll check out the victim's cabin and number four. In the meantime, I want to start interviewing people. Who-all is staying here at the motor court?"

"The floral designer, two bridesmaids, three groomsmen, the matron of honor and her husband, and the best man." Skye paused. "But, as we just discussed, the twins aren't actually here at this moment."

"There are twelve cabins." Wally counted on his fingers. "Taking into account Belle's and the three being used for storage and work space, that leaves one cottage empty. Is the bride or groom in it?"

"No." Skye explained, "Riley's at her mom's house, and Nick, his parents, Jay and Natasha, and his six-year-old half brother, Luca Jay, who's the ring bearer, are staying at the Ritz-Carlton in Chicago. The California guests are arriving by private jet on Saturday. They'll be driven to Scumble River that afternoon, then will spend the night at the Ritz-Carlton and fly home the next day."

"So is number twelve unoccupied?"

"Yes. It's being held for the makeup artist and hairstylist to share when they fly in from L.A. Thursday evening."

"Okay." Wally looked down at his notes. "Let's start with the people currently at the motor court."

"Who do you want me to cover?"

"You take the women and I'll take the men. That's three each."

"Okay." Skye moved to go, then turned back. "I almost forgot. Except for Iris Yee, they all probably have hangovers and haven't had their morning coffee yet. I promised them as soon as we finish questioning them they can go get some." She gave him a little smile. "So they're probably just a tiny bit on edge."

"You're evil." Wally grinned at her. "I like that in a woman."

Skye winked, then headed to cabin nine. She

knocked and said, "It's me again, Skye." She had explained on her earlier visit that she was the police department's psychological consultant.

"Come in." Tabitha flung open the door. "Did you bring coffee?"

"Sorry." Skye edged past her and sat in the only chair, forcing Tabitha to sit on the bed, which put her at a slight disadvantage.

"What do you want to talk about?" Tabitha's bearing was regal and her face impassive.

"How well do you know Belle Canfield?"

"I don't, except as a wedding planner. Is she the one the ambulance came for?"

Skye ignored Tabitha's question. "When did Riley hire her?"

"Mmm . . . Maybe six or eight months ago. Did Belle get mugged or something?"

"I was under the impression that a wedding like Riley's would take a year to a year and a half to put together. I mean, I know Riley only formally announced her engagement here in Scumble River last November, but I assumed she had already put things in motion several months before her visit home."

"And you'd be right," Tabitha confirmed. "Riley's first choice quit, so she went with Belle, since she had done Paige's wedding."

"But Belle told me she's the premiere Hollywood wedding coordinator. Why wasn't she Riley's first choice?" Skye was careful to keep to the present tense so Tabitha wouldn't guess Belle was dead.

"I don't get involved in the drama, but my guess would be that at first Riley was trying to outdo Paige, hiring a planner even higher up on the food chain than Belle." Tabitha shrugged. "Riley's a bit of a hungry tiger."

"Uh?"

"A person who wants attention so bad, they're starving for it."

"Oh." Skye could think of quite a few hungry tigers, but to be fair they were mostly teenagers who would eventually grow into gentler creatures. "How did Riley come to hire Belle at the last minute?"

"Belle isn't as famous as she pretends. Plus, Nick pulled some strings and offered her double her usual rate." Tabitha's eyes twinkled. "Money talks, you know."

"I've heard that, but money and I are not usually on speaking terms." Skye smiled. "That is, until I started working this wedding."

"You too, huh?" Tabitha snickered. "Yes, Nick is the Money Whisperer, that's for sure."

Skye nodded, noticing that Tabitha's lilting Caribbean accent varied depending on her comfort level. "What time did you get back here last night?"

"Around one, I think. I didn't look at the clock."

"Was anyone hanging around the motor court when you arrived?"

"No." Tabitha's smooth expression didn't change. "I caught a ride with Gus and Liam, and Paige and Zach took the twins. Both cars got here about the same time, and no one else was in the parking lot."

"Did you hear anything during the night or this morning?"

"Sorry. I took a sleeping pill. I didn't hear anything until the ambulance siren woke me up."

"Do you know anyone who dislikes Belle or wishes her harm?" Skye asked.

"Well, there was The Incident." Tabitha's brow wrinkled. "A mother of the bride found Belle naked in the back of the limo with one of the wedding party. Rumor has it she chased her around the parking lot with a cake knife."

"Why did the mother care?"

"He was the father of the bride, the mother's husband."

"Oh." Skye made a note. "What was the woman's name?"

"I have no idea."

"Anyone else who dislikes Belle or would want to hurt her?"

"Everybody in the wedding party." Tabitha crossed her legs. "She's a bully."

"Anyone more than the others?" Skye asked.

"If it were me, I'd be looking at the vendors. That's who she really holds power over."

Skye made another note. "Like Iris?"

Tabitha pursed her lips. "You never answered me. Did something happen to Belle?"

"Yes." Skye rose from her seat and moved to the door. "Someone murdered her."

"Oh, my God!" Tabitha leaped off the bed in one fluid motion. "Dat ain't no true."

"Sorry, but it is." Skye noted that Tabitha seemed genuinely upset. Her accent had increased, and she was now dropping the pitch down on the second syllable, and then raising it on the last syllable. "So, who do you think hated her that much?"

Tabitha held her hand to her chest. "Only person you can be sure is innocent is Riley. She'd never kill Belle less than a week before the wedding."

CHAPTER 6

Meeting of the Minds

When Skye emerged from Tabitha's room, Wally was coming out of the cabin to her right. "Any news on the twins?" she asked.

"They're not at the Feed Bag or McDonald's. Quirk is checking the churches now."

Skye wrinkled her brow. She was missing something, but she couldn't put her finger on it. "Did Liam share any helpful info?"

"He and the other groomsman drove Tabitha back here, arriving at one eleven a.m.; then he proceeded directly to his room, where he made several calls and went to bed at precisely two thirty. He went jogging at seven and didn't observe anything unusual when he left. He returned from the park as the ambulance arrived." Wally's expression was dour. "Does that match what Tabitha told you?"

"Yes. Although she wasn't as precise about the time. She claims she took a sleeping pill and wasn't aware of anything until the siren woke her up."

"I'm not sure I buy his story about jogging this morning." Wally crossed his arms. "That would mean he only got four and half hours of sleep after drinking all night."

"Gus did mention last night that Liam is a health nut," Skye offered. "That probably means he didn't drink as much as the others."

"Let's see what the next pair has to say." Wally took Skye's arm and steered them toward the adjoining cottage. "This one's mine. Who's up for you?"

"Iris Yee."

"After I finish with Gus, I'll take the best man over to Charlie's office to question him so you can talk to his wife alone."

"Got it." Skye left Wally in front of number seven and made her way to cottage two. She hoped Iris had calmed down enough to be coherent.

An hour later, Wally and Skye met again. Neither had obtained any useful information. The floral designer had regained her composure and claimed she and Belle had a professional relationship that worked well for them both. Gus and the Hathaways had stated that they knew Belle only in regard to her job and had no idea who would have wanted to kill her.

Just when Skye thought she might avoid being present when her cousin found out that Belle was dead, Riley, her mother, Anita, and her grandmother Dora showed up at the motor court. Skye wasn't surprised to see them; she was only amazed it had taken them so long to hear about the murder. Scumble River's grapevine usually rivaled the Internet for speed and inaccuracy.

Riley helped her grandmother out of the backseat of Anita's Taurus, then spotted Skye and ran over to her. "What's going on here?" She gestured to the police cars filling the parking lot. "We were at twelve o'clock Mass, and I knew something was up because my cell kept vibrating, so I went into the bathroom and I had a gazillion texts from Tab and Paige about some emergency having to do with Belle. So I got Mom and Gram and came right over." The blond bride-to-be took a much-needed breath, then continued. "Please, please, tell me that Belle's okay. There can't be something wrong with her. Not six days before my wedding."

Dora chimed in, "I'm sure it will be fine, baby girl."

"Skye," Anita ordered, "tell us everything's all right."

"Uh." Skye glanced at Wally, who was talking to one of the county crime techs but plainly monitoring her conversation as well. She raised a brow; should she inform them of Belle's death? He nodded, and she said gently, "I'm so sorry, but Belle was found dead this morning."

"No!" Anita screamed.

Riley threw herself in her mother's arms and burst into tears. Dora swayed, and Skye rushed over to catch the elderly woman before she fell. Supporting her great aunt, Skye herded Anita and Riley into the motor court's office.

Once they were all inside and Dora and Anita had settled in the tiny reception area's only two chairs, Skye leaned against the wall, uncertain what to do next. Surprisingly, none of the three women had asked *how* Belle had died, which was good because that information hadn't been released yet.

Riley pulled herself together enough to fetch Dora a glass of water, but as soon as she was sure her grandmother was okay, she put her Frankenbride face back on. Currently she was crying and whining into her cell at her groom, who was en route from Chicago.

Charlie sat behind the counter, ignoring the women and gazing at the TV mounted in the corner opposite him. If the problem didn't concern someone he loved or something he was in charge of, he wasn't interested.

Riley finally clicked shut her phone and stamped her foot. "It's not fair. I've been dreaming of this day since I was six years old. Nick claims even he can't get another wedding coordinator this close to the date, and I want my wedding to be exactly how I planned."

"I can do it, Riley." Anita straightened in her seat. "Mother and I told you from the beginning we could put on your wedding."

"Mommy." Riley's tone was sugarcoated steel. "It's so sweet of you and Gram to want to help me, but you know we talked about that. It's just too much for you two to handle." She zeroed in on Skye. "You'll just have to do it."

"Me! But I can't. I have no idea how to pull together a wedding like yours." Skye was flabbergasted. "I figured you'd postpone the ceremony, or maybe simplify the whole shebang." If Skye had even considered that Riley might try to rope her into taking over, she would have had a good excuse ready.

Anita spoke before Skye could say more. "Miss Canfield's passing is a terrible tragedy, but it really has nothing to do with Riley." She sniffed. "It's not as if she were family."

"But . . ." Skye trailed off, momentarily distracted by a blast of music from the TV set as Charlie channel surfed.

Anita jumped out of her chair, marched over to him, and held out her hand. "Give me that."

Charlie clutched the black plastic device to his chest. "No one touches my remote but me."

Anita stared at him for another second, then strode over to the TV, tore the electrical cord out of the back of the set, and returned to her seat, stating, "Unlike men, women don't need to hold the remote control, because we have real control."

Muttering angrily, Charlie lumbered to his feet and slammed out of the office.

Once he was gone, Dora said to Skye, "Please put on Riley's wedding for her." Moisture gathered at the corners of her faded blue eyes. "This may be my last chance to see my only granddaughter married." Her voice broke. "And I'm not sure your grandma can wait either."

As Skye hesitated, the office door opened and Wally signaled for her to join him outside. She nodded and said, "I'll be right back."

Wally took her hand. "We found the twins."

"Where?" Skye felt her heart in her throat. "Are they okay?"

"They're fine. They decided last night that they couldn't stay at the motor court. It was, and I quote, 'too icky.'" Wally shook his head. "So, after the Hathaways dropped them off here, they borrowed the Hathaways' rental car and drove into the city. They're staying at the Ritz with their father, grandparents, and six-year-old uncle."

"How did you find out?"

"When I called the groom to tell him his kids were missing, he told me."

"Well, at least that's one problem solved." Skye scrunched up her face. "But you'll never guess what Riley just said."

"She wants you to take over for the dead wedding planner."

"How did you know that?" Skye demanded.

"Elementary, my dear Watson. Riley's a spoiled princess who wouldn't dream of letting the death of one of her serfs interfere with her plans." Wally smirked. "And as my grandpa used to say, scratch a dog once and you've found yourself a permanent job."

"What's that supposed to mean?"

"It means she thinks you're a pushover."

"Is that what you think too?" Skye glared at him. "Because you're both so wrong. No way am I trying to put on a million-dollar wedding."

"Really?" Wally raised her hand to his lips. "Even for me?" He kissed the inside of her wrist. "I need to keep everyone together until we figure out what happened to Belle. If Riley postpones the wedding, all the participants will scatter. I can't order them to stay put. I have no evidence against any of them, and their lawyers would be all over me."

"Crap!" Skye paused to gather her thoughts. "Do you know what you're asking me to do? This event is so over the top, I have no idea how to coordinate it."

"I'm sure Belle had notes you can use."

Skye nodded slowly, remembering the huge three-ring binder that Belle had referred to as her bible.

"I bet Jordan would shell out for an assistant or two for you." Wally kissed her palm. "And I bet he'd pay you your weight in gold to do it."

"Are you implying I weigh a lot?" Skye teased.

"Never. You know I like you fluffy." Wally released her hand and cupped the back of her head. "I'm just saying a fool and his money can throw a heck of a party."

After a thoroughly satisfying kiss, Skye stepped out of his arms and said over her shoulder as she went back into the office, "You owe me big-time for this."

"With all my worldly goods, I thee endow."

The sincerity in Wally's voice brought tears to Skye's eyes, and she was still wiping them away when she stepped inside.

Riley rushed over to Skye. "Has something else happened? One more thing and I'll kill myself."

"Nothing bad has happened." Skye resolved to treat her cousin as she would a high-strung kindergartner—with a soothing but firm hand. "You need to pull yourself together if you want me to take over as your wedding coordinator."

"Thank you! Thank you! Thank you!" Riley squealed and enveloped Skye in a huge hug. "You're the best."

"Yes, I am." Skye squeezed her cousin back, then extracted herself from Riley's stranglehold. "Here's the deal. Nick gives me whatever Belle was getting and covers the cost of two helpers." The new no-kill animal shelter that had just opened up in Stanley County would be getting a nice donation out of this, Skye decided.

"We'll give you twenty-five percent of Belle's fees—it's what we still owe her." Riley had suddenly dropped the girlish persona. "And fifteen dollars an hour for each of the two assistants."

"Fine." Skye already knew who she wanted to hire, and both of them would be happy to get nearly twice Illinois's minimum wage. "And if the wedding goes as planned, I want a bonus."

"Name it."

"Nick pays for *any* wedding dress I pick out, *whenever* I get married." Skye figured that if she said yes to Wally, considering his family's wealth, she would need a fancier dress than she could afford on her salary.

Skye and Wally were silent during the five-minute ride from the police station to his house. It had been a grueling twelve hours, and although her hangover was long gone, her head still throbbed —this time from too much caffeine and sugar. The only things edible at the PD came out of a vending machine, and Skye had overdosed on Diet Coke and Kit Kat bars.

They had reinterviewed everyone at the motor court, then moved on to the other members of the wedding party, but had run out of time before getting to the vendors. In her few spare minutes, Skye had called the caterer with the final guest count and studied Belle's notebook.

As Wally turned the squad car into his driveway, she looked at the four-room bungalow. Although Wally was the son of a Texas oil tycoon, he lived modestly, and no one in Scumble River other than Skye knew about his affluent background.

Passing through the enclosed back porch, which contained a washer, a dryer, and an ironing board, they stepped into the homey kitchen, where the tangy smell of barbeque greeted them. When Wally flicked on the overhead light, Skye saw that the table was set with a red-and-white-checkered cloth and heavy white dishes.

She gestured around the room, then pointed to the plate of brownies on the counter and asked, "Dorothy?"

A few years ago, after his divorce, Wally had a hired a housekeeper who came in a couple of days a week to clean and do the shopping, laundry, and occasionally cook a meal. The tricky part was that Dorothy Snyder was one of Skye's mother's best friends, and Skye always wondered whether she reported their every move to May.

"Yes. I called her when I realized that it would be too late for us to eat at the Feed Bag." Scumble

River's only restaurant stopped serving at six p.m. on Sunday. "I asked if she had time to fix us something." He shrugged off his navy nylon Windbreaker embroidered with SCUMBLE RIVER POLICE.

"And I guess she said yes."

"Yep." Wally unbuckled his utility belt and draped it over the back of a kitchen chair. "She said she was bored and would be happy to help us out."

"Let's see what Dorothy's whipped up for us." Skye lifted the lid of the Crock-Pot. "Yum, beef barbeque." Moving to the fridge, she opened the door. "Potato salad and baked beans."

"Sounds good." Wally yawned and rubbed the back of his neck. "She's a great cook."

Skye noticed the exhaustion in Wally's eyes. "You're tired." He'd been up late last night because of her. "You should have let me go home so you could get some rest." She knew he had the eight a.m. shift the next day.

"I'm fine." Wally yawned again. "I just need a shower."

"Why don't you go ahead, then? By the time you're finished, I'll have everything on the table."

"Or you could join me." His voice was a seductive promise. "It'll help you forget about today."

As she considered the invitation, Skye's stomach growled, and she said, "Maybe later."

"Okay." He chuckled and kissed her on the cheek. "I know a hungry girlfriend is a cranky girlfriend." He started unbuttoning his shirt as he walked away.

A few seconds later, Skye could hear him humming and moving around in the master bedroom; then the shower came on. Smiling, she busied herself with microwaving the baked beans and heating up the buns. Ten minutes later, Wally appeared just as she was putting the potato salad on the table. He had changed into faded jeans that clung to his muscular thighs and cupped the tight curve of his derrière. A plain white T-shirt stretched across his powerful shoulders.

Skye's lips parted and the tip of her tongue darted out to moisten them.

His chocolate brown eyes followed the movement, and he gave her a smile that sent her pulse racing. "It's not too late to change your mind about a shower. There's still plenty of hot water."

In her mind, Skye sprinkled the brownies all over his chest and licked them off. Before she could act on her impulse, her stomach growled again. No. Real food first, fantasy dessert later, or maybe just cuddling. They were both exhausted, and the recent murder didn't exactly set the right mood for lovemaking.

Sadness swept over Skye at the memory of Belle's death. She hadn't liked the woman, but no one had the right to take her life. By murdering her, the killer had stolen Belle's chance to mature, to grow, to become a less selfish person.

Skye thrust out her jaw. Whoever had done it would be sorry. They'd picked the wrong place to commit the crime. Scumble River may seem like a hick town, but it had a terrific police department and a darn good psychological consultant, both of which had a nearly perfect record of bringing murderers to justice.

Wally was looking at her funny, and Skye realized she'd been lost in her thoughts. She shook off her gloominess, grabbed a beer from the refrigerator, and handed it to him, asking, "Ready to eat?"

"I was ready five hours ago." He sank into a chair.

"Me, too." She watched him from the corner of her eye as she poured herself a glass of wine. She never tired of looking at him. He was devastatingly handsome and exuded masculinity. Taking a deep breath, she savored the tantalizing scent of his aftershave.

Skye heaped savory barbeque onto a warm roll and took a huge bite. She closed her eyes and nearly moaned as the spicy meat melted in her mouth, then swallowed and brought the sandwich back to her lips. Hearing Wally chuckle, she glanced at him. He had a bemused expression on his face.

Putting down the bun, she demanded, "What? Do I have sauce on my chin?"

"No." Wally tried to hide his grin. "I just enjoy

watching you eat. You have a much more intimate relationship with your dinner than I do."

"Is that bad?" Was he saying she was a glutton?

"Nope. In fact, it turns me on."

"Oh." Skye smiled to herself. "I was hoping you'd say that."

They ate in silence for a while, but after their initial hunger had been slaked, Skye commented, "I haven't seen these dishes before. What happened to your grandmother's Royal Winton china?"

"Dorothy thinks they should only be used for special occasions, so she made me buy these from Wal-Mart." Wally shook his head. "I'm not sure what she considers a special enough occasion—these are all she ever sets out."

"She and my mother are so alike." Skye ate a forkful of potato salad, then added, "Mom won't even let me have the dishes her grandmother left me until I'm married." *Oops!* She didn't want to discuss Wally's proposal. Hurrying to change the subject, she asked, "So, how's your dad been?" Carson Boyd had been hospitalized last October after collapsing, and the doctors had never figured out what was wrong with him.

"Fine. When I spoke to him last week, he was thinking of taking a cruise." Wally took a swig of beer. "I'm not sure what's up with that. I can't remember the last time he took a vacation."

"Maybe he's met someone," Skye offered.

Wally's mother had died the year he'd finished college.

"I doubt it." Wally's tone was serious. "Remember, I told you, Boyd men mate for life."

Skye kept her face impassive. Wally's first wife had left him, so what did his statement mean? Had she been his mate for life and he was making do with Skye? Instead of asking, she said, "Ready for some brownies?"

"I'm stuffed. Maybe later."

"Me, too." Skye got to her feet. "Why don't you go relax while I clean up?"

Wally pushed back from the table and started to clear the table. "We're both tired. Why should I get to rest and not you?"

Skye grinned. Except for the fact that he was older, divorced, and not Catholic—as her mother continually reminded her—Wally was the perfect man.

Fifteen minutes later they settled on the sofa in the living room. The hardwood floor gleamed in the low light of the aquarium—Skye's gift to Wally on his last birthday—and the deep taupe walls created a warm haven.

"Let's see if the murder made the local news." Wally turned on the TV. "I was surprised when you told me Belle's father was a famous hotelier."

"Believe me, she never let anyone forget who her dad was." Skye wiggled into the buttery soft leather couch. "Did you ever get hold of her parents?"

"No. I spoke with dozens of assorted personal assistants and secretaries and housekeepers, but they all claim the Canfields are on their yacht in the Mediterranean and refuse to give me their cell numbers. The employees claim they'll pass on the message that I need to talk to them about an urgent matter regarding their daughter." Frustration edged his voice. "That's one of the reasons I hope the media didn't get wind of Belle's death."

Skye nodded sympathetically.

"I hate cases where famous people are involved. So far we've only dealt with minor celebrities, but Canfield Hotels are famous worldwide."

"Yes, but I don't think Belle was all that famous. I remember the first time I met her, she was moaning that the paparazzi didn't pay as much attention to her as they did to Paris Hilton." Skye patted his arm. "Maybe we'll catch a break and solve the case before a reporter puts two and two together. After all, who would expect someone like Belle Canfield to be working in Scumble River?"

The news ended and Wally clicked off the TV. "Looks like we dodged the bullet so far."

"Do you want to talk about the interviews?" Skye turned sideways on the sofa so she could look at Wally without straining her neck. "Or are you too tired?"

"Well, there are other things I'd rather do." Wally gave Skye a sexy grin. "But it's probably better if we go over the facts while they're fresh in both our minds."

"Okay. Let me get my notes."

"I'll grab mine too."

When they were both resettled on the couch, Skye asked, "Are you thinking that Belle's murderer is probably connected to the wedding?"

"That's the most likely scenario. The wedding party and the vendors are the only ones in the area who know her. So, yes, that's my working theory."

"Hmm." Skye chewed her lip. "How about an ex-boyfriend? She was pretty up-front about sleeping around, and I heard her on the phone begging a friend to make some guy give her another chance."

"What was the friend's name?" Wally asked.

"Shoot! I don't remember." Skye shook her head. "Something cute and girly." She sighed. "I'll ask Riley and the other bridesmaids if they know the names of any of Belle's close friends."

"Good. Tomorrow, I'll have Martinez start calling all the people in the vic's cell phone directory."

"And whenever I get one of the guys in the wedding party alone, I'll see if he had a fling with Belle." Skye made a note, then asked, "So, anyone you talk to a likely suspect or have an alibi?"

"We still don't have a time of death, but we have narrowed it down a little." Wally flipped open his notepad and said, "Jesse Larson told Quirk that Belle was at the Brown Bag from seven to ten Saturday night."

Jesse was the owner of the Brown Bag, a combination liquor store, bar, and banquet hall located across the road from the motor court.

"Was she alone?"

"No. She was with some guy, but Larson didn't know him. The guy kept his ball cap and sunglasses on the whole time, so Larson could only describe him as big with tattoos."

"Maybe he's the ex-boyfriend," Skye said. "Was there anything else Jesse noticed about him?"

"No. They sat in a dark corner, and she was the one who got their drinks from the bar."

"Belle bragged about never sleeping alone, but I just can't picture her hooking up with a local, and there hasn't been a hint of it in the town rumor mill." Skye nibbled her thumbnail. "I can't even think of anyone to question about it."

"Larson said it was the first time she'd been in the bar. He only knew her because earlier in the month she'd rented the banquet hall for the bridal party's dance lessons."

"Did they leave together?"

"Larson wasn't sure," Wally answered. "And we haven't been able to locate anyone who saw her alive after that."

"So that puts TOD at somewhere between ten p.m. Saturday and shortly before eight a.m.

Sunday." Skye murmured to herself. "Does that eliminate any suspects?"

"Any of the bridal party would have had the opportunity to get to Belle after the attendants' party. Even the ones staying in Chicago could have stopped by on their way to the hotel or returned to Scumble River later." Wally shook his head. "The groom claimed he only knew Belle as an employee, and when they were together, they mostly talked about the wedding."

"I wonder if Nick was ever alone with Belle, or if Riley was always present." Skye tapped her fingers on her legal pad. "Belle was a gorgeous young woman, and Nick clearly likes them young and beautiful. Or as my mom would put it—he's a cradle robber."

"Hey. Give the guy a break," Wally teased. "Maybe he just prefers generationally different relationships."

"Tell that to May." Skye winked. "She's upset about the few years between us; Nick is nearly twenty years older than Riley."

Wally cringed and changed the subject. "Can you casually find out from your cousin if Nick and Belle spent any time together without her? It seems like just the kind of topic that would be perfect for a little girl talk."

"I'll add that to my list." Skye chewed the top of her pen. "Okay, how about the twins? Any motive for them?"

"Not that I can come up with. They don't gain anything by her death, and since they've been away at college, they've had the least contact with her."

"True," Skye agreed. "But I get the feeling they aren't happy about this marriage. Maybe they thought killing Belle would stop the wedding."

"That's quite a stretch."

"Maybe." Skye looked up from her notes. "But they're weird, and I'm keeping an eye on them."

"How about Nick's parents? You talked to them?"

"Actually, it's his dad and his stepmother," Skye pointed out. "His mother isn't coming. She's in some ashram or commune or something and can't leave. Anyway, Mr. and Mrs. Jordan said they had never met Belle. They seemed fairly uninterested in the whole affair and only flew in so early to take their six-year-old son to the Museum of Science and Industry, Shedd Aquarium, and Adler Planetarium."

"I take it this Mrs. Jordan is quite a bit younger than Nick's mother?"

"Like father, like son." Skye flipped through the pages of her legal pad. "Nick is forty-five, his dad is sixty-eight, and his stepmother, Natasha, is thirty-six."

"Hmm." Wally jotted that information down.

"Did Uncle Charlie see anything?"

"No." Wally grinned. "He was out with a lady

friend and stayed overnight at her house. He was just getting back when he heard Iris scream."

"I see." Although he'd never married, Skye's godfather had a reputation as quite a Casanova, so it was no shock to hear he had been otherwise occupied on a Saturday night.

"How about the people you interviewed?"

"The only thing interesting was from Tabitha. She mentioned hearing that a mother of the bride from one of Belle's previous jobs went after Belle with a cake knife after finding her in flagrante delicto with the woman's husband. Tabitha didn't know the name, but you might want to check that out."

"I'll ask the vic's secretary when I call her tomorrow." Wally wrote briefly on his pad of paper. "But someone would really have to be crazy to travel all the way from California to kill her here. That's why I'm not too hot on the ex-boyfriend angle."

"You're probably right," Skye agreed. "What did Riley, Anita, and Aunt Dora have to say?"

He summed up his interviews with the trio, concluding, "I'm certain that none of them killed Belle. Now, if she had screwed up the wedding and been murdered afterward, they'd be my prime suspects."

"Great." Skye threw a pillow at him. "And you convinced me to take over for her. You know, there are easier ways to get rid of me than having my cousin kill me for ruining her wedding."

Wally wrinkled his brow in mock concern. "I guess I'll have to be your bodyguard." He gave her a smoldering look. "I sure wouldn't want anything to happen to it."

"Thanks. Good to know what part of me you're interested in." Skye snickered, then got back to business. "There certainly didn't seem to be any love lost between Belle and the vendors I heard her dealing with this past month."

"Yeah. They're first on my list to talk to tomorrow."

"Shall we do that together?" Skye asked. "I have to speak to them anyway now that I'm in charge."

"Good idea." His voice deepened. "Sweetheart, you did a great job today." He put his hands on her waist and drew her to him. "You did everything right."

"Really?" Skye curled a piece of her hair around her finger. "That's so good to hear." She felt herself start to relax for the first time since finding Belle dead.

"Really." Wally's lips brushed hers as he spoke. "The second smartest thing I ever did was to hire you as a police consultant."

Although she remembered him using that line before, she went along with him and asked, "What was the first smartest thing you ever did?"

He tightened his arms around her. "Propose to you."

Skye stiffened. His previous answer had been

"I'll tell you later," which had led to a night of pleasure. Now she was afraid he would demand an answer to his proposal.

To distract him, she traced a hand down his chest; when she reached the waistband of his jeans, she popped open the button and said, "Let's forget about the murder until morning."

"Well, okay. But only if you can you think of something for us to do to keep from getting bored until then."

She slowly pulled down the zipper on his fly. "Does this give you any ideas?"

CHAPTER 7

Two Birds with One Stone

Skye struggled to wake up. She patted the mattress next to her. It was empty, and she felt a twinge of disappointment. Then the enticing aroma of freshly brewed coffee soothed her and she managed to pry open her eyes.

Sunlight poured through the gap in the drapes, and she checked the clock on the nightstand. *Crap!* It was ten after nine. Had Wally already left for work? And if so, how in the heck would she get to her car? She really didn't relish the idea of a walking half a mile to the motor court in high heels.

As tempting as it was to lie back down and go to

sleep, visions of the wedding's to-do list danced in her head, and she reluctantly swung her legs over the side of the bed. After a shower, she dressed in yesterday's outfit, wrinkling her nose at the stale odor. Wally was right. It was definitely time to bring over a change of clothes and fresh under-wear, not to mention a pair of tennis shoes.

In the kitchen, she found a note and a set of keys on the table.

Sugar,

Sorry to leave you, but I knew it was going to be another long day for us and thought you needed your sleep. Here are the keys to the Thunderbird. I had a hunch you wouldn't want to call me at the station for a ride since your mom's working days this week. Once you're ready, come over to the PD and we'll start tracking down the vendors.

Love you,
Wally

Skye appreciated the heads-up that her mother was on duty. May, a police dispatcher, usually took the afternoon shift. Skye loved her mom, but it was best to be prepared when dealing with her. Especially since she'd be ticked off that Skye hadn't called her yesterday to fill her in on all the gory details of the murder.

At least Skye's best friend, Trixie Frayne, was

out of town, escorting a group of high school students through Europe for the month. If Trixie had been home, she'd also have wanted a full update.

Skye thought of the postcard she'd received Saturday from Trixie—a picture of the Eiffel Tower. Maybe Skye and Wally could go to Paris on their honeymoon. Except she still wasn't sure she should marry him. There were so many aspects to consider. Did he want kids? Did she? And what about his father's wealth? If Wally was his heir, that kind of money could change everything. What if he decided to take over the family business? Was she willing to move to Texas with him?

Then there was May's disapproval of Wally, which was why calling for a ride after spending the night with him would be a bad idea on so many levels. Not that Skye's mother wasn't fully aware she and Wally were sleeping together. But May practiced the theory of better living through denial, and Skye wasn't ready to challenge her mother's version of reality.

Skye shook her head; she didn't have time to deal with making a major life decision right now. Instead, after a quick stop at home to change clothes and feed Bingo, she hurried to the PD.

As Skye went inside, she braced herself for her mom's recriminations, but May greeted her at the door and enveloped her in a bear hug. "You're such a good girl."

"I am?" Skye waited for the other shoe to drop.

"Of course." May kissed her cheek and stepped back. "To volunteer to help your cousin like that. I know it'll be a lot of work, but the whole family will lend a hand."

Oh, boy! Skye wasn't sure she wanted the family's assistance, but no way was she telling her mother that. "Uh, that's swell." Something about May's mood made Skye talk as if she were the star of a nineteen-fifties sitcom. "I'll let you know what I need once I figure things out." She certainly wasn't about to burn any bridges. Not when she might need them for a fast getaway.

"What are you doing here?" May asked as she went back to her place behind the counter.

"Wally and I are going to talk to the wedding vendors together since we both need to speak to them."

A crease formed between May's eyes, and she said, "I hope you won't let the investigation get in the way of what's really important."

"The murder isn't important?"

"That woman was a stranger," May snapped. "A Californian." She dismissed Belle as if she were a guest who had worn out her welcome.

"So is the bride and most of the wedding party."

"This is your cousin's big day." As usual, May disregarded any facts that didn't fit her view of the world. "Riley's counting on you. You can't let her down."

Skye understood her brief visit to the land of

Good Daughter was over, and she chose her words carefully. "Of course, the wedding is my first priority, but I also have a commitment to the police department. I can't ignore that obligation."

"You're sleeping with the chief," May said in a voice that could have flash frozen ice cream. "I doubt he'll sue you for breach of contract."

"Uh, sure." Skye nodded. The blinders regarding Skye and Wally's relationship came off when it was convenient for May, but Skye was not about to point that out. "Right." Edging past her mother, she said, "Gotta go."

Without waiting for a response, Skye hurried up the stairs to Wally's office. She found him on the phone and kissed him on the cheek before settling into the visitor's chair.

She listened as he finished up his conversation. "So the ME can't pinpoint time of death either? Damn! Did he find anything we can use? Really? He can? Great. Okay. Let me know if there's anything else. Bye."

"I take it that was Simon?" Skye asked when Wally hung up the receiver.

"Yeah. As you heard, no TOD. But if we find the weapon used to knock Belle out, the ME thinks he can match it to the bruise on her temple."

"So, all we need to do is locate the weapon. Any idea what it might be?"

"No. All Reid could tell me is that it was round, with some kind of embellishment on the surface.

Maybe shaped like one of those oversize waffle cones."

"Hmm." Skye tried to think if she had seen anything like that. "A wine bottle? But the glass would be smooth, not patterned."

"Just keep an eye out when you go through the supplies. The crime techs searched the area, but it would be easy to miss something with all that wedding stuff piled everywhere." Wally pulled a legal pad and a pen out of his top drawer. "And speaking of supplies, run down the list of vendors for me."

"There are other minor vendors involved, not to mention the owners of the venues the various events are being held at, but"—Skye flipped open Belle's binder and read—"the principle ones are . . ." She ran through the list, ending with, "mixologist, ice sculptor, DJ, band, string ensemble, trumpeter, theatrical company, hairstylist, makeup artist, pyrotechnician, butterfly wrangler, cigar roller, linen consultant, engravers, table décor specialist, light tech, lounge furniture rental company, transportation specialist, and photo booth operator."

"You're kidding." Wally whistled. "No three-ring circus or herd of unicorns?"

"Shh!" Skye held a finger to her lips. "Don't give them any ideas."

"When you said million-dollar wedding, I thought you were exaggerating."

"I'm not sure of the exact price. I doubt anyone knows at this point, but I'm betting it will be close to seven figures." Skye shook her head. "Can you imagine spending that kind of money on one day?"

"Is it mostly Riley's idea?"

Skye nodded. "But Nick's picking up the tab."

"Then I understand." Wally leaned toward her. "If that's the kind of wedding you wanted, I'd sure as heck try and get it for you."

Skye felt her throat close. "Thank you." Why was she hesitating? She'd never find anyone as wonderful as Wally. "Uh. That's really sweet of you." Not knowing what else to say, she changed the subject. "So what's the plan for today?"

"I had no idea there were so many vendors involved." Wally laced his fingers behind his head and gazed at the ceiling. "I guess we'll have to prioritize. Besides the floral designer, were any of them in Scumble River Saturday?"

"Yes." Skye scrunched her face, trying to remember. "Belle was meeting with the tent-and-rental guy to show him the venue, and with the linen consultant, and the photographer and the DJ were driving in from Chicago to firm up the picture and song lists."

"Are any of these people local?"

"No." Skye snickered. "Belle thought any business south of I-355 was run by yokels. Most of the vendors she hired are from Chicago or the burbs, and several were flying in from California."

Skye consulted the binder, flipping to the contact information page. "Of the ones Belle met with yesterday, the tent-and-rental company is located in LaGrange; the rest are in the city."

"This is going to take a lot longer than I thought." Wally sounded resigned. "What was on Belle's agenda for today?"

"The groom and his men have an appointment in Chicago at noon to try on their tuxedos, and in the afternoon they have reservations to play golf at Cog Hill in Lemont. The women's fitting is at four, also in the city. Prior to that, they are shopping at Water Tower Place." Skye bit her thumbnail. "Belle was scheduled to be at both fittings, but I can skip the guys and meet the girls at the dress shop."

"I'm surprised that someone as wealthy as Nick doesn't have his own tux." Wally teased, "A rental tux—how uncouth."

"He does have his own, as do all his groomsmen, but, sadly, they don't match."

"What's not to match on a black tux?" Wally's eyebrows drew together.

"They all have different buttons." Skye smirked. "And who said anything about renting? Nick is buying them for his men."

"Well, damn." Wally shook his head. "And I thought my father's Texas friends were into excess. Obviously, California takes that prize."

Skye was silent. She'd quit trying to wrap her

mind around the amount being spent on the wedding. If she thought too long about what that money could do for people struggling to put food on the table, she'd be forced to smack someone.

"Okay, here's what we'll do." Wally interrupted her thoughts. "You call all the vendors who were in Scumble River on Saturday and explain you're the new wedding planner and I'm your assistant. Say we have to talk to them today."

Skye nodded.

"Don't tell them Belle's dead, just that you're taking over," Wally instructed. "Later, I'll have Quirk formally interview them and inform them that Belle was murdered."

"So that we can see how their stories differ and how they react, right?" Skye guessed.

"Right." Wally nodded. "Schedule the first appointment with that company in LaGrange, then the ones in the city."

"Okay." Skye was scribbling notes as he talked.

"If you can't fit them all in before you're supposed to try on your dress, I'll drop you off and interview the rest while you're at the store. I'll get my officers to start questioning the other vendors to see if any of them can account for their time from ten Saturday night until eight Sunday morning."

"Sounds good." Skye reached for the phone. "Just let me call Riley first and let her know that I'm meeting the group at the shop."

• • •

It was nearly noon by the time Skye and Wally pulled into the tent-and-rental company's parking lot, and the showroom was empty when they walked through the double glass doors. A few seconds later a huge man with acne-scarred skin and a crew cut lumbered out of an office. He wore jeans and a short-sleeved denim shirt with the company name and logo stitched on the pocket. His muscular arms were decorated with tattoos.

As he crossed the showroom Skye clutched Wally's biceps and whispered, "Do you think he was the guy with Belle at the Brown Bag Saturday night?"

Before Wally could answer, the man joined them. He held out his hand. "You must be Ms. Denison; I'm Brian Cowden, the crew leader in charge of your event."

Skye nodded and introduced Wally as her assistant. Although she knew that the police were allowed to lie to suspects, she felt a tiny niggle of guilt.

Brian gestured for them to be seated at a table surrounded by four chairs. "What can I do for you, Ms. Denison?"

"As I said on the phone, I've just taken over as the new coordinator for the Erickson-Jordan wedding." Skye took out her pad. "Since my predecessor left unexpectedly, I need to get up to speed on what's been ordered and the timeline for the job."

"Sure thing." The crew leader turned one of the empty chairs around, straddled it, and rested his beefy forearms on the back. "Too bad Ms. Canfield didn't quit before Saturday. I spent three hours down in Scumble River going over every detail with her."

"That is a shame." Skye cheered inwardly; he had given her the perfect opening. "But at least she took you for drinks at the Brown Bag afterward."

"Where did you get that idea?" The crew leader scowled. "We were at the country club the whole time. It was strictly business between us."

"Of course it was, Mr. Cowden," Skye agreed, forcing a sincere tone. "I didn't mean to imply otherwise. It's just that three hours is a long time, and I thought you might have wanted some refreshment before your long drive home. But then, Belle wasn't exactly concerned with her employees' well-being, was she?"

"Call me Brian." His dark eyes were cautious. "She was focused on things being perfect, but we pride ourselves on providing exactly what the client wants, so that wasn't a problem."

"And I'm Skye." Her friendly smile didn't reveal her thoughts. "I see from Belle's notes that you're putting up a twenty-two-foot gabled tent and a Plexiglas dance floor over the country club's pool." This guy wasn't straying from the party line. She hoped going over the details would lull him into a false sense of security. "When will those be installed?"

"I understand the bride wanted them done in time for the rehearsal, so we'll begin setting up tomorrow."

"Good. This is the first wedding of this size I've been in charge of, and the couple is very particular." Skye allowed a vulnerable note to enter her voice. She often found that by letting people underestimate her, she came out ahead in the long run. "You're also supplying us with chairs and tables, correct?"

"That's right." Brian's posture became slightly less rigid. "Five hundred Chaivari chairs, fifty large round tables for the dining room, and twenty-five high-tops for the outside cocktail party, which will be delivered Friday. The venue is supplying the miscellaneous tables for gifts, place cards, et cetera, and the chairs for the ceremony, but we're providing the two special spandex-covered illuminated tables for the wedding and groom's cakes."

"And you're aware that the bride wants a sweetheart table in the center of the tent rather than a head table?"

"Yes."

"How about the lighting?" Skye checked her list. "I understand it's really important, and, at this price, it must be amazing."

"Our lighting tech is a genius," Brian bragged. "He can do anything. He's got the chandeliers,

LEDs, and cans ready to go. Miss Canfield approved it all Saturday, so he'll be doing his part on Thursday and Friday."

"Did he meet with Belle when she agreed to his plans?"

"No." Brian explained, "I'm the only one from the company that dealt with her. She said she preferred one person to blame if there was a problem." He shot Skye a quizzical look. "Do you want to talk to him?"

"No. Let's continue on the way Belle started." Talking to the lighting guy would only expose her ignorance. "This must be a huge contract for you," she probed, glancing at Wally, who nodded slightly, indicating his approval with her line of questioning.

"One of our biggest ever. This event will put us in the black for the rest of the year." Brian grinned. "Which is why, whatever Miss Canfield wanted, we were happy to supply."

"Oh." Skye pretended to make notes. "Did she ask for anything out of the ordinary?"

Brian glanced at Wally. "Could you give us a few minutes alone?"

Wally nodded, got up, and walked toward a display of various-size lattice arches. Skye noticed that he slipped his cell phone from his pocket, held it toward Brian for a moment, then turned his back on them.

Brian eyed Skye calculatingly. "I assume our

deal with Ms. Canfield will remain the same with you."

"Uh." Skye had no idea what he meant. "Yes." Her voice was uncertain. "I hope so."

"So the amount stays the same?"

"It had better." Skye tensed, figured he was testing her to see if he could charge her more. "I have the list right here. Tent and floor are a hundred and twenty thousand, chairs and tables are ten, and lights thirty, with late penalties if you don't meet your deadlines." She had read all the vendor agreements earlier.

"Right. For a total of one sixty. That makes your cut eight thousand."

"My cut?" Skye blurted out before she could stop herself. It took her a moment to pull herself together, then she asked as coolly as she could, "Is that what Belle was getting?"

"Yes. Five percent." Brian wiped his head with a red handkerchief. "I told her, and I'm telling you. That's the best we can do."

"That seems like a fair amount," Skye reassured him. "Did Belle ask for more?"

"She originally asked for ten, and maybe that's what she gets in L.A., but here in Illinois we don't usually have to pay commissions to coordinators, so five is our limit."

"Don't worry about it." Skye hid her skeptical reaction. Chicago had invented machine politics and the art of payola, but if Brian wanted to blame

California for Belle's lack of ethics, she wasn't about to argue. "I don't do business like that, so you don't owe me a thing. If you get it all installed on time and it's perfect, that's enough for me."

CHAPTER 8

Picture Imperfect

"Can you believe she was demanding a kick-back?" Skye asked Wally once they were back in his Thunderbird, driving toward the city for their one-thirty appointment with the photographer. She had repeated the conversation he had missed. "Is that even legal?"

"More to the point, was she demanding it from all the vendors, and did one get angry enough to kill her?" Wally asked.

"Good question." Skye wrinkled her brow. "Do you think Brian was the tattooed guy at the Brown Bag even though he denies being there?" Skye asked.

"We can't rule him out, but there are a lot of big, tattooed guys in Stanley County." Wally skillfully merged into the heavy I-55 traffic. "I snapped a picture of him with my cell phone and sent it to Quirk to show Larson, but since he didn't see the guy's face, I doubt he'll be able to identify him. It's too bad he can't describe the tattoos, but he said he never got a close look."

"Crap!" Skye pursed her lips. "But Brian *is* a suspect?"

"Uh-huh. I told Quirk to bring him in later this afternoon, and I'd question him when we get back."

"You don't want me there, right?"

"Right." Wally nodded. "I'll tell him I forced you to bring me along to your meeting with him. We don't want him to know that you're part of the investigation."

"That's what I thought." Skye gripped the dashboard as a semi cut in front of them with only inches of clearance to spare. "Back to the commission Belle was demanding. How are we going to get the other vendors to admit she was shaking them down for a cut of their profits?"

"Same way you got Cowden to tell you."

"You mean dumb luck?"

"No. I mean good interrogation technique." Keeping his eyes on the road, Wally reached over and squeezed Skye's hand. "Do exactly what you did with Cowden. Open the door and let the suspect walk through it."

Parking was a nightmare, and it was one thirty-five when they entered Yves Galois's studio. Skye had hoped to duck into a restroom to comb her hair and put on some lipstick, but there was no time. When the photographer's lip curled as he inspected her, she wished she had taken a few minutes to freshen up regardless of the delay.

He sat behind an imposing Italian Renaissance Revival desk, and not bothering to stand, he snapped, "The tardy Mademoiselle Denison, I presume."

"Yes." Skye stepped toward him and offered her hand. "I'm sorry we're late. I always forget how much time it takes to park in the city." She gestured to Wally. "This is my assistant, Walter."

Yves appeared more impressed with Wally than he had been with Skye. "Have you ever modeled?" Wally shook his head, but the photographer persisted, "You have a rugged *Brokeback Mountain* look that's very in right now."

"I've never been interested." Wally stuck his hands in the pockets of his black jeans. "And still am not."

Skye bit back a giggle as she watched Wally's ears turn red. Taking pity on him, she pointed to the corner of the desk where calla lilies and white roses were arranged in a beautiful glass vase, and said, "Wow. That's a gorgeous piece."

"Thank you. It's an original Moser." Yves's smile was smug.

Skye was impressed. She had learned about antiques and collectables a few years ago when she'd coordinated the Route 66 Hundred Mile Yard Sale, and she knew a vase by that artist didn't come cheap.

"Please sit down." Yves gestured impatiently to the visitors' chairs. "I only have a few minutes until my next client." Skye and Wally sat as the photographer continued, "I'm not clear why we had to meet today. It's too late to change anything. Belle and I agreed on the photo list Saturday. All the locations, poses, and groups have been decided."

"As I told you on the phone, Belle is no longer the wedding coordinator for this event. I am." Skye ignored his pout. "And as such, I need to make sure everything is proceeding as it should. I couldn't find the list you mentioned. Did Belle have one?"

"Yes." He fingered his thin black mustache. "She insisted on making a copy right then and there. Most planners allow me to mail it to them."

"Oh." Skye waited, and when he remained seated and silent, she said, "Could you give me the list?"

"I suppose." He reluctantly stood, picked up a folder from his desktop, and walked into a back room. He returned in a couple of minutes and handed her a sheaf of papers. "Try not to lose this one."

"*I* didn't lose the last one," Skye corrected him. "Belle's notes indicate that you'll be present for the bachelor and bachelorette parties, the evening of the rehearsal, and from ten a.m. on the day of the wedding until the last guest leaves."

"Yes, damn it." Yves's answer was clipped. "How many times must I go over this?" Irritation was starting to crack his smooth facade. "I will make the endless drive to the godforsaken town this garish affair is being held in three more times, I will take pictures of drunken revelry at the parties, and I will remain until the last bumpkin has gone back to the barn on Saturday."

"It sounds as if you aren't happy with the arrangements." Skye stated the obvious. "Why did you agree to them?"

He rubbed his thumb and forefinger together. "Because of all that lovely, lovely cash, of course."

"Yes, I see you're being paid a tidy sum." Skye paused, hoping he would mention Belle's cut. When he didn't, she said, "Still, I know you have expenses. It's not as if you'll take home the whole amount, so why agree to something you aren't happy about?"

"So I'm not wildly enthusiastic. Belle made me see that it was worth my while." Yves's tall, lean body tightened. "A gig's a gig. All weddings are a pain in the derrière." His smile was forced. "I signed the damn contract, didn't I?" His long, thin fingers drummed on the chair arm. "What more do you want from me, blood?"

"I'll pass on that." Skye eyed him thoughtfully; he did look a little like a vampire.

Yves stood and Skye realized she was running out of time but couldn't think of a smooth way to make him admit he was giving Belle a kickback.

So she went for the obvious. "I take it that the five percent you agreed on with Belle still stands with me?"

"Of course."

Bingo.

Yves herded Skye toward the door. "Is that why you brought your muscle?" He nodded toward Wally, who had taken Skye's arm.

"Of course not." Skye backpedaled quickly as the photographer's hand reached for the knob. Was there anything else she should ask? She glanced at Wally, who shrugged.

"So, I'll see you Thursday at the bachelor and bachelorette parties," Skye said, stalling. "Do you know the time?"

"Yes." Yves's hand was on the small of her back, and he firmly propelled her over the threshold. "Seven sharp."

She had time for just one more question. "Were you surprised when Belle asked for a commission on your fee?"

"No." Yves's tone was even, but his eyes indicated his irritation. "Nothing surprises me. The wedding business is murder."

"Yves didn't agree to shoot the wedding for the money," Skye announced as she put on her seat belt. "The job doesn't mean the same thing to him as it does to the tent-and-rental company."

Wally handed his parking receipt and a twenty

to the man in the booth, then asked, "What makes you say that?"

"His studio is on the Gold Coast, he advertises himself as a VIP photographer whose clients include the city's glitterati, and his desk alone is worth more than all the furniture in my entire house. Thirty-two thousand is a lot of money, but I'm sure he could make just as much photographing an event in Chicago. Especially since June is the high season for weddings."

"So why did he take the job?" Wally asked as he accepted his change—six whole dollars.

"That's what we need to find out." Skye flipped down the visor and combed her fingers through her curls. In her hurry this morning, she'd allowed her hair to dry without straightening it. "I'm guessing from what he said that Belle had something on him." She applied pale peach lip gloss. "She was extremely good at finding out what motivated people and using that knowledge to her advantage. As she did with Riley, when she threatened to move the wedding to California if she didn't produce an assistant for her in Scumble River."

"Interesting theory." Wally pulled out of the garage, then glanced over to Skye. "What did she have on you?"

"The usual." Skye's cheeks reddened. "Family loyalty and Catholic guilt."

Since the photographer had practically thrown them out of his studio, they were a bit early for their meeting with the linen consultant. Wally had barely entered the woman's office when she marched over to him, not stopping until she was nearly stepping on his toes, and demanded, "What are you doing here?" A petulant expression marred her heavily made-up face and produced a querulous line between her overplucked eyebrows. "I told you I'd call you when I was finished."

Skye stepped from behind Wally and said, "Hello, I'm Skye Denison. If you're Angela Beckman, I believe we have an appointment."

"Oh, I didn't see you there. Yes, I'm she." The linen consultant put a hand to her chest. Turning to Wally, she explained, "I thought you were someone else." She blew out a puff of exasperation at Skye. "You're not supposed to be here for fifteen minutes."

Angela wore a short black skirt and a lace spandex empire-waist top. A pink bow rested below the vee of her considerable cleavage. The outfit looked expensive but too young for the fiftysomething-year-old woman.

Skye gestured to Wally. "This is my assistant, Walter. Would you like us to wait somewhere until you're ready?"

"No." Angela sank stiffly into a chair and motioned Skye and Wally to sit on the matching settee. "Since I had to postpone my plans when you called and insisted on seeing me, I'd prefer to get this over with as quickly as possible."

"Who were you expecting?"

"Excuse me?" Angela's expression was abruptly guarded. "How is that your business?"

"Just curious." Darn. Skye had hoped the woman would let something slip.

"That can be a career-limiting trait in this business."

"I'm sure you're right." Skye struggled to regain control of the conversation. "Anyway, as I explained on the phone, I'm the new bridal planner for the Jordan-Erickson wedding." She paused. It was odd that not one of the businesspeople she'd talked to had asked what had happened to Belle. "And as you may recall, I'm meeting with all the vendors to bring myself up to speed."

"Yes. I'm not so ancient that I can't remember a conversation that took place less than four hours ago."

"Of course not." Skye wondered why the linen consultant was so prickly. "So, where are we with the linens?"

"I just went over this with Belle Saturday afternoon," Angela complained. "Can't you get the information you need from her or her notes?"

"I prefer to start fresh and make sure we're on the same page."

"Fine." The woman glanced nervously at the door. "The bride has selected gold satin tablecloths. They are finished and ready to be transported."

"Then you have them in your possession?"

"I just said I did." Angela smoothed a wrinkle near her eyelid with her pinky. "You seem to think that because I'm a few years older than you, I'm not in full possession of my faculties."

Skye ignored the woman's touchiness and asked, "How about the pink lace overlays?"

"They're coming today. They had to be hand beaded to match the design on the bride's train."

"What else has arrived?"

"The napkins, but I'm still waiting on the napkin treatments." At Skye's blank look, Angela explained, "The pink lace bows that the spray of miniature orchids will be tucked into."

"When do you expect them?" Skye felt a quaver of alarm shoot up her spine. "You realize that you have a failure-to-fulfill clause in your contract?"

"Of course I do." Angela blew out a puff of exasperation. "They had to be specially dyed to match the bridesmaids' dresses, which took a bit longer than planned. But they'll be here tomorrow or the next day. Guaranteed."

"Good." Skye studied her notes. This might be an interrogation, but she still had to make sure everything was ready for the wedding. "How about the chair covers and sashes?"

"We couldn't get five hundred of the moiré fabric the bride wanted." Angela's tone was wary. "But Belle approved the chiffon substitution."

"Did Riley agree?"

"I assume so." Angela's expression was hard to read. "I have Belle's signature, so if the bride is unhappy, that's your problem, not mine."

"May I see it, please?" Skye had worked in public education too long to take anyone's word for anything. No "the dog ate my homework" excuses for her.

Angela shook her head in disgust. "I'll get the file."

When linen consultant left the room, Skye whispered to Wally, "What do you think?"

"Try to draw this out. I'd like to find out who she thought I was when we first came in."

"Okay." Skye wasn't sure how to stall. "But I have to be at the dress shop by four."

"Don't worry." Angela's aqua blue eyes were sharp as she returned with the paper Skye had requested. "We'll be done long before then."

Yikes! How much had Angela overheard? Skye recovered. "I was talking about tomorrow. We have plenty of time today."

Angela tucked a strand of long blond hair behind her ear. "But I don't."

Skye studied the letter of agreement. "I see Belle did consent to the substitution." She looked up. "Have the chair covers arrived?"

"Yes. They got here a couple of days ago, and the rhinestone clips for the sashes came yesterday."

"Great. I'd like to take a look at them and the tablecloths, since you have them both."

Angela opened her mouth to object, then gave an irritated shrug. "Back here."

Skye took as long as possible examining the supplies, but finally she had to finish. She had less than half an hour to get to the dress shop.

As she and Wally walked to the door, she said to Angela, "I noticed the linens are costing us forty-three thousand and your fee is twelve thousand, so I can expect my check to be two thousand seven hundred and fifty, correct?"

"I was hoping that deal was off now that Belle is out of the picture." Angela's lips formed a bitter line.

Skye shrugged. "Well, if everything is perfect, it's possible that I might waive my commission."

Angela's expression was skeptical as she looked Skye in the eye. "Anything is possible if you don't know what you're talking about."

Huh? Skye glanced at Wally to see whether he understood Angela's parting shot, but he appeared equally confused. Maybe she meant that perfection was impossible to achieve.

Skye nervously checked her watch as Wally drove her to the dress shop. Riley would have a cow if she was late, and, worse, Anita would be on the phone complaining to May before Skye could say a word. Too bad they didn't have Wally's police car. They could really use the lights and siren about now.

While they were stopped at a red light, Wally asked, "What's your impression of Angela Beckman?"

"As a psychologist, I'd say she has age issues." Skye wrinkled her nose. "Which is not unusual in our youth-oriented society."

"I noticed a couple references to her not being *that* old. Anything else you picked up on?"

"The outfit she was wearing was too young for me, let alone someone twenty years older than I am. And that Alice in Wonderland hairstyle . . ."

"It did seem like something you'd see on a teenager, but, hey, I don't keep up with the latest hairdos." The signal turned green and Wally put the Thunderbird into gear. "Do you think that means anything?"

Skye considered the question. "This is purely a guess, but the wedding industry deals primarily with twenty- to thirty-something brides."

"And?"

"And according to the clippings in Belle's file, Angela has been the leading linen consultant in Chicago for a long time, but she's gotten a lot less press over the past year or so." She tapped her chin with her index finger. "Maybe her ideas have gotten out of date."

"Yeah. Everyone's always looking for the next big thing," Wally agreed.

"But working a platinum wedding like Riley's could put her back on top."

"Which means Belle could make or break her career."

Skye gasped as a pedestrian darted in front of the car, then, when she could speak again, said, "What I'm confused about is that it appears Belle was shaking down all the vendors. If her father's so wealthy, why would she need to do that? In fact, why would she even be working?"

"Maybe she wants to be independent and earn her own living." Wally slowed as brake lights flashed in front of them. "You know, show she's not just another spoiled rich kid."

"Or, and this fits better with her personality, she wants to be famous in her own right. Be the celebrity wedding planner she claimed to be." Skye recalled Belle's jealousy of Paris Hilton. "But she still wants to live in the style to which she has grown accustomed."

"If I ever get to talk to her parents, I'll ask them." Wally double-parked in front of the dress store. "So, who do you think the linen lady mistook me for?"

"I wonder. She sure was nervous about whoever she was expecting." Skye shrugged. "Maybe it was Dr. Botox or someone bringing her the newest fountain-of-youth pill."

"Or the hit man she hired to off Belle coming to collect his fee." A horn blew and Wally said, "Call me when you're finished here and I'll come pick you up." They had agreed that he would tackle

113

the DJ on his own while Skye attended the dress fittings.

"Okay." She leaned over and kissed him on the cheek. "Good luck."

"You, too."

Skye watched the Thunderbird disappear into afternoon traffic, then reluctantly crossed the sidewalk and pulled open the door to the shop.

She'd barely stepped inside when Riley threw herself into Skye's arms and sobbed. "You've got to do something." The young woman's beautiful face was contorted, and streaks of mascara ran down her cheeks. "She isn't here and she's going to ruin everything."

CHAPTER 9

Dressing the Part

Skye guided her hysterical cousin through the deserted main showroom to a white velvet love seat in the rear of the salon. Once they were seated, she heard high-pitched voices coming from behind the back wall and guessed the other women were hiding from the furious bride.

"Natasha sent a message that she's not coming today," Riley howled, and collapsed next to Skye. "She says she found a dress in California she likes better, and she isn't wearing the one I picked, so there's no need to be here for the fitting."

Skye had already guessed that Riley's future stepmother-in-law was the cause of the problem, and putting her arm around the distraught blonde, she asked, "Does it really matter that she won't be dressed the way you want?"

"Yes!" Riley wailed, tears welling up again. "You don't know her. I'm sure she picked a gown that isn't in the color palette I've selected, and, no doubt, one that will put the spotlight on her instead of me."

"No one can outshine you." Skye dug in her tote bag, pushing aside a notebook, a canister of pepper spray, and her cell phone, until she found a packet of tissues. Handing one to Riley, she soothed, "We can't force her to wear the dress you chose, but we can make sure she's not in any of the pictures, except the ones of the family, and I can put her table at the reception out of the lighted area. Does that sound like a solution?"

"No." Riley blew her nose. "I have a better idea." The dewy young girl suddenly turned into a scheming vixen. "I want you to spill a glass of something hideous on her before the ceremony. Then we'll happen to have the original dress I chose available, and unless she wants to spend the day with a giant stain across her chest, she'll just have to wear it."

Skye opened her mouth to protest, but the look in her cousin's eye stopped her, and instead she said, "Fine." There was no way she was spilling a drink on Natasha. Skye could only hope that on the day of the wedding, Riley would be too preoccupied to notice. "Shouldn't we start our fittings now?"

"Right." Riley sniffed, and then nodded. "I won't let that awful woman ruin my day."

"Thatta girl." Skye paused. "By the way, since I'm new to the business, is it customary for the wedding consultant to meet with the groom by himself or only with the bride and groom as a couple?"

"Well, I don't know what's customary"—Riley stood, wiping away the last of her tears—"but my friends told me never to let Nick and Belle meet without me. Not that I would ever leave Nick alone with a gorgeous girl like Belle anyway. Though, if you want to talk to him without me, feel free." Apparently not realizing she had just insulted Skye, Riley took her cousin's hands and pulled her to her feet. "Now, let's go have some fun. I love trying on clothes, don't you?"

"Sure." Skye wrapped her arms around herself. "Who doesn't?" The store was freezing, which was good. Didn't objects contract in the cold? Maybe the low temperature would help her fit into her dress. She just prayed it wouldn't take butter and a miracle to get the zipper up.

"Wait until you see what I picked for you all to wear," Riley squealed. "It's fabulous."

Skye shuddered. Since her cousin's bridesmaids were from different geographical areas, and Riley had chosen the bridesmaids' dresses without them, she'd had the women phone in their measurements. So this was the first time anyone other than the bride would see her selection.

Undaunted by Skye's silence, Riley chattered on, "Madam Olga says these dresses are the hottest style this season, and they flatter any figure."

"And I bet we can use them again after the big day, right?" Skye had been in enough weddings to know all the platitudes that brides and dress-shop owners used to persuade the bridesmaids to pay big bucks for hideous ensembles.

"Why would you want to do that?" Riley blinked. "Everyone will have seen you in it already."

"Of course." Skye hid a smile. "How gauche of me."

Skye followed Riley, intent on getting through the fittings as fast as possible. When they entered the waiting area, Riley's mother and grandmother were seated on matching armchairs, while Tabitha and Paige shared a sofa. Hallie was curled up on a settee all by herself, looking miserable. Skye speculated that the girl had trouble functioning without her twin.

An elegant lady in her early sixties stepped forward and offered Skye her hand. "I am Madam Olga. You must be the missing maid of honor."

"Yes. Skye Denison." The older woman's skin was smooth and soft, but her grip was firm. "Sorry for the delay. Did Riley explain that I've taken over for Belle?"

"Yes," Madam Olga said after a moment. "Such a shame when someone so young passes away."

"Isn't it?" Skye wondered whether the salon owner knew that Belle had been murdered or had been told she died some other way. "We're all saddened by her untimely death."

After a moment's silence, Madam Olga clapped her hands together and a young woman appeared. "Patricia, please show these ladies to their fitting rooms." She gestured toward the row of doors lining a hallway behind her. "Your gowns are waiting for you. Patricia will help you into them."

"Yes, ma'am." Skye sent up a silent prayer of thanks. At least they each had their own rooms. She'd been afraid she would have to strip in front of the other bridesmaids.

Madam Olga indicated Anita and Dora. "I'll take care of these ladies personally."

"What about me?" Riley screwed up her face. "Who's going to help me?"

"My dear, after you've approved your wedding party's attire, we'll turn our full attention to you," Madam Olga responded in a regal tone. "Everyone assists the bride. Meanwhile, one of my staff will bring you some refreshments."

"Lovely." Riley sank down on one of the vacated chairs. "That's more like it."

Skye was shown into a ten-by-ten space containing a raised dais in front of a three-way mirror. The bridesmaid's dress hung from an elaborate gold hook on the wall, and she cringed as she examined it. It was very, very pink, the bodice consisted of two swathes of shirred silk that formed an X between the breasts, and the dress was completely backless.

Shit! Shit! Shit! How in the world was she going to wear it? Skye was amply endowed. There was no way she could go without a bra, and even a strapless one would show underneath this dress.

"You know"—Patricia stood in the doorway watching Skye's reaction—"it has built-in support."

Skye nearly sank to her knees in relief. "Really?" Now, if the dress just fit, she'd be a happy camper. She'd even be willing to overlook the fact that the enormous skirt's ruching resembled the inside of a casket lid.

"Yes." Patricia tilted her head. "We can also use double-sided tape to make sure you don't pop out at an awkward moment."

"Like there would ever be a good time to pop out," Skye muttered as she sat on the bench to take off her shoes.

Patricia snickered, then said, "This dress makes a real fashion statement."

"If I wanted to make a statement, I'd wear a sandwich board."

Hiding a smile with her hand, the sales assistant

closed the door after saying, "I'll be back in a moment to assist you."

Surprisingly, when the woman returned and zipped up the dress, it was actually a little too big. She tsked. "Did you add a couple of inches to your measurements when you phoned them in?"

"No." Skye's cheeks reddened. "Well, maybe a smidge. Just to be on the safe side."

"You girls never tell us the truth." Patricia tsked again. "Either you tell us the size you wish you were or add a little so it won't be tight."

"Sorry." Skye turned her head to see the back of the dress. "But it's fine."

"Fine is not good enough at Madam Olga's. We will take it in. Wait here while I send the seamstress to you."

"No, really." Skye tried to stop the departing saleswoman. "What if I gain weight?"

Patricia shot her a stern look. "Don't."

Once Skye was pinned and her appearance approved by Riley, she changed back into her regular clothes and sat in the waiting area with her cousin. A couple of minutes later, Tabitha and Paige joined them, followed by Hallie, who immediately pointed to her cell phone, mouthed the words *Excuse me,* and disappeared.

As they waited for Dora and Anita to finish, Riley popped a finger sandwich into her mouth and chewed reflectively. "I'm not sure I like the bridesmaid's dresses." She furrowed her brow, then took a sip of Perrier. "I suppose it's too late to change my mind."

"Yes," Skye squeaked, alarmed at the thought of trying to get four new gowns by Saturday.

"I guess you're right." Riley paused and turned to look at Tabitha and Paige. "Do either of you not like the dresses?"

Paige's lips parted, but Skye frantically shook her head, and the redhead closed her mouth.

"Soooo." Riley drew out the single syllable, indicating her annoyance. "Do you love them?"

"They're perfect for your Pink Fantasy Fairy Tale theme," Skye offered.

"Yes." Riley nodded, satisfied. "They are." She bit into a petit four. "Did you know that Belle tried to change them behind my back?"

"No. How did you find out?" Tabitha asked.

"'Cause I overheard her on the phone." Riley licked frosting off her fingers. "She was telling Madam Olga to say they were unavailable when she talked to me."

"Did you confront her?" Skye questioned. When Riley nodded, Skye asked, "What did she say?"

"At first she tried to deny it, but when I wouldn't back down, she claimed she just thought the other dresses I had been considering were better and wanted to make sure my wedding was perfect."

Paige had been silent while Riley talked, but suddenly she said, "She really was a conniving witch."

"I think that's because when she was running around being the Canfield heiress she always got her own way," Tabitha offered. "These past couple of years, actually working for a living and having to cater to rich brides, must have been tough for her."

"Maybe." Riley shrugged, clearly losing interest in the conversation.

Skye frowned. Why *had* Belle been working for a living? She and Wally had come up with some theories, but if Belle really didn't like her job, why didn't she go back to being a socialite? Skye would be interested to see what Wally found out when he checked on that. In the meantime, she needed to catch Madam Olga alone and see what the shop owner had to say about Belle's attempt to switch the bridesmaids' dresses. What was the real story behind that?

A voice interrupted Skye's thoughts. "Riley, Madam Olga is ready for you now."

Riley glared at the doorway. "Mom, why don't you have your dress on?" Anita was wearing her street clothes and wiping her forehead with a tissue. "You know I wanted to see you in it."

"Sorry, honey." She sank into a chair. "Don't worry, it looked fine, but I had a terrible hot flash and I didn't want to stain it with sweat, so I took it off."

"Poor Mom." Riley handed her mother a tumbler of ice water. "Anything I can do?"

"I'll be fine in a minute." Anita held the glass to her forehead.

"Where's Grandma?" Riley asked. "She didn't show me her outfit either."

Anita took a gulp of water, then answered, "Mom's not feeling too well. This outing was too much for her. She's resting in Madam Olga's private parlor and will be out a little later."

"Should I go check on her?" Riley wrinkled her brow. "Should she be alone?"

Skye marveled at the sudden appearance of the "nice Riley." Her cousin switched personalities faster than most women changed clothes. "I'll check on Dora," she offered.

"What a good idea, dear." Anita fanned herself. "That way Riley can try on her dress."

"Great." Skye was glad for an excuse to be alone for a moment. And maybe she'd be able to nab Madam Olga for a little chat.

"Don't take long," Riley ordered. "I want you all here for my grand entrance."

"I won't." Skye kept her face expressionless. "I wouldn't miss it for anything."

Skye and Riley went opposite ways in the hallway. Skye wasn't sure where Madam Olga's parlor was but figured it was away from the fitting areas. The first room she tried was obviously a work space. Racks of garment bags, a couple of sewing machines, and a large table took up most of the area.

She was about to close the door when a container of bright silk rectangles caught her attention. Why would the dress shop have a box of loose labels? The dresses should come with labels already sewn inside.

Glancing over her shoulder to make sure no one was around, Skye slipped inside. Next to the carton of labels, which all bore famous designer names, was a dress with its original label neatly removed and new one pinned in its place, ready to be sewn. Was Madam Olga selling counterfeit designer clothing? And if so, had Belle somehow been involved?

As Skye stepped out of the workroom, Madam Olga appeared at the end of the hallway. She quickly closed the space between her and Skye and said, "What were you doing in there? That room is off-limits to clients."

"Sorry." Skye struggled to maintain an innocent expression. "I was looking for Mrs. Erikson."

"I don't believe you. You didn't have to go inside the room to see she wasn't there." The older woman's mouth tightened. "You're a trouble-maker, just like your predecessor."

"Belle was a problem?" Skye quickly regrouped, recognizing this as a chance to question the dress-shop owner. "Speaking of her, why did she try to make Riley switch her choice of bridesmaids' dresses?"

"Pff. She was greedy." Madam Olga shook her

head in disgust. "There was a higher profit margin on the ones Riley decided against and thus Belle's commission would be bigger."

"Oh, so she was getting a cut from you?" Skye asked. "Is that usual?"

"It is not uncommon."

Skye decided to press her luck and ask about what she had seen in the workroom. "How about sewing designer labels into dresses. Is that a common practice, too?"

"Ah." Madam Olga smiled thinly. "You thought you saw something, but you saw nothing." She took Skye's elbow and steered her down the hall. "Mrs. Erikson is in here." As Madam Olga opened the door, she hissed, "Silly little girls should mind their own business." She released Skye, turned, and marched away.

After checking on Dora—the older woman insisted she'd be fine and adamantly refused to be taken home—Skye returned to the waiting area. Hallie was back, pacing in a tight circle. The others sat silently munching on refreshments.

"Has Riley come out yet?" Skye eyed the group thoughtfully. Did any of them know more about Belle than they were admitting?

"No. You're safe." Paige smiled reassuringly.

"Good." Skye plopped down on the sofa and reached for a cookie. "I didn't have time for lunch, and I'm starved."

"Hardly."

Hallie's voice surprised Skye. The girl hadn't said two words since she'd arrived. "Excuse me?" Was Hallie commenting on Skye's weight?

"You are not starved. You may be hungry, but no one here is starving. Not like those poor children in Haiti." Hallie's tone was accusatory. "You all disgust me. The money being spent on this stupid wedding could support a whole village over there for ten years."

"The money isn't yours to say how it should be spent," Paige snapped.

Hallie's shoulders sagged and Skye asked, "Have you spoken to your father about this?"

"He won't listen," Hallie sobbed. "He just says that he's worked hard and the poor people should too."

"That's his privilege." Skye got up and handed the girl a tissue from her purse. At this rate she should invest in Kleenex stock. "Everyone has to make their own decisions in life. If you want to give your money to the poor or volunteer your time in third world countries, that's your right. If your father doesn't see it your way, that's his. Maybe he supports a cause you don't know about."

Hallie features were pinched. "None of you understand." She was clearly not convinced.

"No. I'm sure we don't." Skye remembered her own view of the world when she was Hallie's age. She'd joined the Peace Corps, sure she could make a difference. And even though she was disillusioned by her failure to see much progress, she'd become a school psychologist for the same reason —because she was sure she could save the world. That hadn't worked out exactly as planned either, and now she worked on helping one person at a time. "Maybe you can explain it to Riley, and she could help you persuade your father to make a significant donation."

"I'd like that." Hallie's expression was odd. "But I doubt Riley would care."

"Hasn't she been nice to you?" Skye asked, wondering if Riley was the stereotypical evil stepmother.

"It's not that." Hallie shook her head. "Hale and I are nearly nonexistent to her, which is how she wants it. Either we're at college or Dad sends us on some trip to get us out of the way. It's just that she's a user, you know, just like that wedding planner of hers."

"Did you know Belle?"

Hallie twitched her shoulders, but before Skye could press her for an answer, Riley swept into the room, and everyone's attention focused on her.

The wedding dress she wore was breathtaking. The A-line gown was made of pearl-colored silk with jewel-encrusted straps whose beading extended downward and joined to form a vee under the bustline.

As if the wedding march were playing, Riley walked the length of the room, revealing the intricate organza flowers twining around the Swarovski-crystal monogram on her train. She slowly turned and struck a pose before saying, "Isn't it fabulous? It's a Badgley Mischka."

Skye wondered whether it was really made by the designer whose tag was sewn into it but decided not to open that can of worms. Better Riley was happy with a beautiful fake than demanding that Skye find her the genuine article less than a week before the wedding.

Anita, apparently recovered from her hot flash, piped up, "It cost twelve thousand dollars." She rose from her chair, walked over to Riley, and fingered the veil. "This is one of a kind. It's embroidered with real gold thread and cost two thousand all by itself."

Skye cringed, afraid of Hallie's reaction, but the girl only moaned softly and bit her lip.

Riley pulled the skirt up and stuck out her foot. "I'm not sure I like these."

They all stared silently at the high-heeled sandal the bride was brandishing. Everyone was plainly afraid to comment.

Finally, Skye asked, "Are they really important? Your dress completely covers them. No one will even see them."

"The right shoes can change your life," Riley declared and crossed her arms.

"You're kidding me!" Hallie blurted out. "You don't really believe that?"

The bride put her hands on her hips. "Look at Cinderella."

"But she's not real," Skye said gently.

"Neither is Riley," Hallie muttered.

Skye held her breath, waiting for her cousin to explode, but Madam Olga stepped forward and said, "I have several other wonderful pairs of shoes in your size. Why don't you go back to the dressing room and Patricia will get them for you."

"Do you have any Louboutins?" the blonde asked excitedly.

Skye didn't relax until Madam Olga nodded and guided Riley down the hall.

What seemed like hours later, Riley decided on a new pair of shoes and decreed that they could leave.

As they walked out of the salon, Hallie put a hand on Skye's arm, drawing her back a little from the others, and whispered, "I'd like to talk to you alone. Can I see you tonight?"

"Sure," Skye agreed. "I'll be at the motor court working until at least ten."

As she climbed into the Thunderbird beside Wally, Skye thought about Hallie's request. What did the girl need to discuss with her—alone?

CHAPTER 10

Off Center

"No! Oh, shit!" Frannie's scream made Skye jump, and she lost her footing on the slick porcelain of the motor court's bathtub.

Frannie Ryan had been one of Skye's students at Scumble River High School but now attended Joliet Junior College. Yesterday afternoon, after agreeing to be Riley's wedding planner, Skye had hired Frannie and her boyfriend, Justin Boward, as her assistants. They had started work a few hours before, when Skye had gotten back from Chicago.

"Help, Ms. D.!" Another shriek burst through the bathroom door just as Skye regained her balance.

This scream sounded more frantic. Skye grabbed the shower curtain, which instantly clung to her like syrup to a waffle. As she wrestled with the cheap plastic, an image of the murderer returning to the scene of the crime and attacking Frannie popped into her head.

Skye succeeded in peeling the curtain from body, but as she leaped out of the tub, she slipped on the linoleum floor and slid into the toilet. Furious at herself for leaving Frannie alone while Belle's murderer was still walking around free, she ignored the pain shooting from her shin down her leg and snatched a towel. What if the killer was intent on stopping Riley and Nick's wedding by getting rid of anyone who was working on the event?

Adrenaline pounding, Skye dashed into the cabin's main room and skidded to a stop in front of the girl, who was kneeling by an open carton, yelling at its contents.

Crap! This was getting old. How many times did she have to rush in to rescue someone who didn't need her help before she learned her lesson?

"Look at these." Frannie stood and held out a menu card topped with a pink tulle bow. "Just look at these." The girl was a little taller than average, and, like Skye, a lot curvier than was fashionable. "They all have Riley's name spelled wrong." Frannie dug through another bundle. "The programs are misprinted, too."

Skye stood dripping, clutching the towel to her breasts with one hand and holding the offending square of pasteboard with the other. Frannie was right: *Riley* was spelled *Riled.*

"Holy smokes!" Skye quipped. "That'll definitely rile the bride's temper."

Frannie joined in, "Yep, no way she's not getting riled up about that."

After they stopped giggling, Frannie said, "You're not dressed." She had apparently just noticed Skye's appearance. "And you're dripping on the carpet."

"Really?" Skye glared at the girl. "I guess that's

what happens when you're in the shower and someone screams for help as if they're being murdered."

"You were in the shower?"

"I told you I couldn't stand the stench any longer and needed to wash up."

Skye and Frannie had been sitting on the floor unpacking the latest UPS shipment when Frannie had dropped a carton full of perfume bottles meant for the bachelorette party's goody bags. She'd been able to roll out of the way, but Skye hadn't been as fortunate. A wave of fragrance washed over her like an incoming tide, drenching her T-shirt and bra. She smelled as if she had been marinated in rose cologne.

"Oh, yeah." Frannie held her nose with her fingers. "That stuff is nasty."

"Yes, it is." Skye turned to go back into the bathroom to get dressed, thankful that she always kept a change of clothes in her car. You never knew when a three-year-old would pee on your lap during a preschool screening, or an older student would vomit all over you during an evaluation. Not to mention the occasional lunchroom incident.

"Why do you think Riley picked it?"

"I have a feeling she chose it more for the color than the scent," Skye answered Frannie, then added over her shoulder before she closed the bathroom door, "Which is why I had you put the rest of it in the trash outside."

"Speaking of that," Frannie shouted through the thin plywood, "when are they going to empty that Dumpster? It's so jam-packed, I could barely squeeze in the carton, let alone close the lid."

"Garbage day is tomorrow, I think." Skye returned wearing a fresh pair of jeans and a T-shirt.

"Why's it so full?"

"Partly because of all the packing material we've been shoving into it. But also, all of the supplies Belle rejected are in there."

"You mean she threw away good stuff?" Frannie twisted a glossy brown lock around her finger, stared at it as if she'd never seen it before, then let it unwind. She had cut her nearly waist-length waves when she entered college, and her hair now hung in a straight curtain to the middle of her back. "Why?"

"She claimed the quality wasn't what she was promised." Skye pulled on socks and laced up her tennis shoes. "It's shocking how many companies would rather have you toss their merchandise than pay for return shipping." She pulled her wet curls back into a ponytail. "And it seemed that no one was willing to incur the wrath of Belle by refusing her demands."

"It sounds as if Belle was a pain."

"I thought so, but dealing with the bride today put Belle's behavior in a whole new light."

"Riley gave you a hard time?"

"Not me so much, but she expects perfection."

Skye thought about her cousin's behavior at the dress salon. "And she isn't afraid to cry—or to make other people cry—to get her own way."

Skye wrinkled her forehead. That reminded her; she'd forgotten to tell Wally about Madam Olga and the phony designer labels. His account of the DJ's interview had taken most of the drive from Chicago to Scumble River. And since they both had too much to do to have a leisurely dinner together, he'd dropped her at the motor court as soon as they got back to town.

"Tantrums never work for me." Frannie narrowed her brown eyes. "Why do they work for her?"

Skye hesitated, but Frannie wasn't her student anymore, and she *had* decided to treat the girl more like a friend than a responsibility, so she didn't try to soften what she had to say. "Sad as it is, between Riley's beauty and Nick's wealth, people behave a lot differently toward her than they do you or me."

"That's not fair."

"You're right," Skye agreed. "But that's reality."

"But it sucks."

"I agree with you." Skye shrugged. "But, for this week at least, Riley is the queen, and we're the drones." She handed Frannie paper and a pen. "Now, make a list of everything that hasn't arrived yet or that we need to replace, so you can start making calls tomorrow morning."

"Okay." Frannie sighed, then seemed to forget the world's injustices and took the legal pad. "I'll compare the inventories against what's here."

"Great." Skye checked her watch. It was close to eight thirty. "Any idea what's taking Justin so long?" She had sent him to get a pizza more than forty minutes ago.

"Want me to call his cell?" Frannie offered.

"No. I guess I'm just hungry." Skye shook her head. "It does take a while to get over to Clay Center and back. I sure wish someone would open up a pizza place in Scumble River."

"Ms. Bunny was talking to Simon about adding a takeout window at the bowling alley." Frannie worked part-time at the bowling alley's grill.

"Hmm." Skye's response was noncommittal. Like May, Frannie desperately wanted Skye to go back to dating Simon. Frannie's father, Xavier, was Simon's assistant at the funeral home, and Frannie considered Simon her big brother.

Frannie and Skye worked in silence until the door to the cottage opened and the enticing scents of pepperoni and cheese preceded Justin into the room. He was juggling a large, flat box, a six-pack of Diet Coke, and a stack of napkins, and as soon as he cleared the threshold, he announced, "Dinner is served."

At eighteen, Justin topped six feet, but his weight had not caught up with his height, and his skinny build induced any woman with a smidgen of

135

maternal instinct to try to feed him. His hair was military short and he hid his long-lashed brown eyes behind thick glasses. He wasn't an attractive teenager, but Skye suspected that he would grow into a nice-looking man.

"Thank goodness. I thought you'd gotten lost." Skye relieved Justin of the box. "I'm starved." As soon as she uttered the words, she remembered Hallie Jordan's reaction to them earlier that afternoon. Would the young woman show up tonight for the private talk she wanted? And if she did, what would she say?

"Me too." Frannie took the plastic bucket from the nightstand. Charlie had removed the beds from the cottages they were using for storage but had refused to take away the rest of the furniture. "I'll go get ice."

Justin dropped the napkins and sodas on the desk. "I'll give you a hand."

Skye opened her mouth to say that it didn't take two people to get ice but immediately closed it. If Frannie and Justin wanted a few minutes of privacy, she wasn't about to stop them. Besides, it was probably better that neither was alone at night around the motor court.

As soon as the teenagers were gone, Skye snatched a slice of pizza and took a huge bite. A nanosecond later her cell rang. She put the piece down, wiped her fingers on a napkin, and grabbed her purse.

Skye tried to remember to put the phone in an outside pocket of her bag but rarely did so. This time she found it near the bottom, tangled up with a terrycloth headband, a grocery receipt, and her key ring.

Flipping it open, she hurriedly said, "Hello."

No one answered.

"Hello." Skye wondered whether whoever had been calling had given up. "Is anyone there?" When Justin got back she'd have him show her, again, how to check for missed calls.

As she fumbled to turn off the phone, she detected the sound of breathing.

"Can you hear me?" Scumble River didn't have the best cell phone reception.

More breathing; then, as she was about to close the phone, a genderless voice said, "Keep your nose out of other people's business and your mouth shut about things you don't understand or this might be the last wedding you organize."

Unnerved, Skye returned the phone to her purse. Her heart was pounding and her knees were shaking. Whom had she ticked off today? Shoot! Every vendor she'd talked to was unhappy with her for one reason or another. Before she could narrow the list down, she heard Frannie and Justin returning.

As the teens burst into the room, both were flushed and a little giggly. Justin was saying, "So she was all, like, whoof, and then, you know, I was all, like, whatever."

Frannie answered, "Gah!"

Skye had no idea what the teens were saying and didn't mention the threatening call to them; she'd talk to Wally about it later.

Justin put the ice bucket on the desk and scooped up a slice of pizza. In between bites, he said, "You'd better tell Mr. Patukas that some animal's gotten into his garbage."

"Was it a raccoon?" Skye took a swig of soda. "I hope it wasn't a coyote. I've heard there's a real problem with them this year."

Frannie shrugged. "We didn't see it, just heard some noise by the Dumpster."

"I'll let him know." Skye finished eating and put the debris in the trash can.

Once Justin and Frannie were full, they all buckled down to work and unpacked the remaining boxes with no more interruptions.

Just before ten, Skye told the teens they were through for the night, instructing them to meet her back at the motor court at nine a.m. and reminding them to keep track of their hours.

After Frannie and Justin had gone, Skye gathered up her things, turned out the lights, and headed for her car. As she stepped off the pavement, she spotted Hallie and Hale getting out of a bright yellow cab parked in front of cabin ten. Hale handed the driver a wad of cash, and the taxi left in a squeal of tires.

As it passed her, Skye noticed that the cab was

from Chicago, and whistled under her breath. Scumble River was seventy-five miles south of the city, and she could only imagine how expensive that fare had been.

When she turned her attention back to the twins, she saw that they were having an intense discussion, and she immediately squatted down, concealing herself behind her Bel Air. Even though she didn't really believe the siblings had killed Belle to stop the wedding, she had a hunch that something was going on with them.

Having heard Hallie's views on her father's lavish spending, she was afraid they might be plotting some sort of protest. After all, PETA threw blood at women who wore fur. Maybe Hallie was planning on turning the reception dinner into a soup kitchen for the homeless. And as the new bridal consultant, it was Skye's duty to be prepared.

They were speaking too quietly for her to hear from where she was. Keeping the vehicles between her and the siblings, she duckwalked until she was beside Tabitha's rental car. Hale and Hallie were just on the other side of the Acura.

Leaning against the cool metal, Skye heard Hale say, "I still don't understand why you want to spend the night here rather than at the hotel with Dad and Grandpa. I promised Luca Jay we'd take him to the new Disney movie."

Skye edged toward the rear of the sedan and peeked around the bumper. The twins were standing facing each other, and Hale was bending forward, intent on his sister. Their similarity was eerie. In the dim light, they appeared two halves of a whole.

Hallie answered, her voice so like his it almost sounded as if Hale was talking to himself. "You didn't have to come with me." She hunched her shoulders and stuck a hand in the pocket of her jeans. "I asked you not to."

"But why?" Hale's tone was troubled. "We always do everything together."

"Maybe it's time that changed." Hallie nibbled at her thumbnail. "Maybe we should spend some time apart, like your therapist said."

Hale's normally pale complexion turned red. "Do you have someone in mind?" His tone forbade her from saying yes. "Who is it? That guy in our philosophy class?"

Skye frowned. Hale sounded more like a jealous boyfriend than a brother.

Hallie turned as if to go into the cabin but paused and said over her shoulder, "At least he's a nice guy, unlike the witch you hooked up with."

"Belle wasn't that bad," Hale said, but his tone wasn't convincing.

Belle Canfield! Skye lost her balance and sat abruptly on the asphalt. The idea of someone as worldly as Belle having an affair with a boy like

Hale was difficult to believe, but then everyone said opposites attract.

Determined to see Hale's expression without revealing her presence, Skye crept forward. But he had followed Hallie to the step in front of the cabin. Now Skye couldn't even hear them.

Skye poked her head around the bumper and strained to hear what was being said, but their voices were too low. She chewed her lip. She had to get closer, but how could she without being noticed? She spotted a large bush near the door. If she went along the rear of the neighboring cottage, she might be able to slip behind the evergreen without being seen. Darting from the shelter of the Acura to the side of cabin nine, she jogged around the structure, then inched forward until she was hidden by the shrub.

Hallie held the door of her cabin open, one foot over the threshold. "You know I want you to have a girlfriend, just not someone shallow and mean like her."

"She's wasn't my girlfriend. We had sex a few times." Hale shoved a hand through his hair. "She made it clear I wasn't good enough for her to really date. I'm not handsome or powerful." His lips pressed together in a bitter line. "And I'm not rich, since Dad refuses to set up a trust fund for us."

Skye wrinkled her brow. Hale sounded sincere, but she'd worked with enough adolescents to know that wasn't a good enough reason to trust anyone. A teenager could be caught red-handed with a bottle of vodka at his lips and still vow that he had never taken a sip of alcohol in his life.

Skye moved a little closer, not wanting to miss a word, and heard Hallie say, "Why would she lie?"

"She was a twisted woman." Hale's voice was edged with annoyance. "It amused her to toy with us. She knew you disapproved of her, and she liked that she dumped me but could still make my life miserable."

"That *would* be something she found entertaining. And she thought we were stupid not to be able to talk Dad into giving us any serious money."

"So do you believe me?"

"Yes, I guess so."

"Do you still want to spend time separately?"

"Yes." Hallie turned away. "I think your therapist is right. And he's right about you needing to find a real girlfriend, not just keep hooking up with women you know will use you, too."

"Maybe." Hale crossed the grass to his cabin. "Good night."

When Hallie stepped into her cottage and closed the door, Skye counted to sixty, then eased out from behind the bush, marched up to number ten, and knocked.

"Go away, Hale." Hallie's voice was impatient. "We'll discuss it more in the morning."

"It's Skye. I noticed your light and remembered you wanted to talk to me. Is now not a good time?"

"Oh, sorry." Hallie swung open the door. "I thought you were my brother."

"Can I come in?"

"Sure." Hallie's expression was resolute. "After I said I wanted to talk to you, I sort of chickened out, but your showing up just proves what Reverend Hill said. God wants me to do the right thing."

"People often feel better after they tell someone what's bothering them." Skye sat in the desk chair.

"I know. I'm a psych major."

"And I'm a school psychologist, although I also work as the psychological consultant to the local police department."

"Yeah." Hallie nodded. "Riley's mother mentioned that, which is why I thought talking to you would be easier than talking to the one of the officers."

"Sure." Skye kept her voice neutral. "I understand." Was Hallie about to confess? Had she killed Belle to get her out of Hale's life? That would be weird even by Scumble River standards.

"The thing is, I really, really don't want anyone to know I told you this." Hallie wrinkled her brow. "If my brother knew, he'd have a meltdown."

"Well, I can't promise anything." Skye hated having to say that, but she couldn't lie to the girl. "If what you tell me has anything to do with the murder, I'll need to share it with the chief."

"That's fine." Hallie glanced toward her twin's

cabin. "Just don't tell Hale. His therapist says not to upset him right now."

"I can promise that." Skye nodded. "Unless, of course, you're confessing to Belle's murder."

"Not a chance. But I did hear her arguing with someone Saturday night when we got back here after the attendants' party."

"Why didn't you tell anyone this before?" Skye questioned.

"I didn't want to get involved." Hallie studied her shoe, avoiding Skye's gaze.

"And your minister changed your mind?"

"Yes. I spoke to him on the phone this morning, and he said it was my Christian duty to tell the police what I heard." Hallie's attention moved to her intertwined fingers. "He said I could never minister to the poor if I put myself first."

"I see." Skye nodded. "He sounds like a wise man."

Hallie nodded, then took a deep breath and said, "You know that after we got back to the motor court from the attendants' party we borrowed a car and drove into Chicago?" When Skye nodded, she continued, "While Hale was getting the keys, I took a walk over by the floral refrigerator."

"Okay," Skye encouraged her. "Is that when you heard Belle arguing with someone?"

"Yes. Inside cottage four, the one you're using for storage."

"Belle and who else?"

"I couldn't tell." Hallie shook her head. "It was too far away."

"Any idea if it was a man or woman?"

"No. The only reason I knew one of the people arguing was Belle was because I recognized her laugh—you know, that high-pitched hee-haw—but I couldn't hear what she or the other person was saying."

"And this was around what time?" Skye asked.

"Close to one fifteen. We left here at one twenty."

"Why did you take a walk in the first place?"

"Well." Hallie bit her lip. "The truth is I told my brother I had to go to the bathroom, but I was smoking. That's why you can't tell him any of this."

Before Skye could respond, the cabin door was thrust open, and Hale exploded into the room.

CHAPTER 11

Something Old

Y ou know, for a second, just before she told me what happened, I thought she was going to say that her brother had killed Belle." Skye sat with her back to the carved oak headboard of Wally's king-size bed, telling him about her conversation with Hallic. "Then, after she reported what she'd heard and Hale came bursting into the cabin, I thought we would have another murder on our hands."

"I'm still not clear on the logistics, or, for that matter, why she was so concerned that her twin would be mad." Wally lay on his right side facing her, his head supported on his hand. "Why was it such a big deal that she took a walk and had a cigarette instead of going to the bathroom?"

"The brief explanation is that Hale is abnormally possessive and keeps Hallie on a short leash." Skye raised an eyebrow. "Which is fairly odd considering he's her brother, not her husband."

"So, she just needed a few minutes away from her twin because he doesn't approve of her smoking. Was that her excuse?"

"I guess. Once Hale arrived I couldn't ask a lot of questions." Skye smoothed a wrinkle in the bedspread. "I felt like it would be better to speak to her again when I could get her alone." She looked at Wally. "Do you think that was a mistake? After all, she who hesitates . . ."

"Is probably right," he assured her. "From what you told me, Hallie wouldn't have talked openly with Hale there." A deep line formed between Wally's eyebrows. "Although, I'm sorry to say, getting her by herself is going to be even tougher now that her brother is on full alert."

"I know, and I understand his concern about her health, but she's twenty-one and if she wants to smoke, I don't see how he can stop her."

"Yeah, imagine having to sneak away from your brother to have a cigarette."

"I guess I should be thankful I only have Velcro Mom and not Super Glue Brother." Skye rolled her neck. She was exhausted, and she still had four days to get through until the wedding.

"Definitely," Wally agreed, then said, "Back to what Hallie witnessed."

"As we already knew, Saturday night—well, actually Sunday morning—when she and Hale got back to the motor court after the attendants' party, they—and by *they*, I'm thinking Hale, since Hallie wants to be a missionary—decided that the cottages were 'just too icky' and borrowed a car to drive into Chicago so they could stay at the hotel where their dad is staying."

"So, when Hale went to get the keys to the Hathaways' rental, Hallie told him she had to use the bathroom and went into her cottage." Wally half closed his eyes, recapping what Skye had told him. "Then Hallie slips out of number ten, walks over to the floral refrigerator in front of number three, and lights up."

"Yes." Skye adjusted the pillow behind her back. "She wants to be far enough away so Hale won't see her or smell the smoke. She's puffing away and she hears Belle and someone else yelling from inside cottage four."

"Too bad Hallie couldn't tell who was arguing with Belle or what they were fighting about."

147

"Yeah." Skye made a wry face. "Instead of being nosy and finding out what was going on—as I would have done—she crushed out her cigarette, slipped back into her cabin, then joined her brother when he pulled up in the Hathaways' rental car."

"How was it that Hale didn't notice she smelled like smoke?"

"Hallie's not dumb, despite some evidence to the contrary. She keeps perfume and mouthwash in her purse to use after she sneaks a cigarette."

"It sure would have been nice if she told us this when she was interviewed after the murder." The skin across Wally's prominent cheekbones tightened. "Since her information narrows down the time of death, maybe we could have eliminated a few more suspects."

"Possibly. We know Belle was put in the refrigerator sometime between one twenty and three a.m. because Simon said it would take close to five hours for her to suffocate, and I found her a little after eight. But I doubt many people will have an alibi for that time period, because most of them were probably in bed." Skye pressed her fingers to her temples. "We just can't get a break in this case."

"It sure seems that way." After a moment, Wally said, "So what happened when Hale burst in while you were talking to Hallie?"

"It turned out that Hale saw me going into his sister's cabin and wanted to know why I was visiting her at that time of night, so he eavesdropped. The walls are pretty thin, and he heard our whole conversation."

"And he heard Hallie admit to smoking and went ballistic." Wally finished Skye's thought.

"Yep." Skye half smiled. "Not only had she broken her promise to quit; she had also lied to him about where she was and what she was doing."

"He sounds a little psycho."

"His possessiveness is extreme." Skye put her elbows on her knees and rested her chin in her hands. "From what I know about the psychology of twins, it's not unusual for them to be extremely close, even to the exclusion of other friends, but his behavior is bordering on the pathological, and Hallie did mention he's in therapy. I'm guessing for anger-management issues among other problems."

"And you did say Belle had dumped him. So, if he's already feeling betrayed that his sister wants more independence . . ." Wally trailed off.

"Still, when would he have murdered her?" Skye pointed out. "The drive to Chicago would have taken at least ninety minutes, so even if he immediately turned around and came back, he couldn't have gotten to the motor court before four thirty."

"So he's out as a suspect, as is Hallie." Wally frowned.

"Yep." Skye stretched. "But wait until you hear about Madam Olga's little scheme."

After Skye finished telling him about the dress labels being switched, Wally whistled. "That sure gives her a motive to kill our vic if Belle threatened to expose her."

"Except . . ." Skye wrinkled her brow. "From what we've learned about Belle, she'd be more likely to blackmail Madam Olga than rat her out and turn her in."

"There is that," Wally conceded. "I'll have to ask the city attorney to check the law, but I suspect counterfeiting labels might be a federal crime, since crossing state lines is probably involved. If that's the case, I'll pass on your information to the proper authorities."

"Good. I hate to think she's taking advantage of vulnerable young women at a time when they're too excited to be cautious." Skye thought for a second, then went on to the next matter on her mental list. "What did Brian Cowden say when you questioned him?"

"He claims he left Belle at the country club, and since Larson couldn't ID him and we didn't have a motive for him, there wasn't anything we could hold him on."

"Isn't being shaken down by Belle a motive?" Skye asked.

"No, because he offered you the same deal. If he killed her in order to not have to pay her, why would he be willing to give you money?"

"Nuts!" Skye gnawed on her thumbnail. "Did

Martinez or Quirk find anything while we were in the city?"

"No." Wally shook his head. "Martinez called every number in the vic's cell phone directory, but no one admitted to knowing anything about a bitter ex or Belle begging for a second chance. Most said she didn't have relationships; she had hookups and publicity dates."

"Publicity dates?" Skye had never heard that term before.

"From what I gather, it's someone who goes out with a celebrity to get their picture taken by the paparazzi," Wally explained. "You said she was upset she didn't get the media exposure Paris Hilton gets. This was her way to be photographed more."

"Oh." Skye wasn't surprised. Nothing about the California crowd shocked her anymore. "How about Quirk's interviews this evening with the vendors we spoke to in the afternoon?"

"They didn't yield anything either."

"Nuts!" Skye felt defeated.

"And no luck reaching Belle's parents. Their employees insist they've passed on the message to contact me about an urgent matter regarding their daughter, but neither Mr. nor Mrs. Canfield has called back." Wally shook his head. "The only positive thing about not being able to get in touch with her folks is that it gives us a good reason not to release the name of the victim."

"Because the next of kin hasn't been officially notified, right?" Skye asked. When he nodded, she added, "Not that everyone around here doesn't know, but at least the national media hasn't found out."

"Thank goodness." He ran his fingertips along her inner arm. "I'm glad you decided to stop by tonight rather than waiting to tell me tomorrow."

"Me, too." Skye was silent for a moment. "Oh, one more thing. I almost forgot the call I got tonight when I was working at the motor court."

"What kind of call?"

Skye told him what had been said, ending with, "Too bad I couldn't tell if it was a man or a woman, and the caller ID read 'unavailable,' but it would have to be someone I gave my number to, which is pretty much just the vendors."

"Not necessarily. Between caller ID and the Internet, getting a phone number is remarkably easy nowadays. I'll check with your carrier and see if they can trace the call. Too bad it's not as easy as those TV shows make it seem."

"I still think it's one of the vendors we talked to today."

"Telephone threats usually amount to nothing, but I'll follow up tomorrow to make sure." Wally frowned. "Although, to be safe, you'd better stay here tonight."

"I'm fine," Skye said, but her tone wasn't convincing. She hated to admit that she dreaded being by herself in her big old house after all that had happened. It wasn't that she was scared. It was more a deep sense of sadness for Belle and for all the people involved. She'd been trying to think of the murder as just another case, but she knew that once she was alone, she couldn't stop herself from dwelling on the personal aspects of Belle's death. "I have a long day tomorrow."

"I'll set the alarm for six," Wally coaxed.

"Then you'll turn it off and sneak away like this morning." Skye refused to meet Wally's eyes, knowing one look into their warm brown depths would persuade her to stay against her better judgment.

"I promise to be ruthless." Wally put a hand over his heart. "No matter how much you beg for five more minutes or how cute you look."

"Well . . ." Skye wavered. "I am tired, and if I stayed, I could go to sleep faster."

"Who said anything about snoozing?" Wally's grin was devilish. "You didn't think I meant *sleep* when I referred to begging, did you?"

Wally woke Skye with a kiss and a cup of tea. She had seen a bumper sticker that read: I LIKE MY MEN LIKE I LIKE MY COFFEE, SWEET AND STRONG. She smiled to herself; Wally fit that description to a T.

As she sipped, he told her his plans for the day. "First, I'm going to interview Hallie, and while I do that I'll have Martinez and Quirk determine if any of the suspects have an alibi for the newly narrowed-down time of death. After I finish with Hallie, I'll talk to more of the businesses involved with the wedding. How about you?"

"Since questioning the vendors and sorting through the deliveries ate up most of Monday, I couldn't touch base with the venue or the other people working the event, so that's on my agenda for today." Skye put the mug on the bedside table and stood. "But the top of my list is to call the engravers and get new menus and programs made up." She explained about the misspelling.

"Good thing Frannie spotted that error."

"Definitely. And on the positive side, Belle used a local company, so the new stuff won't have to come all the way from California. Plainfield is considerably closer than Los Angeles."

"That's a lucky break." Wally leaned against the doorframe and watched Skye pull on her jeans.

"And the bridal party is out of my hair until after lunch."

"Oh?"

"Yes. They're all going to Tiffany's at Oakbrook to shop for wedding jewelry. Belle's inconvenient death messed up Riley's original plan to shop there on Sunday, so to make it up to her, Nick's taking the whole group along. Riley adores having an audience. They should be leaving Scumble River by nine."

"Then I better get going so I can catch Hallie before she takes off." Wally kissed Skye good-bye. "Call my cell if you need me."

Following a quick pit stop at home, Skye arrived at the motor court freshly showered and dressed in khaki shorts and a white sleeveless cotton blouse. Grabbing her purse and Belle's binder from the passenger seat, she hopped out of the Bel Air, glad to see Frannie and Justin waiting in Frannie's car, a secondhand Ford Focus.

The teenagers met her on the cottage's front step. "Ms. D.," Frannie said as Skye fumbled with the key, "we were wondering if sometime today, during one of our breaks, we could interview you about the murder."

"Sorry." Skye had told Frannie and Justin to call her by her first name now that they weren't her students anymore, but they couldn't seem to bring themselves to do so. "I can't talk about an ongoing investigation."

Justin held open the door and waved Skye and Frannie inside before complaining, "But this story could be our in for JJC's student newspaper." Both teenagers were journalism majors.

"Yeah," Frannie added. "We have to submit a portfolio, and Ms. Steele says she'll run our stories, so we'd both have a great clipping to include."

Kathryn Steele, the owner of the *Scumble River Star*, the local weekly paper, had left Skye several messages asking for information about the murder. Clearly, when Skye hadn't returned her calls, she had gone with Plan B.

"Sorry, kids." Skye picked up the phone on the desk. "You already have lots of clippings. The best I can do is to give you an exclusive interview after the case is solved."

"But, Ms. D., what if Ms. Steele doesn't want it then?" Justin whined.

"Kathryn will want it." Skye dialed. "Now, how about you two get to work? The flowers are arriving tomorrow, so Iris needs all the boxes in cottage three unpacked and the materials sorted out."

"Okay," Frannie conceded. "Do you need us to do anything here before we go?"

The engravers answered, and Skye held up a finger to the teenagers, indicating that they should wait. "Hi, this is Skye Denison. I'm the new coordinator for the Erickson-Jordan wedding."

"What happened to Ms. Canfield?"

"She couldn't finish the job, so I'm taking over." Skye hedged, knowing Wally wanted to keep Belle's death a secret as long as possible.

"Oh. Okay. What can I do for you?"

"I'm afraid you'll have to redo all the menus and programs." Skye's tone was firm but pleasant. "You misspelled the bride's name. It's Riley, not Riled."

"We engraved what we were given." The

woman's tone was equally firm but not as pleasant.

Skye fumbled with the binder, looking for the order. When she couldn't find it, she said, "I don't have the original, but I'm positive Ms. Canfield would not make that kind of error." She hadn't expected the engravers to try to blame Belle, but she should have. This would be an expensive order to redo, and the business wouldn't want to foot the bill.

"It was sent digitally. You need to find the computer file." The woman's voice was impatient.

"Right. I'll do that and get back to you. In the meantime, you need to redo the order. Do you have a sufficient quantity of the Crane pearl white paper?"

"Yes. That's no problem."

"And I need everything no later than Thursday." Skye inwardly cringed, afraid the engravers would say two days was impossible.

"We can do that, but there'll be a rush fee."

"Only if it wasn't your mistake, I assume," Skye quickly added.

"Yes." There was a long pause. "Of course, but it wasn't our fault."

As she hung up, Skye frowned. She had no idea how to find a file on someone else's computer. It really was time for her to stop traveling at 33 rpm in an iPod world. When the wedding was over, she would sign up for a computer class.

But first, she had to solve the more immediate

problem, and the answer was staring at her with an impatient look on his face. She had nearly forgotten that she had a computer whiz on the payroll.

"Justin, there's a change of plans. I need you to find a file on Belle's laptop."

"Awesome." He grinned and cracked his knuckles. "Where is it?"

Damn! "I don't know." Skye started dialing again. "Let me check with the chief and see if the crime techs took it, and if they didn't, if it's all right for us to go in Belle's cabin."

After speaking to Wally, Skye said to Justin, "The techs have it, but if you go to Laurel, Chief Boyd is clearing you to use it there."

"Should I go now?"

"Definitely." Skye handed Justin her keys. "Here. Use the Bel Air. It has a full tank of gas." She knew Frannie's father had forbidden her from loaning out her car.

Once Justin was gone, Frannie moved toward the door, a pout on her face. "I guess that means I'm on my own unpacking the floral stuff."

"Yep. I need to go out to the country club and make sure everything is going smoothly with the ceremony and reception setups."

"How are you going to get there?"

"Crap!" Skye smacked herself on the forehead. "I forgot about that when I loaned Justin the Bel Air."

"Guess you'll need someone to drive you."

Frannie smirked. "If you and I both unpack, it'll go quicker; then I can take you to the country club."

"You win." Skye briefly considered calling around to borrow a car but figured it would be quicker to do it Frannie's way. "Let's get cracking."

CHAPTER 12

Something New

Shoot. Who knew so much junk was involved in arranging a few flowers?" Frannie looked around at the boxes stacked five deep in cabin three.

"None of this is junk." Iris Yee stood in the open doorway with her hands on her nonexistent hips, glaring at the teenager. "And I'm doing a hell of a lot more than arranging a few flowers."

Skye stepped in front of Frannie. "Of course you are, Iris. Belle said your creations are legendary."

"Really?" Iris's delicate features, a blend of Asian and European, were impassive. "I'm flattered. I would have never guessed she felt that way."

"Well, I doubt she would have brought you all the way from the West Coast if you weren't the best."

"Perhaps."

Frannie glanced pointedly at the wall clock, and

Skye asked, "Is there any special way you want the supplies unpacked?"

Iris gestured to the worktables positioned against the four walls. "Sort the materials according to whether they're for the tall gold centerpieces, the low crystal centerpieces, the ceremony arch, or the body flowers."

"How will we figure out what is what?" Frannie made a sweeping motion with her hands. "I wouldn't know a philodendron from a gardenia."

"Here's the list and the inventory." Iris handed the pages to Skye. "I'll be back to check on you in a bit."

"Wait a minute." Skye stopped her. "You mentioned the centerpieces and body flowers; those are the bouquets, right?" Iris nodded and Skye continued, "But how about the dragonwood branch trees for the cocktail party and the floral hedges that are supposed to line the aisle for the ceremony?"

"My assistant is flying in with them on Friday." Iris shook her head. "You don't have a clue."

"I'm doing the best I can in difficult circumstances." Skye kept her tone even, believing that a good time to keep your mouth shut was before you put your foot in it. She couldn't afford to offend Iris. It wasn't as if she could do the arrangements herself, and where would she get another floral designer at this late date?

"This event will be a disaster," Iris moaned.

Skye noticed a panicky expression in the woman's eyes and said soothingly, "It'll be fine if we all pull together." The last thing she needed was a vendor meltdown.

"Who knew working without Belle would be worse than working with her?" Iris continued as if Skye hadn't spoken.

"Oh. I thought you said you and Belle had a terrific relationship."

"Yes. Of course we did. What are you implying?" Before Skye could answer, Iris turned on her heel and marched away, saying over her shoulder, "If you're done interrogating me, I have calls to make."

After the floral designer left, Frannie asked, "What was that all about?"

"I wish I knew," Skye murmured to herself, then said to Frannie, "I'm sure it's nothing. Let's get to work. We have a lot to do today."

"Okay. If you want to be that way." Frannie shrugged. "But if you let me, I could help you with the investigation *and* get a terrific story for my portfolio."

They worked in silence, speaking only when they had to figure out on which table a strange piece belonged.

They were down to the last row of cartons when Frannie held up a silver conical object. "Ms. D., what do you think this is?" The teen put it on her head. "A party hat?"

Skye giggled, then plucked the odd item off Frannie's skull and looked it over. It was heavier than she expected. After checking both the pages Iris had left and the inventory, she said, "I don't see it on either of these lists."

"What in the heck is it for?" Frannie asked.

"I have no idea. It looks like an antique. Or at least a collectible." Skye examined the object more closely, running her finger over the intricate design of flowers and vines embossed into the metal, but stopped when she felt a depression. "Anyway, it's damaged." She showed it to Frannie. "See the dent right here?"

"Yeah, it's a big one. That must be why someone tossed it behind the boxes." Frannie held out her hand. "Give it to me and I'll put it in the trash."

Skye was about to pass it to Frannie when she paused. Something was nagging at her. Something she'd heard recently.

It came to her in a flash. Wally had said to watch out for an object with a raised pattern that was shaped like an oversize ice cream cone. *Holy mother of God!* She was holding the weapon used to knock out Belle.

Skye left Frannie to finish the unpacking with the excuse that she needed to use the facilities. The teen nodded but raised her brows when Skye took the unidentified item with her. Once inside the bathroom, Skye put it carefully on the floor, then dialed Wally's cell.

He answered on the first ring. "Hello, sugar. I hope you're calling to ask me to lunch."

"I wish I was, but I'm too busy to eat." Skye relaxed at the calming sound of his voice. "Still, I think you'll be happy I phoned."

"I'm always happy to hear from you." Wally's tone was light, but Skye could hear the underlying tension. "I'd be euphoric if you said you'd figured out who murdered Belle Canfield."

"Well, I haven't done that, but I might have found the murder weapon."

"The actual murder weapon was the refrigerator. Do you mean the thing she was knocked out with?"

"Yes."

"You're kidding."

"No." Skye smiled. "Frannie and I were unpacking the floral materials in cabin three today, and she found a metal cone-shaped object with a dent."

"I'll be right there." Wally hung up before Skye could respond.

Frannie was flattening empty boxes when Skye returned to the main room of the cottage. As soon as Skye appeared she said, "I'm almost through here. Do you want to go to the country club now?"

"It's eleven thirty. I'll do the rest of the cartons. You go get some lunch. Meet me back here in half an hour."

The girl looked at her suspiciously but shrugged. "Okay. Do you want me to bring you anything?"

"No." Skye shook her head, wanting Frannie gone before Wally arrived. "I'm fine."

Frannie had barely driven away when Wally pulled into the parking lot. He left the squad car running when he got out and strode swiftly over to where Skye was standing on the cottage's top step. "Put it in this." He held a large plastic evidence bag toward her.

"Here you go."

He sealed the top, then dated and signed the front. Once he was finished, he asked, "Where's Frannie?"

"I sent her to lunch."

"Does she know this might be a weapon connected with the murder?"

"No. That's why I sent her away." Skye explained, "Kathryn Steele wants her and Justin to write an article about the murder for the paper."

"Son of a b—" Wally cut himself off. "That woman is a thorn in my butt."

"She's just doing her job."

"Too bad hers makes mine harder." Wally shook his head. "Okay. Show me where you found the thing."

Skye led him into the cabin. "It was there between a box and the wall." She pointed to the right of the door. "How did the evidence techs miss it?"

"They only searched number four; none of the other cabins appeared to have been disturbed."

"That makes sense." Skye nodded. "We didn't see it until we had nearly all the cartons unpacked. They were five deep."

"Where's the box?"

She gestured to a lone carton in the middle of the room. "This one. I was able to stop Frannie before she dismantled it."

"Good. I'll take it and the possible weapon over to Laurel so the techs can test them." Wally ran his fingers through his hair. "We have your prints on file, but we'll have to get Frannie's since she handled it too."

"What are you going to tell her?"

"I'll think of something." Wally walked back to the police car. "Who besides you and Belle had access to this cabin?"

"Iris Yee." Skye trailed after him and leaned against the fender, watching him lock the evidence bag in the trunk and pull on a pair of rubber gloves.

"Didn't Tabitha Urick mention Iris as someone who didn't get along with Belle?"

"Yes." Skye drummed her fingers on the hood of the cruiser. "And Iris let something slip today. When I talked to her right after the murder, she claimed she and Belle were the best of friends, but this morning she said something about Belle being a pain to work with."

"If this thing turns out to be the weapon the

perp used to knock Belle out, I think that comment and Iris's access to the cottage where it was found win her an all-expense-paid trip to the PD's interrogation room."

"Shoot." Skye slammed the door of the squad before following him back to the cottage. "If she's the killer, what am I going to do with fifty thousand dollars' worth of flowers and no one to arrange them?"

"Sorry." Wally carefully picked up the carton by one flap and carried it to the police car. "Solving a murder trumps putting on a wedding."

"That depends on who you're talking to." Skye cringed at the thought of informing Riley and Anita that they would need another floral designer. "When will you know if that thing is the weapon?"

"Probably later today or tomorrow at the latest." Wally slid into the driver's seat. "It's not as if the county crime lab has any other murders ahead of ours." He put the squad in reverse. "I'll call your cell when I have some news. Meanwhile, mum's the word."

"Yeah. Right," Skye muttered. "That's one of the few flowers that isn't being delivered here in the next twenty-four hours."

Riley's wedding and reception were being held at the Thistle Creek Country Club located halfway between Scumble River and Laurel. When Frannie turned into the long drive, she pointed to a man pounding the ground with a five iron and said, "Will you look at that?"

"Well, long ago when men cursed and beat the earth with sticks, it was called witchcraft." Skye snickered. "Nowadays we call it golf."

"You are so not funny." Frannie shook her head.

Skye shrugged. Trying to make a teenager laugh was like trying to amuse a cat—you never got the result you were hoping for.

As they continued down the winding road, Skye was astonished by the number of golfers present. How come there were so many people able to take off from work on a Tuesday in the middle of June? Then again, the lush, green, gently rolling hills spoke of privilege, not laboring at a nine-to-five job.

Frannie broke into Skye's thoughts. "What are you smirking at, Ms. D.?"

"Just trying to picture my father or cousins dressed in lime green plaid pants and pink polo shirts, hitting a little ball from hole to hole."

"Not going to happen. Unless they can shoot it, gut it, and have it for dinner, no way will your relatives waste their time on it." Frannie parked in front of the clubhouse, a cream-colored brick building with huge floor-to-ceiling windows. "Who do you need to talk to here?"

"The events manager." Skye got out of the car. "You can go hang around the pool if you want. I'll find you when I'm ready to go back."

"Okay." Frannie headed toward the back of the structure. "Take your time. I've got a book in my purse."

Skye waved and went inside. To the right were the golf shop and offices, and to the left was the ballroom where the ceremony would be held.

A woman dressed in a blue linen suit approached her immediately. "Ms. Denison?"

"Yes. Please call me Skye."

The woman held out her hand, and Skye noticed that her put-together image was ruined by nails bitten down to the quick. "Good afternoon, I'm Allison Waggoner, the events coordinator for Thistle Creek."

"Thank you for meeting with me on such short notice."

"No problem. The Erickson-Jordan wedding is my top priority. Normally we don't allow bridal parties to start setting up until the day before the wedding. But Mr. Jordan agreed to pay us for an entire week." Allison motioned down the hall. "Would you like to see what's been done so far?"

"That would be great."

"I was sorry to hear about Ms. Canfield's death," Allison said after she and Skye entered the ballroom.

Although no formal announcement about Belle's murder had been made, by Monday morning the news had leaked out through the Scumble River grapevine. They were just lucky that no one had

168

connected the wedding planner to the famous Mickey Canfield.

"It was a shock." Skye scanned the woman's face, trying to read her expression. Was she truly sorry that Belle was dead, or was she relieved not to have to deal with the difficult wedding planner anymore?

"Do they have any leads?"

Skye shrugged. "Not that they're sharing with me." Was Allison's question idle curiosity, or was she asking because she was the killer?

"But you consult with the police, don't you? And, of course, you're dating the chief, so I'm sure if anyone knows what's going on, you do."

"Are you from around here?" Skye asked, ignoring Allison's comment.

"I'm from Laurel, but my mom lives in one of the new senior apartments in Scumble River."

"Oh." That explained why Allison knew so much. She could tap into the small-town gossip network. "Does she like it there?"

"Loves it." Changing the subject, Allison swept her arm around the room. "What do you think?"

Although they still had a long way to go, the chairs had been set up, as had a partially constructed colonnade of ten-foot-tall Corinthian columns against a fairy castle backdrop. "So far, so good." Skye consulted her binder. "Are those Chaivari chairs?"

"Yes. Just as Ms. Canfield specified."

"Great." To Skye they looked like a version of the ladder-backs in her own dining room—except these were smaller and painted gold. But Belle's notes indicated that Riley had specifically requested all the chairs used in her wedding be Chaivari. Considering the ones for the reception would be covered in fabric and no one would see them, Skye was baffled as to why having this particular kind was so important.

"It was hard to locate so many since the tent-and-rental company you've hired is our usual source, and they're using their supply for the five hundred needed for the dinner. But as I said, this event is my top priority."

"I appreciate your efforts on our behalf." Skye was an advocate of positive reinforcement. Also, considering she had already received one threatening phone call, she wasn't taking any chances of being next on the murderer's hit list. "When will the rest of the room be completed?"

"The structure will be done this afternoon. The carpenter is at lunch right now, but he'll be back any minute to finish the crown top."

"Terrific." Skye checked her binder again. "And the fabric people are scheduled for tomorrow?" Nine hundred yards of white silk and chiffon would be swathing the reception tent from ceiling to floor. The colonnade would be framed with pink voile, and Iris would fill the top with clusters of roses, hydrangea, and golden branches. "I understand our caterer is using your facilities and waitstaff; is that correct?"

"Yes. That's all taken care of." Allison consulted a notebook she pulled from her blazer pocket. "Although the catering company is from Chicago and has a mobile kitchen, so they only need ours as a staging area."

"Can you show me where the bride and her party will get ready?"

"This way." Allison led Skye toward the other end of the building. "We've equipped two of the empty meeting rooms—one for the bride and the other for her attendants—with mirrored vanity tables, chairs, comfy sofas, and a small fridge."

After Skye inspected the two dressing rooms, she and Allison went outside, where several workmen were laying Plexiglas over the pool to create a dance floor, and a gigantic tent was being constructed next to the patio. The plan was for the ceremony to take place in the ballroom; then everyone would move to the patio for the cocktail party, then on to the tent for dinner, and back to the pool and patio area for dancing.

Skye spotted Brian Cowden directing the men and called, "Hello."

He waved but didn't join her.

"Wow." Skye glanced around. "This is truly amazing."

"It's the biggest, most elaborate event we've ever hosted." Allison nibbled on a fingernail.

"This is our chance to really get the club on its feet financially."

"Oh?" Skye questioned. "I hadn't realized Thistle Creek wasn't doing well."

"It's doing fine, but an enterprise like a country club is a huge investment and takes a while to show a profit."

"And this wedding could push the club into the black?"

"Exactly." Allison's eyes held a mixture of hope and fear. "But it's a lot of responsibility, especially since there are so many details."

"That must be hard on you." Skye studied the event coordinator. "It sounds as if the owner is really depending on you."

"Yes, he does count on me." Allison's cheeks turned red. "And I'd hate to let him down. He's such a special man, and he's put every penny he has into this place." She picked at a flake of dry skin near her thumbnail. "That's why the contract Ms. Canfield had us sign is so worrisome."

"Because of the penalties it imposes if anything is late or not to specifications?" Skye guessed.

"Precisely." Allison gazed into Skye's eyes. "Ms. Canfield was holding a sword over our heads, since it all came down to whether she signed off at the end. And no matter what I did, she was never happy."

"I'm certain that's not the case." Skye's tone was encouraging. "Belle was probably just nervous herself. I'm sure she wasn't really that bad deep down inside."

"Maybe." Allison shrugged. "But you're young, and it sounds as if you still think there's good in everybody. Trust me—if you believe that, you just haven't met everybody."

CHAPTER 13

Razzle-dazzle

Once Allison went off to admonish a workman whose pace was lagging, Skye took out her phone and dialed Wally. She'd used her cell more often this past month working on the wedding than she had since she'd gotten it, and she was finally beginning to understand why the device was so popular.

It rang and rang, and she was figuring out what message to leave on voice mail when Wally answered, "Hi, sugar. Sorry it took me so long. I was on the landline with County."

"Did they figure out if that thing Frannie found was the weapon used to knock Belle out?" Skye couldn't decide which answer she wanted to hear. If Wally arrested Iris, Skye would be up a floral river without a designer.

"No. They're still running tests. They probably won't know until tomorrow."

"How about fingerprints?"

"There were a slew of them on the box, so it'll take a while to match them all, but they weren't able to get any usable prints off the possible weapon because of the raised pattern on the metal."

"Shoot."

"At least they know what it is."

"Is it a Victorian bouquet holder?" Skye had been turning the question over and over in her mind and thought she had come up with the answer.

"Very good." Wally's smile was evident in his voice. "One of the crime tech's parents owns an antique shop and she recognized it. She says she's pretty sure it's authentic, not a reproduction."

"Now that we know what it is, do you want me to casually ask Iris about it?" Skye dug out the floral designer's list of inventory. "It's not mentioned on the sheets she gave me, so it would be natural for me to bring it up."

"It would probably be better not to give her any advance warning that we found it." Wally's tone was thoughtful. "Let's wait and see if the dent matches the vic's wound."

"Sure," Skye agreed. "Then I'll keep working on wedding stuff, and you can call me if you need anything."

"Will do," Wally approved. "I've got Martinez watching Ms. Yee, and, up to now, she's been acting normal and hasn't left the motor court."

"Well, that's a good sign." Skye was still hoping Iris was innocent. "Anyway, the reason I called is about the owner of the country club."

"Kent?"

"Do you know him?"

"Slightly. He seems like a good guy. What about him?"

"I don't think I've met him, but the club's event planner gave me an earful about how much they need the money from this event." Skye filled him in on the details.

When she finished, he asked, "But wouldn't that mean that both Kent and the event planner would want the wedding to go on as planned? Which would mean keeping Belle alive."

"True. Unless Belle threatened to use one of the contract stipulations to stiff them." Skye explained, "They're getting paid in three installments. They got twenty-five percent when the venue was booked, another twenty-five at the beginning of May, and they won't get the remaining fifty percent until Saturday night."

"Great. More suspects." Wally sounded discouraged. "Just what we need."

"Sorry."

"Not your fault," he assured her. "At least I cleared that mother of the bride who went after Belle with the cake knife. She's divorced and honeymooning in Acapulco with her new husband."

"Was she ever a viable suspect?"

"No, but it's good to cross her off the list."

"At this point any step forward is a good one. Even a baby step."

After saying good-bye to Wally, Skye opened her binder, trying to decide what she should do or whom she should see next. As she skimmed the list, her heart sank. She'd been blocking the upcoming activity from her mind.

Riley had insisted that the entire bridal party have a dance lesson before the wedding, and it was today at two thirty. Skye shuddered. She had no sense of rhythm whatsoever, and she looked like a squirrel in a clothes dryer when she danced. She knew this for a fact from her two previous experiences in taking dance lessons.

Her first had been in second grade, when her mother had made her take ballet. The other students had been dancing since they could walk, and those sweet little girls were not happy when a newcomer was added to their troupe. They taunted Skye mercilessly, saying she looked like a hippopotamus, and that her tutu was really a "fourfour."

Those baby ballerinas had terrorized Skye until she finally locked herself in the bathroom. She came out only after her mother promised she wouldn't have to attend any more sessions.

Although Skye had lost weight in sixth grade, she never forgot that experience, and when she took her second set of dancing lessons five years ago during her engagement to Luc St. Amant, the scion of a wealthy Louisiana family, she still associated dancing with those cruel seven-year-olds.

Mrs. St. Amant had not been pleased with her son's choice of fiancée and had tried to scare Skye off in various ways, one of which was to enroll her in a debutante dance class. Luc had begged Skye to humor his mother, and she had given in, agreeing to attend.

The fact that Skye was several years older than the other young women, and a damn Yankee who had snagged one of New Orleans's most eligible bachelors, did not make for a pleasant learning environment. Skye lasted through the twelve-week course but vowed never to put herself in that position again.

And that was before she had had an epiphany and had given up her diet, realizing that rice cakes made better packing material than snack food, sugar-free Jell-O was gummy water, not dessert, and chocolate was God's way of saying he wanted women to be happy.

Now that she was no longer willing to suffer the deprivation of the eight-hundred-calorie-a-day diet she'd stuck to for more than fifteen years, and had gained weight, Skye wanted to take another dance lesson about as much as she wanted to stick a straight pin in her eye.

Nevertheless, she had no choice. Unlike the other members of the bridal party, who had free will, Skye was on the payroll, and Nick and Riley were shelling out big bucks for her to do what they wanted.

On the bright side, it would give her a chance to chat with the male half of the wedding entourage. The men had only been formally questioned about Belle's death. Who knew what they might reveal in the heat of a tango? Especially if Skye could manage not to step on their toes.

It was already one thirty. She had only an hour to get back to Scumble River, check with Justin and see if he had found the electronic file, show Frannie what to do next, and go home to change into a skirt and high heels, the mandatory dress code for the afternoon activity.

As Frannie drove them to the motor court, Skye gave her a rundown of what she wanted her to do the rest of the afternoon, then called Justin's cell.

"Yeah." Justin's voice crackled. "I found the order, but you won't like what it said." He cleared his throat. "The engraver was right. Ms. Canfield made the mistake, not them."

"Shoot!" Skye felt a headache starting up. That meant they'd have to pay the engraver for the second order, as well as the rush fee. Good thing Riley and Nick thought money was no object. "Thanks anyway. Are you still in Laurel?"

"No. I'm about ten miles from Scumble River," Justin reported.

"Great. Meet us at the motor court. We should be there in fifteen or twenty minutes."

When Skye flipped her phone closed, Frannie asked, "Bad news?"

Skye nodded, searching her purse for an aspirin. She dry swallowed the pill and said, "I'm going to close my eyes and try to get rid of my headache."

"Sure, Ms. D." Frannie's glance was sympathetic. "You rest. Everything will be fine."

When they were all back at the Up A Lazy River, Skye got the teens started on the place cards. The calligrapher had finished inscribing the guests' names and had delivered the cards that morning. Now they needed to be assembled and sorted for the reception. Skye instructed Frannie and Justin to call her if they ran into any problems, then hopped into the Bel Air and sped home.

While she changed into a dress and heels, Skye thought about what she had learned about Belle so far. On the one hand, the wedding planner was a greedy witch who made the life of those who worked for her miserable. On the other hand, she seemed intent on producing a perfect event. What was wrong with this picture?

Bent over, one foot halfway inserted into her pump, Skye paused. Why would a rich, society fashionista care so much? It wasn't as if she needed the money or the job. Was it because she wanted to be famous? Or was Wally right about Belle wanting to prove something to her parents?

Maybe she just enjoyed the power. Even though she had to take orders from the brides, ultimately their weddings were in her hands. Or was the rush of spending hundreds of thousands of dollars nearly every day the attraction? Skye shrugged and finished putting on her shoes, but somewhere in the back of her mind she knew that if she could unravel Belle's motivations, she would be a lot closer to solving her murder.

Several members of the wedding party, including Riley's mother and grandmother, were already at the banquet hall when Skye arrived. Anita and Dora gestured for Skye to join them.

"You need to go talk to Riley," Anita said, her color high. "The poor thing is hysterical."

Skye's left eye began to twitch. Riley might be the apple of her mother's eye, but she was the core of nearly all of Skye's problems.

"That awful woman is messing up things again." Dora's thin voice quavered.

"What woman?" Skye asked, afraid she already knew. Only one person wasn't kowtowing to Riley's demands.

"Nick's stepmother." Anita shook her head. "I just can't understand why she's acting this way. It's almost as if she's deliberately trying to spoil things."

"I think Natasha is used to being the center of attention," Skye explained. "And now a younger, more beautiful woman is stealing all her thunder."

Before either Dora or Anita could reply, a woman whom Skye assumed was the dance instructor clapped her hands and announced, "We only have two hours, so let's get to work." Skye realized the rest of the party had arrived and they were ready to begin.

As Skye took her place on the dance floor, she heard Riley say to Nick, "If she doesn't show up for the lesson, you have to make sure she doesn't participate in the family dance at the reception. She'll ruin everything."

"But, honey, she was a professional dancer before she married Dad. She'll be fine."

Skye held her breath. Nick had not responded in the correct manner, which would have been to agree with his bride to-be and trash his stepmother. Would Riley explode?

To Skye's relief, Nick received only a dirty look for his error. Then Riley strode to the front of the hall and announced in a rah-rah voice, "Everyone find your partner. This is going to be so much fun!"

While everyone paired up, Skye kept an eye on the bride. She didn't believe for a minute that her cousin would let Natasha get away with not falling in line with Riley's wishes.

The bride continued, "The first dance at the reception, after Nick and I finish our sweetheart dance, will be a waltz." She pointed to the instructor. "Charisa will show you how it's done."

Skye turned toward her partner, groomsman

Gus Zeitler, and said, "I need to apologize in advance. I have less rhythm than a penguin."

"No problem." Gus wiggled his bushy eyebrows. "I have less rhythm than the stone the penguin stands on."

"Then we're the perfect pair." Skye held out her arms the way Charisa indicated. "Shall we count together?"

"Or we could slip out to the bar and have a drink," Gus whispered.

"Sorry, but I like my head where it is, and Riley would bite if off if she caught me sneaking away."

"Yeah, there is that," Gus agreed. "But after two and a half hours of jewelry shopping, I need a beer."

As Skye struggled to follow the instructor's directions, she asked, "What did they end up buying?"

"The bride got a Di Modolo pink and white diamond ten-karat necklace, with matching five-karat bracelet and ten-karat earrings."

"Wow."

"Two hundred and fifty thousand big ones."

"Wow again." Skye couldn't even imagine spending that kind of money on something she'd wear only a few times a year.

"Nick bought the groomsmen gold cuff links, and the bridesmaids all got pink pearls to wear with their dresses."

"Nice."

Skye and Gus grew silent as Charisa turned on the music and said, "Now we waltz."

They were doing pretty well— Skye had stepped on Gus's silver-toed snakeskin cowboy boots only twice, and he'd bumped them into another couple only once— so she thought it was safe to attempt a conversation. "I hear that Belle was pretty hot stuff."

"Who's been talking?" Gus grinned. "One of the girls jealous?"

"No. Belle was pretty open about her love life." Skye arched a brow. "Did you two ever hook up?"

"Nah." Gus shook his head. "I wasn't rich enough, handsome enough, or famous enough for her."

As Skye opened her mouth to ask about Liam, she heard someone hiss, "I don't know why you're mad. I took care of the problem."

"No, you didn't. You made it worse. I had to fix your mess."

Skye craned her neck. "Did you hear that?" In the crowd of couples, she couldn't tell who was speaking.

"Hear what?"

"Something about a problem." Skye danced them toward Riley and Nick, but they were silent.

"Hey," Gus protested. "I'm supposed to lead."

Skye ignored his complaint and waltzed over to Tabitha Urick and Liam Murphy, who seemed to be having a lively discussion, but before Skye got close enough to hear what they were saying, Charisa announced, "Now we're going to change partners. Ladies, please move one to the right."

Skye ended up with Zach Hathaway, who asked, "How are things going with the wedding planning?"

"Fine." She forced a smile. "Thank goodness Belle left meticulous notes."

"She seemed like a person who paid attention to details." Zach's expression was unreadable.

"That she was."

Skye was about to ask Zach if he had known the wedding planner well when Charisa said, "Now we'll learn the bossa nova."

"Damn!" Skye muttered. She hadn't realized they would have to learn more than one dance.

"Not a fan?" Zach asked.

"No rhythm," Skye confessed.

The bossa nova was a lot more difficult than the waltz, and Skye had to pay attention to her feet rather than question Zach further. After the first hour was up, Charisa called a ten-minute break and Riley made a beeline to Skye.

Pulling her aside, she demanded, "You have to do something about Nick's stepmother."

"Uh." Skye had been hoping that Riley would let that issue go. "Like what?"

"Talk to her. Make her see how important it is that she cooperates."

"Riley, I wouldn't have any idea how to do

that." Skye was still thinking about what she'd overheard on the dance floor and didn't have a quick excuse at the ready.

"You're a psychologist." Riley stamped her foot. "Psych her out."

Skye winced. Why did so many people believe her degree in school psychology gave her magical powers? If that were true, did they really think she would be working in public education, making less money than the garbage collectors? And would she have had to take the job as Belle's assistant to get her house fixed up?

Before Skye could explain the limits of a school psychologist's abilities, Riley whirled around and marched off, demanding Nick's attention.

A few seconds later, Charisa called the group back to order. This time Skye was paired with Liam, who looked nearly as uncomfortable as she felt.

When Liam took her in his arms, she said casually, "So, how's everyone handling Belle's death?"

"I don't think any of us knew her on a personal level." Liam's response was formal. "I'm sure everyone is saddened by the loss, but it's not as if she were a friend."

"But I hear she was very friendly with a lot of men—at least one night at a time." Skye watched the lawyer carefully. "Did you ever hook up with her?"

"No." He looked down his nose. "Her promiscuity was common knowledge. I would never take the chance on catching some disease." He shuddered. "Condoms break, you know."

"Of course." Skye nodded, remembering Gus's remark about Liam's health consciousness.

"Do you know how much longer this nonsense will last?" Liam asked.

"Forty-five minutes. It sounds as if you're not fond of dancing either."

"I don't mind dancing, but I haven't been able to get any work done today." Liam edged them toward the door leading to the bar. "Would you mind if we sat this one out?"

"Not if you take the blame when Riley catches us." Skye gave in. She really needed to rest.

Liam selected a table at the back and sat down. "It's only one thirty on the coast, so I can still reach some people."

"Fine with me."

Liam took his BlackBerry from his pocket.

"I'll just take a breather." Skye sat down, hoping to overhear something useful.

Liam nodded and turned his attention to his phone.

Within minutes, the lawyer's droning voice nearly put Skye to sleep. She didn't understand most of what he was saying, and what she could figure out didn't seem to pertain to anyone involved in Riley's wedding.

Skye was close to drifting off when fingers bit into her shoulder and she yelped.

"What are you two doing in here?" Riley stood in front of Skye, glowering. "The lesson isn't over yet."

Liam slipped his cell back into his pocket and said smoothly, "Skye twisted her ankle. Since there's so much to do for the wedding, she wanted to make sure she could walk on it tomorrow and wouldn't have to cancel any appointments."

"I see." Riley crossed her arms. "Then at least come back where you can watch."

Liam and Skye both jumped up. "Sure."

"The rest must have helped your ankle." Riley herded the two of them toward the banquet hall. "You don't seem to be limping."

"Yes." Skye gritted her teeth. "My ankle feels much better."

"Good." Riley's voice held a hint of satisfaction. "Then let's get back on the dance floor. We're not paying you to sit around."

"Right." Skye gave her cousin a weak smile. "No sitting around. Got it."

"I don't know what's wrong with you people," Riley complained. "You're all acting as if I'm asking you to dig ditches." As she walked away, she said over her shoulder, "Everyone should be thanking me for such a wonderful time. After all, weddings are the champagne of life."

"Yeah," Liam muttered once Riley was out of earshot. "It's just too bad that marriage is the hangover."

Five minutes later, as Skye struggled to learn the tango, she was seriously considering faking another injury. This time she'd been paired with Hale, and there was something so creepy about the young man, she could barely stand for him to touch her.

When she stumbled for the eightieth time, Skye looked up and froze, mesmerized by the infuriated glare on his face. She quickly mumbled, "Sorry."

"If you'd lose some weight, this wouldn't be so hard for you," Hale snapped.

Skye yanked her hand from his grasp, having reached the end of her patience with the rude young man. "Remind me, are you the good twin or the evil twin?"

Hale's face turned magenta, and he yelled, "You women all think you're so perfect, but none of you are."

"That does it." Skye narrowed her eyes. "Go finish puberty somewhere else."

Hale opened his mouth, then snapped it closed, whirled around, and stomped out of the hall.

As everyone watched him slam the door behind him, Skye wondered just how mentally unstable Hale really was.

CHAPTER 14

Something Borrowed

Skye pondered Hale's behavior as she walked back to the motor court. His comment about all women thinking they were perfect had to refer to Belle. After all, at Skye's first meeting with the wedding planner, Belle had been quick to point out her perfection. There was also Hale's sister, who was bucking for sainthood. Not to mention Riley, his soon-to-be-stepmother, another woman who acted as if she farted perfume. Skye nodded. Yep. He probably meant all three of them.

The sound of Frannie's voice greeted Skye as she opened the door to the cabin where the teens were working. "No, I'm sorry, she's still not here."

As Skye walked in, Frannie looked up, then said into the receiver, "Wait one second; she just got here." Frannie turned to Skye and demanded, "Why isn't your cell on?"

"I have no idea." Skye didn't remember turning it off, but then again, she didn't remember not doing it either.

Frannie held out the phone to Skye. "It's Simon. He's been calling every ten minutes."

"Take a message." She so didn't want to talk to her ex-boyfriend right now. She was too busy dealing with a wedding and a murder to have time to discuss their past relationship. She probably should have sent him a thank-you for the flowers he'd had delivered to her on Monday. His note of apology for the snarky remarks he'd made at the crime scene on Sunday had been sweet.

Frannie grunted and shoved the receiver into Skye's unwilling hand.

Skye gave in and spoke into the handset. "Hi, Simon. It's me."

His usual laid-back tenor was gone, replaced by an agitated rumble. "Bunny's in trouble."

Simon's mother, Bunny Reid, had arrived in Scumble River two and a half years ago after a twenty-year absence from his life. At the time, she'd been addicted to painkillers she'd been given when she hurt her back and was on probation for trying to forge prescriptions to obtain more of them.

To stay out of jail, she'd had to attend Narcotics Anonymous meetings, find work, and establish a permanent address. Simon had helped her with the last two by purchasing the local bowling alley and allowing her to live above it while she managed the business. Since then, Bunny had mostly cleaned up her act, but she still occasionally contributed a few gray strands to Simon's auburn hair.

"What did she do?" Skye questioned.

Frannie and Justin sat on the floor and stared at Skye, not pretending to do anything but listen to her conversation.

Skye gave the teens an exasperated look and attempted to stretch the phone cord as far as the bathroom, but it wouldn't reach.

"I hope nothing." Simon's voice cracked. "But Boyd took her in for questioning a couple of hours ago."

Skye gasped. "Why?" What in the world had happened while she was wasting her time learning to boogie?

"I have no idea." Simon blew out an exasperated breath. "The bartender called and told me the cops had taken her away. I went straight to the PD, but no one would tell me anything."

"Is my mom there?"

"No. She worked the day shift and was gone by the time I got here." He paused, then continued, "I don't know the man who's working, but he must be one of the new dispatchers."

"Have you talked to Wally?"

"No. I haven't been able to persuade anyone to get Boyd for me, and I can't get into the back of the station. Being the county coroner isn't cutting any ice with the dispatcher." Simon sighed. "I'm sorry to drag you into this, but I can't think of anyone else who can help."

"That's okay." Skye liked Bunny and thought the high-spirited redhead was good for Simon, who tended to be a little stuffy. "I'm glad you called me."

"So, you'll help?"

"Of course," Skye said. "Let me try Wally's cell."

"I tried it, but maybe he'll answer if it's you."

"Do you want to hang on?"

"Yes." Simon's one-word response was clipped.

Skye took her cell phone from her pocket, turned it on, and punched in Wally's number. When the call went immediately to voice mail, she hung up and said to Simon, "Sorry, he's not picking up."

"Can you come down here?" Simon asked. "I know you're busy, but I need you."

"I'll be there in five minutes." Skye was touched. In all the years they'd dated, she couldn't remember Simon ever admitting he needed her, or anyone else for that matter. "Meanwhile, call my mom. Maybe she knows something or can at least intercede with the dispatcher for you."

"I'll do that right now." Simon's tone was hesitant. "I don't want to cause any trouble between you and Boyd, but I really appreciate this."

"No problem," Skye said immediately, then paused, wondering whether Wally *would* take issue with her for helping Simon. She shrugged. If he did, that was just too bad. She and Bunny were friends, and it was past time for Wally to get over his jealousy of Simon.

Turning to Justin and Frannie, Skye said, "When you're done assembling and tying the ribbons on the place cards, arrange them in order in these." She pointed to a stack of eight-by-ten boxes with the numbers one to fifty written in black Magic

Marker on the lids. "One set per table. When you're done, you can call it a day."

"What did Simon want?" Frannie scooted between Skye and the door. "Where are you going?"

"I'll be in town." Skye edged past her. "If you need me, call my cell."

"Wait a minute." Frannie ran after her. "Is Simon in trouble?"

"No." Skye got into the Bel Air and slammed the door before Frannie could ask any more questions.

When Skye arrived at the police station a little before five, half a dozen cars were parked in the lot it shared with the city hall and library, which wasn't a good sign. Business hours ended at four, and the library closed at noon on Tuesday, so there should have been only two vehicles—the dispatcher's and the on-duty officer's. What kind of trouble had Bunny gotten herself into this time?

As Skye pushed open the glass door, she could see Simon pacing back and forth in the tiny waiting room. His appearance was a shock. He usually looked as if he had stepped directly out of the pages of *GQ*, but today his hair was uncombed and he was wearing stretched-out sweatpants, a paint-stained T-shirt, and holey tennis shoes.

He greeted her with, "No progress here. Your mom wasn't home."

"That's odd," Skye murmured. "She and Dad should be just sitting down to supper. And she didn't mention going anywhere when I talked to her yesterday. It's so unfair; if I'm not where she expects me to be, she freaks, but she gets free range." She shook her head. "Mothers."

"At least yours isn't under arrest."

"Good point." Skye walked over to the glass partition that separated the radio area from the lobby. "Let me see what I can do about yours."

"Yes?" The dispatcher, whose name tag read LONNY, spoke through the intercom.

"Hi. I don't know if you remember me." *Shoot.* Lonny was a substitute who was called in when none of the regular dispatchers were available, and Skye had met him only once. "I'm the PD's psych consultant. Could you buzz me through please?"

"Uh." Lonny scrunched his face. "The thing is, I was told not to let anyone in."

Skye pasted on her most reassuring smile. "I'm sure that doesn't include me."

"Well . . ." Lonny fingered his mostly nonexistent mustache. "I don't know. They said no one."

"They who?"

"Sp—I'm not supposed to say."

"I understand." Skye made eye contact. "How about you check with Chief Boyd, then?"

"He said he didn't want to be disturbed. To refer anything that came up to the officer on duty."

"Okay." Skye needed to remember to ask Wally

194

for a key so she could avoid the third degree by coming and going through the garage. "Then ask him."

"She's on her supper break." Lonny shook his head. "I'm only supposed to call her if it's an emergency."

"Okay." Skye dug through her tote, pulled out her wallet, found her ID card, and pressed it against the glass. "See, I work here."

"Anyone could print up one of those." Lonny's tone was stubborn.

Taking a deep breath to calm down, since shouting would not get her what she wanted, she said, "Check on the chief's desk. There's a picture of him and me there that should convince you that, no matter what, he'd want you to let me in."

It didn't feel right to use her relationship with Wally to help Simon, but Skye reassured herself that she was really helping Bunny, which was a different story.

When the dispatcher returned, his tone was both apologetic and annoyed. "Why didn't you just say you were Chief Boyd's girlfriend?"

Skye didn't answer. Even after five years of living back home, it was sometimes hard to remember that some Scumble Riverites thought a woman's entire identity came from the man she was married to or dating.

As Lonny buzzed her in, she said to Simon, "I'll let you know what's going on as soon as I can." She was positive she couldn't talk the young man into letting Simon in, too.

"Thanks." Simon nodded his understanding. "I'll be right here."

Skye took a few steps down a short hallway, stopping in front of the coffee/interrogation room at the end. The blinds were shut on the double windows, but she could hear voices behind the closed door.

"I'm going to ask you again: Where did you get the hundred-dollar bills you deposited in the bank today?"

Skye frowned; that wasn't Wally speaking. And she was fairly certain it wasn't any of the other Scumble River officers, either.

"Why are you asking me again?" Bunny's tone was coy. "Do you really think I'll give you a different answer than the one I've been giving you for the past hour? Or the one I gave Chief Boyd for the hour before you got here?"

"Ma'am," the stranger answered, "you don't seem to understand your situation. We can and will lock you up."

"So?" Bunny didn't sound the least bit intimidated. "Then I guess the fellows at the county jail and I will just have to have a little party." Her usual soprano slipped down into a sultry alto range. "After all, the deputies are all good friends of mine."

"Who said anything about the county jail?" The

196

stranger's voice was cool. "I'm talking about federal prison."

Prison? Skye quickly knocked on the door. She was uncertain about the best way to approach the situation, but she had to get in there before Bunny flirted her way onto a chain gang.

The door opened a crack, and Wally's irritated gaze swept over Skye. He stepped out of the room, closing the door behind him, took Skye by the elbow, and steered her into the nearest cubicle.

"What's wrong?" he asked. His posture was stiff and his shoulders tense. "Are you okay?"

"I'm fine," Skye assured him. "But I heard you arrested Bunny. Why?"

"She's not under arrest. We just have some questions for her." Wally frowned. "How did you hear about it anyway? There was nothing over the radio, and we took her out the back door of the bowling alley."

"The bartender saw you." Skye was hoping to avoid mentioning Simon.

"The bartender called you?"

"Not exactly." Skye tried to steer the conversation back to where she wanted it to be. "What are you questioning her about?"

"If he didn't call you, who did the bartender call?" Wally refused to be sidetracked.

"Her son," Skye hedged.

"Reid." Wally's expression grew darker. "You can say his name."

197

"Sorry." She was handling the situation badly but didn't know what to do to make it better. "Yes, Simon."

"And Reid called you?"

She nodded.

"Why?"

"The dispatcher wouldn't let him back here, you weren't answering your cell, and May wasn't home."

"So you came running to help him." Wally's voice was dangerously calm. "I should have guessed."

"Not help Simon." Despite her effort to keep it out, a sheepish note crept into Skye's voice. "I came to help Bunny. She *is* a friend of mine, you know."

Wally paused while considering what Skye had said; then he shrugged. "Maybe that's true, or maybe that's just what you've convinced yourself is true. But this makes me wonder if you still have feelings for Reid, and that's why you won't give me an answer to my proposal."

Skye was silent, not altogether sure Wally wasn't right. "Can we talk about this later?" She wasn't ready to have this discussion. "You still haven't told me why Bunny was brought in for questioning."

"Are you asking as the psych consultant"—Wally crossed his arms—"or her friend?"

"It can't be both?"

"No. One is sworn to keep confidentiality and the other isn't."

"In that case, the psych consultant." Skye hoped she was telling the truth. "So what's so hush-hush?"

"I'm not kidding about this being classified." He sounded worried. "If you tell anyone, both of us could be in trouble with the feds."

"The feds!" Skye squeaked. "What in blue blazes did she do?"

"Early this afternoon she deposited two thousand dollars' worth of counterfeit bills in the bank."

"Holy mackerel!"

Wally grunted his agreement.

"You don't think she knew that they were counterfeit, do you?"

"Probably not." Wally's voice was low. "She's too much of an airhead to pull off something like that."

"She's not an airhead." Skye tried to lighten the mood. "She's just reality impaired."

Wally ignored Skye's joke. "When the bank called me, I had no choice but to notify the Secret Service."

"I thought the FBI was in charge of counter-feiting." Skye was confused. "Isn't the Secret Service the one that protects the president?"

"Yes, but they're also responsible for national security, which is the heading counterfeiting falls under." Wally ran his fingers through his hair. "In today's climate, we're just lucky Homeland Security isn't involved."

A flare of panic ran through Skye as she realized that Bunny might be in deeper trouble than she'd originally thought. "Is the Secret Service questioning her now?"

"Uh-huh." Wally leaned against the desk. "I called the Chicago field office and they instructed me to bring her in on the QT. The last thing they want to get out is news of counterfeit money floating around."

"Scumble River isn't the best place to try to keep anything under wraps. Around here a secret is just something you tell one person at a time."

"I explained that to the two special agents they sent, but they pointed out that only the bank president and I know, so it would be fairly simple to track down any leaks."

"Well, I won't mention it to anyone," Skye assured him. "But once Bunny's released, I can't imagine her keeping it quiet."

"*If* she's released."

"That bad?"

"She's really pissing them off." Wally's mouth tightened. "And I haven't been able to convince her that this isn't something she can flutter her lashes and giggle her way out of."

"Can't you explain to the Secret Service agents that she doesn't mean any harm? That Bunny's one of a kind?"

"I tried. I told them that they broke the mold after they made her." Wally shook his head. "But the senior guy said they should have arrested the artist and sued him for faulty merchandise."

"Oh." Skye sagged.

"They've been here since four, and they aren't getting anywhere with her."

"Maybe she really doesn't know anything."

"Could be," Wally agreed. "But I have a hunch there's some reason she's afraid to tell what she does know."

"Do you think the phony money could be tied in with Belle's murder?" Skye hadn't made the connection before.

"It's possible. After all, two serious crimes, days apart, occurring in a town this size . . ." Wally twitched his shoulders. "What are the odds of that?"

"True. And this wedding has brought in a lot of outsiders," Skye reminded him.

"Exactly." Wally straightened. "Bunny had better quit messing around and tell us what she knows."

"Can you get the agents to let me talk to her?" Skye was pretty sure she could persuade Bunny to come clean. Whatever the redhead was afraid of, it probably had more to do with a scheme she didn't want Simon to know about than any knowledge of the murder.

CHAPTER 15

Something Blue

The Secret Service agents had reluctantly agreed to allow Skye, aka the Scumble River Police Department psychological consultant, to question Bunny. It had taken Wally half an hour to convince them, and it had taken Skye even longer to persuade the three men to step out of the room while she did so. If the PD had had a two-way mirror, they might have been less averse to the idea. But it didn't and they weren't.

Consequently, it was nearly six thirty when Skye walked into the coffee/interrogation room, a utilitarian space resembling the teacher's lounge at the high school. A counter with a sink ran the length of the sidewall, a long table took up most of the center area, and a couple of vending machines occupied the rear.

Skye had had nothing to eat since breakfast, so her stomach was growling and her temples were pounding. She wasn't sure if the headache was from hunger or stress—probably both. But she knew it was nothing a thick steak and a week away from Scumble River wouldn't cure.

Bunny was seated and squinting into the small mirror of a gold compact. The contents of her handbag were dumped out on the table, and she was fluffing her bright red curls with a rattail comb.

Skye was surprised that Bunny had been allowed to keep her purse. Maybe the agents were trying to soften her up since she looked like a pushover, but, boy, were they barking up the wrong bimbo.

As soon as Bunny noticed Skye, she popped out of her chair and grabbed her in a hug, saying in one breath, "Skye, honey, what brings you here? Did you come to straighten out those silly men?"

Bunny was dressed in Lycra stirrup pants; the matching silver halter barely contained her surgically enhanced breasts. Over the outfit she wore a black leather jacket, unzipped to show off her bellybutton ring.

Skye didn't even blink. Bunny had been a dancer in Las Vegas for twenty years, and some things, like her taste in clothing and her predilection for getting into trouble, would never change.

Not waiting for Skye to answer her first two questions, Bunny continued, "Do you want a soda?"

"No, thanks. I—"

"Well, I sure as hell need one. Do you have any money on you? Those assholes took my wallet."

Skye dug a dollar out of her pocket and handed it over. As Bunny fed the bill into the vending machine's slot, she appeared to have no idea how much trouble she was in.

After Bunny had had her first sip of sugar and

caffeine and was settled back in her chair, Skye said, "So, where did you get the counterfeit money?"

"I don't remember." Bunny waved her hand, the long silver nails catching the light like tiny daggers. "Do you remember where you got every dollar in your wallet?"

Skye stared hard into the redhead's big brown eyes. "Cut the crap." Her expression was just too innocent to be real, and Skye was in no mood for Bunny's usual coquettish behavior. "We're not talking about a couple of bucks here. There is no way on God's green earth you don't remember where you got two thousand dollars."

"You know . . ." The older woman set down her soda can and toyed with the rhinestone bangles on her wrist. "Sometimes my mind wanders."

"Really?" Skye raised a skeptical eyebrow. "Well, today it appears to have left you completely."

Bunny blinked, then said with a fake catch in her voice, "Not everyone is as smart as you are, Skye."

Skye crossed her arms. "Maybe not." She wasn't buying the poor little dumb Bunny routine. The redhead was silly and immature and impulsive, but she wasn't stupid. "But you do understand that counterfeiting is a serious offense."

"Yeah." Bunny grimaced. "It's a class C felony, and I can get up to twelve years in prison or be fined as much as two hundred and fifty thousand dollars."

"How in the heck do you know that?" Skye wondered whether the special agents had told her.

"Oh, I'm a walking storehouse of facts." Bunny's smile was lopsided. "It's just that sometimes I can't remember where I put the key to the storehouse door."

"It's time to find it." Skye hid her grin; giggling at the redhead's jokes would ruin the tough-guy image she was trying to project. "Because with your prior record, the judge wouldn't be lenient."

"Well." Bunny snapped shut her compact. "If I were assured Sonny Boy would never, ever hear what I had to tell you, maybe my memory would improve."

Skye smiled to herself. She knew it. "That might be arranged." The fake money had something to do with some scam Bunny didn't want Simon to know about. "But I can't promise until I know what's going on."

"But if I tell you and you decide you have to tell Sonny Boy, I'm screwed." Bunny pouted. "You have to promise first."

Was the redhead setting Skye up, or was she just being Bunny? Skye crossed her fingers and hoped she wouldn't have to go to confession for breaking her word. "I promise."

"Hmm." Bunny gave Skye a calculating look. "The question is, can I trust you?"

"Of course." Skye attempted her own version of an innocent expression. "Have I ever lied to you?"

"If you haven't, you'd be the first one."

Skye felt a stab of guilt but pushed it aside. "Come on, just tell me so we can both get out of here." She was doing this for Bunny's own good.

"Okay." Bunny's mood shifted, and she wagged her finger at Skye. "But remember, you might still end up marrying my son, and you wouldn't want me to be a monster-in-law."

"Bunny." Skye's tone held a warning. "Tell me or I'm leaving. And if I walk out of here, they're locking you up and throwing away the key. They don't even have to charge you. They can just claim you're a threat to national security."

"Okay, already." Bunny shrugged. "Don't get your thong in a twist. It's not that big a deal."

Skye shuddered inwardly at the thought of wearing a thong but nodded encouragingly.

"Well, that wedding planner, the one who went and got herself killed the other day . . ."

Skye winced. "Belle Canfield." Shoot. This was looking more and more like it was tied to the murder.

"Yeah, her." Bunny teetered to her feet, balancing precariously on four-inch silver stilettos. "She wanted to use the bowling alley for a combined bachelor and bachelorette bash."

"Yes." Skye had suggested the venue, figuring that if everyone would be drinking, it would be best to keep the party local. "And?"

"She wanted it on Thursday night."

"And?" Skye still couldn't see why Bunny would want to keep this a secret from Simon.

"Thursday night is the mixed-doubles bowling league. Our biggest group. They use all the alleys."

"So? I doubt the wedding party would want to bowl." At least not early in the evening when they were still sober, and the league would be finished by nine thirty, ten at the very latest.

"Maybe." Bunny frowned. "But she wanted the whole building. Said it had to be a private party. I offered her the bar or the grill or the basement, but no, Miss High-and-Mighty would only make the deal if I closed the place down."

"And when you said no . . ." Skye squirmed. This story couldn't end well.

"She offered me two thousand in cash, above the fee for the party."

"So you said yes."

"A little voice told me to." Bunny tilted her head. "It whispered in my ear, 'It's tax-free money; Sonny Boy won't have to know anything about it. You can finally get those Botox injections you've been wanting.'"

"You know that voice isn't real?" Skye questioned, worried that Bunny had finally slipped over the edge.

"It may not be real, but it has some pretty good ideas." Bunny tossed her curls. "So I took the dough, booked the party, and told the league we were fumigating that night."

Yikes! Skye cringed. Simon would not be happy that Bunny was ousting the locals, who were his loyal customers, in favor of out-of-towners. Or that she was going behind his back to do it. Or that she was planning on cheating on her income taxes.

"When did Belle give you the cash?" Skye asked.

"Saturday afternoon."

"Why did you wait until today to deposit it?"

"The bank was already closed when I got it Saturday, and it's closed on Sunday; then I forgot Monday," Bunny explained. "Which reminds me, if money doesn't grow on trees, why do banks have branches?"

Skye ignored Bunny's non sequitur and questioned, "So, the hundred-dollar bills that Belle gave you are the same bills that turned out to be counterfeit?"

"Yep." Bunny's shoulders drooped, and she suddenly looked every one of her fifty-seven years. "Trust me to be the one to get stuck with funny money when I decide to take a bribe. I should get SUCKER tattooed on my forehead."

Skye informed the feds and Wally about what Bunny had revealed, then gave Simon a modified report, telling him only that there was some problem with the deposit the wedding planner had given his mother to reserve the bowling alley for the bachelor/bachelorette party. She left out the parts about counterfeit money, bribery, and tax evasion. Even with the sanitized version, Skye was glad she wasn't along for the ride when he drove Bunny home.

Once Simon and his mother left, Skye waited for Wally while he conferred with the special agents. After a half hour, he told her to go ahead and leave since he had no idea how much longer he would be. The feds believed that Belle had brought the counterfeit money into Illinois from California, but they wanted to track down a few details before they left Scumble River.

As Skye hurried out of the police station toward her car, intent on dinner and a relaxing bath, a hand came down on her shoulder. She shrieked and whirled around.

"Whoa." Simon put up both hands. "Did I frighten you?"

"Yes. You nearly scared me to death." She wished people would quit accosting her in parking lots. "What are you doing back here?"

"Sorry." His tone was sheepish.

"That's okay. I just thought you had left with your mother."

"I did. But once I dropped her off, I realized I hadn't thanked you for helping me."

"You didn't have to come all the way back here for that." Skye noticed that Simon had changed clothes. He now wore pressed khakis and a moss green polo shirt. "You could have called and left me a message." She set her purse on the hood of her car, opened it, and began digging for her keys.

"I could have." Simon plucked the key ring out of her bag, but instead of giving it to her, he tossed it in the air and caught it. "But I didn't want to."

"Oh." Tilting her head to look at him, she asked, "Why not?"

"Uh." A discomfited expression stole across Simon's face. "Well, you see, I . . ."

"Yes?" Skye was confused. The Simon she knew was rarely uncertain or at a loss for words.

"Are you hungry?"

"Yes." The question caught her by surprise.

"Good. So am I." Simon put her keys in his pocket. "Let me take you to dinner."

Skye refused to think of this as a date. She and Simon were just grabbing something to eat together, like they did after church on most Sunday mornings. It wasn't as if she hadn't tried to refuse. He had nearly shoved her into his Lexus.

Still, she wished she looked a little nicer. She had on the dress and heels from her dance lesson, but it had been close to twelve hours since she'd put on her makeup, and she couldn't remember the last time she'd combed her hair.

Simon's voice interrupted her thoughts. "Since the Feed Bag closes at seven, I thought we'd go to a new restaurant a little south of town along the river."

"There's a new place?" Would it seem tacky if she got out her makeup bag and fixed herself up? "I wonder why I haven't heard about it."

"It's only been open a couple of weeks, and you've been tied up with the wedding and all."

"True," Skye agreed. "I haven't read the *Star* in a month. I have a stack of them in my sunroom, but I fall asleep before I get past the front page."

"Believe me, you haven't missed much. Unless you want to know whose dog is barking or whose teenagers got arrested for DUI."

Skye gazed at Simon's handsome face. The moonlight streaming through the windshield bathed him in a golden glow, and being alone with him like this made her think about all that had happened since they'd broken up. It saddened her that things had turned out so badly between them.

They rode in silence until Skye said, "It's really sweet of you to take me to dinner, but totally unnecessary. You know, I love Bunny, and I was happy to help her."

"This isn't about Bunny." He glanced at her, his amber eyes smoldering. "And sweet is not the way I feel about you."

Uh-oh! Skye didn't know how to respond, so she didn't. What had brought this on? Simon's passion had always been limited to the bedroom. Had he changed, or had she underestimated him from the beginning?

Neither of them said anything more until they

arrived at the restaurant. Only a few other customers were present, which at eight thirty on a Tuesday was what Skye would have expected. Not many locals would be out this late on a work night. Even on weekends most people around here had eaten by seven.

Once they were seated, a server arrived to take their drink orders. Simon shocked Skye again by ordering a bottle of wine without consulting her. He knew she seldom drank, and certainly not when she had to get up early the next day. What had gotten into him? It was almost as if he'd been a black-and-white movie in the past, and now he'd been colorized by Ted Turner.

After the server left, Skye and Simon sat in silence. Their table was next to a large window overlooking the Scumble River. Water lapped the shore, and Skye gazed at the reflections of stars twinkling on its inky surface.

The stillness grew uncomfortable until finally Simon asked, "How are—?"

At the same time Skye said, "Do you—?"

They both stopped and Simon said, "You first."

"No, you go ahead," Skye insisted. "What were you about to say?"

"I was just about to ask how Frannie and Justin are working out as assistants."

"Great." Skye fiddled with the napkin in her lap. "They're a lot of help."

"They're both good kids. And although I know

Xavier is disappointed that Frannie transferred from Loyola to JJC, I think it was for the best."

"Yeah." Skye nodded. "Some teens aren't ready to make such a huge leap from small-town high school to big-city college."

"Right. Change is hard for a number of people." Simon took a sip of water. "What were you going to say?"

"Uh. What was I going to say?" Skye gave a nervous laugh. "Oh, yeah. Have you been here before? The waitress seemed to know you."

"Connie and her husband own the place. They're friends of mine."

"That's nice." Skye bit her lip. She and Simon never used to have any trouble finding things to talk about, but tonight the atmosphere around them crackled with an underlying tension that dried her mouth and emptied her mind.

Before she could think of a topic of conversation, Connie arrived with the wine. She smiled at them both as she poured, and asked, "Special occasion?"

Simon stared at Skye and said, "I hope so."

Skye gazed into her glass. What did that mean?

Connie's grin widened. "Would you like to relax first, or are you ready to order?"

"I'd like the duck, please," Skye blurted out. Sitting around sharing a bottle of wine with her ex-boyfriend now seemed a little too intimate, and she was eager to eat and go home.

213

Simon ordered steak Diane. After quizzing them about the rest of their choices, Connie left, and Simon and Skye went back to staring out the window.

At last, Simon cleared his throat, opened his mouth, then paused as if he had changed his mind. Finally, he asked, "How do you like the wine?"

"It's good." She smiled at him. "You remembered I don't like it too dry."

"I remember everything about you."

His sexy tenor sent a shiver down her spine, and Skye choked on her next gulp of wine. *Holy moly!* She so shouldn't be here, and she definitely shouldn't be getting turned on by another man when she had Wally's ring in her purse.

She struggled for a response and finally said, "You always did have a remarkable memory. That's why it was so scary being your bridge partner. You knew every card that had been played. I was constantly worried I'd lose the game for us and you'd be mad."

"Did I give you the impression that a game was more important to me than you were?" Simon furrowed his brow. "Do I really come across as that kind of guy?"

Skye twirled the liquid in her glass until she had formed a tiny red tornado. "Yes." It was time to be truthful with him and herself. "You do, or at least you did."

"I see." The corner of his mouth twisted downward. "Why did you stay with me for so long?"

"I thought I loved you." She felt panic building at the back of her throat and swallowed it down. "And I thought you loved me."

His voice was heavy with remorse. "I did." He was normally a careful man, but that veneer was starting to crack. "I still do."

"Really?" Skye stared into his golden hazel eyes, trying to understand the bewildering array of emotions rushing through her. "That certainly wasn't my impression from what you said to me at the diner eighteen months ago."

"I was wrong." Simon reached across the table and captured her hand. "And I was afraid."

"Of me?"

"Of how you made me feel."

"I don't understand." Skye tried to remove her hand, but he held on tight. "I thought I made you feel good."

"Too good." Simon's tone was raw. "As it got better and better between us, I kept wondering how I could stand it when you left me. And then when you suspected me of cheating, a part of me said, 'Fine. Let Skye leave me now, because later it will hurt even more.' "

Skye had to lean forward to hear the rest.

Simon stared down at their clasped hands and whispered, "As it did when my mother left me."

The pain in his voice tore at her. "I think I understand now." She took a deep breath, afraid she would start crying. "What happened to make you change your mind? Did you go into therapy or something?"

"No." Simon shook his head. "It wasn't any one big revelation. Just a lot of little ones over time."

"Oh?" Skye wasn't convinced. Surely something had had to happen to set his change of heart in motion. "Like what?"

"It started last October when you were nearly killed by that psycho." Simon's voice hardened. "Before that, in the back of my mind, I always thought we'd get together again once you got over your infatuation with Boyd. Realizing that I could lose you forever before that happened was a real eye-opener. That's when I started 'accidentally' running into you after Mass." He smiled sadly. "I was sure that, given enough time, once we started talking again, you'd see I was the one for you. But you didn't."

"I thought you just wanted to be friends." Skye frowned. Hadn't she? "So you've been leading up to this moment for eight months? Why didn't you say anything sooner?"

"I was sure the chemistry between you and Boyd would burn out." His hopeless stare drilled into her soul. "But tonight, when I saw you march into battle for my mother, I knew I couldn't wait any longer."

"So, then you really didn't mean it when we had

our big fight and you said the relationship I want doesn't exist? That I was deluding myself by wanting a soul mate?"

"No. I was the one deluding myself." Simon's expression was bleak. "Now I know there *is* only one person who completes me, and it's been hell since she's been gone."

Skye sat, stunned. She had never expected to hear those words from Simon.

When she didn't respond, he said, "I know you're involved with Boyd. And I know our breakup was my fault—"

"Wait." Skye interrupted him. She had to tell Simon about Wally's proposal before he said something he might regret. "Wally has asked me to marry him."

"Have you answered him?"

"Not yet."

"Then there's still time." Simon produced a faint smile.

"For what?"

He stared into her eyes. "For you to give me a second chance."

CHAPTER 16

Flower Power

Every instinct in Skye's body told her to roll over, pull up the covers, and go back to sleep. Her legs and back ached, probably from the dance class, and it felt as if she'd lain down only five minutes before, even though her alarm claimed it was six a.m. and she knew she'd gone to bed at ten thirty.

Of course, she hadn't fallen asleep until after three, having tossed and turned, her thoughts leap-frogging from the wedding preparations to the murder to Simon.

His astonishing plea for a second chance had left Skye speechless, and she had finally told him that she couldn't even think about what he was asking for until after the wedding was over. Simon had said he understood, and after they'd finished their meal, he'd dropped her back at her car, announcing that he'd see her Sunday to find out her verdict. The irony that Sunday was the same day she'd promised Wally a decision about his proposal was not lost on her.

Then there was the little matter of Kathryn Steele. As Skye and Simon were leaving the restaurant, Skye noticed Kathryn watching them from a corner table. Skye knew that the probability of meeting someone you know increases exponentially when you're with someone you don't want to be seen with, but it was just her luck that that someone was the owner of the local newspaper. No doubt, a report of Skye's dinner with Simon would be in next week's "Talk of the Town" gossip column.

Skye groaned, then decided she needed to channel her mother and pretend none of it had happened. If this was during the school year, rather than three days before a million-dollar wedding for which she was solely responsible, she would have called in sick. But since she was the boss, she had to get up.

Skye staggered to the bathroom and stared into the mirror over the sink. She looked awful. Her hair gave the impression that she had spent the night in a Cuisinart, but her face argued that she'd been sleeping on a waffle iron. Would a shower help, or since she looked like the Wicked Witch of the East, would she just melt under the water? She decided to find out.

Having survived bathing, and feeling marginally better, Skye threw on a pair of shorts and a T-shirt, then gathered her hair into a ponytail. She didn't have time to mess with her appearance today.

Before getting her own breakfast, Skye fed Bingo and cleaned his litter. She'd found out the hard way that if the box wasn't immaculate, the finicky feline refused to use it and would choose somewhere more to his liking—like her most expensive pair of shoes or the middle of her bed —to do his business.

Finally, cradling a precious cup of tea as if it were a baby bird, Skye took a seat at the kitchen table to plan her day. First on the list was to make sure she still had a floral designer. If Wally arrested Iris, the shit would hit the fan, and the fallout would not be evenly distributed.

Taking a legal pad and pen from the kitchen drawer, she wrote:

8:00 a.m.—Call Wally.
8:30 a.m.—Motor court—Check supplies for favors / Show Frannie and Justin how to put together the boxes
10:00 a.m.—Drive to country club / Consult with fabric drapers
1:00–4:00 p.m.—Call caterer, baker, etc.
5:30 p.m.—Dinner with Wally
7:00 p.m.—Bridal shower—be there at 6:30

Skye checked the time: eight ten. Rats! She was already running late. Scooping up the phone, she dialed Wally at home. When his voice mail message started, she hung up and tried his cell, then his private line at the PD. *Shoot!* Where could he be? Exhaling noisily, she pushed the buttons for the station's general number.

Her call was answered immediately. "Police,

fire, and emergency department. How may I help you?"

Skye recognized the voice. "Thea, it's Skye. Is Wally around?"

"Hi, hon. Nope. He got a call a couple of minutes ago from County, then took off. Said he needed to talk to that florist over at the motor court."

"Shit!"

"Skye," Thea tutted. "Do you kiss your mother with that mouth?"

"Sorry. If Wally checks in, ask him to call me."

"Sure thing, hon."

"Thanks."

"Oops!" Thea yelped. "Gotta go. My other line is ringing. Bye."

So much for Skye's schedule. Now the top priority on her to-do list was find Wally and pray she still had a floral designer. If not, she would have to take a crash course in Flower Arranging 101, and she knew that wouldn't turn out well. Her eighth-grade home-ec project had ended up looking more like a compost heap than a centerpiece.

Skye grabbed the breakfast of champions—a can of Diet Coke and a brown-sugar-cinnamon Pop-Tart—and flew out the door. She made record time, and it was only a little past eight thirty when she pulled into the motor court.

The bad news was that a squad car was parked in front of Iris Yee's cabin. The good news was that the floral designer was not locked in its backseat.

After pulling in next to the cruiser, Skye jumped out of the Bel Air and headed toward Iris's cabin. A few steps before she got to the entrance, she stopped, unsure of her next move. Should she knock, wait for them to come out, or what?

While she vacillated, the door opened and Wally emerged. His well-muscled body moved with an easy grace, and as he came toward her, she could see his broad shoulders straining against his navy uniform shirt. Even at a time like this, she couldn't help but notice how hot he was. Regrettably, the frustrated expression on his handsome face did not add to his attractiveness.

When he spotted her, he said, "Getting a late start today?"

"Yeah. I had a hard time waking up this morning." Skye noted that his greeting wasn't as warm as usual, but she figured he was preoccupied with the investigation. "I called to ask if you had heard anything about the bouquet holder yet, and Thea said you were here talking to Iris."

"Yeah. County called the minute I walked into my office this morning." Wally glanced around the parking lot. "Let's sit in the squad so we're not overheard."

Skye barely waited until the car doors were closed before she asked, "Are you arresting Iris?"

"No." Wally hit the steering wheel with the heel of his hand. "Damn it! Everything that connects her to the bouquet holder is circumstantial."

"What did County find out?" Skye was torn—relieved Iris was still free to work the wedding but discouraged they weren't making any progress on the case.

"The bouquet holder does match the wound on Belle's head, and they even found a strand of her hair caught in the seam, but with no usable prints we don't know who wielded the weapon."

"I'm guessing that because the bouquet holder wasn't on the invoice, Iris claims she has no knowledge of it."

"Exactly." Wally's nostrils flared.

"How did Iris explain what she'd said about Belle being a pain?"

"She maintains that while the vic *was* difficult to work for, she made more money off Belle's weddings than any three or four other planners' events put together."

"So why kill the golden goose?" Skye tapped her chin. "That would be true for all the vendors."

"Maybe the California ones, but for the local businesses this is a one-shot deal."

"True."

"Also, the method makes it look like an unplanned murder. A heat-of-the-moment killing."

"Right." Skye nodded. "Whoever did this wasn't prepared. Something Belle did or said must have set him—or her—off. Which means it could be anyone. She had a knack for finding a person's sore spot and poking at it until they screamed."

"What do you mean?"

"She knew Riley was intent on having the wedding in Scumble River, so Belle threatened to move it back to California if she didn't get a local assistant. And with Iris, Belle continually questioned her creative vision just to see her squirm."

"This last month has been tough on you." Wally's voice was cool.

"I'm used to handling mean people. I work in public education, remember?" What was he getting at?

"But this is your vacation. Your time to recover from being poked at." Wally frowned. "If you'd let me help you out, you wouldn't have to take these summer jobs. I could lend you the money to fix up your house."

"I already have one home-improvement loan. I don't want to get in over my head. Besides, I might not be a good investment," Skye teased. "You could lose your shirt."

She had no idea how much money Wally had. His father was a multimillionaire, but because Wally refused to work for his dad, she didn't know whether he had only his chief of police salary, or some sort of trust fund. It seemed mercenary to ask him before she accepted his proposal, but the whole money issue was one of the big reasons she couldn't decide whether to marry him or not. She'd been engaged to one wealthy guy, and that hadn't worked out very well.

"I'm sure you're a great investment," Wally said flatly. "But you're not sure if I am."

"That's not true," she protested. "It's just—"

"But I guess I shouldn't complain, since I was the one who talked you into filling in for Belle so you could help me out."

"Yes. You did." Skye jabbed him in the chest with her index finger. "You owe me big-time for that."

"You're right. I do." Wally's tone was thoughtful. "And I had to renege on dinner last night, too. I hope you weren't too disappointed."

Skye felt her heart sink. Did he know about her dinner with Simon? Should she tell Wally what he had said? Wally had enough on his mind, and he'd have a fit when he heard. He was already jealous of her ex-boyfriend.

"Skye? Are you there?"

"Sorry." Great. She had hesitated too long, and now he was looking at her funny. "I was just thinking."

Wally raised an eyebrow. "So, did you go right home last night?"

"Well, actually, no." *Shoot!* He definitely knew something. Skye bet that the newspaperwoman had called him, told him she had seen Skye and Simon together, and offered him the details for an exclusive about the murder. Skye was pretty sure Wally wouldn't make that deal, but she realized she'd better fess up. "Simon took me to get a bite to eat to thank me for helping his mother."

"Was Bunny with you?"

"Uh." Skye bit her lip. "No. She was probably too tired after all she'd been through."

"Bunny Reid? Too tired to go out? Are we talking about the same woman? Red hair, fake boobs, about five-seven?"

"Very funny." Skye's swatted his biceps. "Okay, so Bunny wasn't too tired. Maybe Simon was tired of *her*."

"That's a lot more likely, but my guess is he wanted to be alone with you."

Skye made a noncommittal sound. She hadn't decided if she should reveal what Simon had said.

"Where did you eat? The Feed Bag was closed. Did you go to McDonald's?"

"No. Did you know there's a new restaurant a few miles south of town on the river?"

"Yeah. A couple from Clay Center opened it up a few weeks ago. It's called the Moonstone."

"The food was good, and it has a really pretty view." Skye tried to distract him. "We should go sometime."

"I have reservations for us for Sunday." Wally stared at her with angry eyes. "I thought it would be a nice place to celebrate our engagement. That is if you're *finally* ready to forget the past and start our future together."

"Oh." Skye studied her left hand, which was bare of Wally's ring. He had a right to be angry about her indecisiveness. "I know you're right."

"But I think I'll come up with somewhere else now." Wally's mouth had formed a thin white line.

"I'm sorry."

"I don't want to go to a place you associate with Reid."

Skye nodded, feeling terrible. Wally was a good man, and she loved him. She pressed her fingers against her temples. Should she just tell Simon it was too late and tell Wally yes right now? She opened her mouth, but nothing came out.

After a few seconds of silence, Wally sighed, seeming to resign himself that he'd have to wait a few more days for her decision. "Well, I should let you get to work."

"Right. Frannie and Justin will be here any second, and there are five hundred little pink boxes with their names on them."

"I need to go over to Laurel and put a fire under the crime tech's butt." Wally started the car. "He still hasn't identified all the prints on the carton the bouquet holder was hidden behind."

"Any other leads?"

"No. Our most credible suspects are Iris and the tent-and-rental man. I'm not convinced he wasn't the one with Belle at the Brown Bag the night of her murder. You told me she claimed that she never went to bed alone, and a lot of women are attracted to those big, tough, tattooed guys."

"True. At least for a one-night fling. And from what they said yesterday during the dance lesson, it doesn't look as if any of the groomsmen were involved with her. And Riley said she never allowed Nick to be alone with Belle," Skye reported. "Tonight at the shower I'll ask the bridesmaids if one of Belle's exes might have wanted to see her dead."

"Sounds good," Wally agreed. "That pretty much leaves the photographer, the linen consultant, and the dress-shop owner as the most viable secondary suspects. They all have obvious financial motives."

"Now, if we could only find someone who saw one of them in Scumble River late Saturday night."

"I've got Quirk and Martinez showing their pictures around town, but no luck so far." Wally shook his head. "At least the vic's parents are due back today. There's something funny about them not responding to any of my messages."

"Do I see a trip to California in your future?" Skye tilted her head. "I bet you'd look good in surfer gear."

Wally grunted. "I can just imagine trying to get the city to pay for that."

"Yeah. The only way that would fly is if they all got to go with you."

"And brought their wives." Wally kissed her cheek. "I've got my cell on if you need me."

"Okay." Skye slid out of the cruiser. "I'll put mine on, too."

"You be careful today. We still have no idea who killed Belle or why, The feds may be convinced it was the counterfeiters, but I'm not so sure."

"Yes, sir." She gave him a mock salute. "See you tonight at five thirty."

By the time Frannie and Justin arrived at nine, Skye had unpacked one carton of each of the favor's four components and set up an assembly line. She showed them how to put together the gift boxes, place the wine-bottle stopper and corkscrew set inside, attach the tiny heart-shaped thank-you card to the ribbon, and tie the bows.

Once the teens were busy, she went to see how Iris was doing. Skye found her knee-deep in roses and orchids. Apparently the deliveryman had offloaded the flowers on the curb and left.

"Hi." Skye waved. "Need a hand?"

"Please." Iris hefted a huge white plastic bucket of long-stemmed pink roses. "These need to get into the floral refrigerator as soon as possible."

As they went back and forth with the containers, Skye commented, "I've never seen this many flowers in one place before."

"Yes." Iris placed a pail of orchids on a shelf in the rear of the cooler. "Normally there would be half this many, maybe even a third, but your cousin and her fiancé wanted something lavish."

"I can believe that." Skye wiped her brow. "Scumble River will be talking about this wedding for the next fifty years."

"Riley's exact words were that she wanted the décor to be 'jaw-dropping.'"

"Knowing what's planned, I'd say Riley should be able to hear the chins hitting the floor."

"She'd better or I'll be in trouble." Iris didn't sound as if she was kidding.

"Even with Belle out of the picture?" Skye asked. When Iris shrugged, she added, "I bet this is the first event you've ever worked at that had the preparations interrupted by a murder."

"Yes. Thank goodness."

Skye glanced at the tiny woman as she said, "Although I'm sure some of the people working for Belle in the past have wanted to kill her."

"Maybe." Iris shrugged again.

"I know since this wedding isn't local, Belle is using a lot of new vendors, but how about the ones she arranged to come from California?" Skye pretended to focus on a pail of greenery. "Do you think any of them got fed up with her demands?"

"Besides me, you mean?"

"Of course."

"The other regulars aren't arriving until Friday," Iris answered.

"Oh." So much for that theory. As the two women worked in companionable silence, Skye said, "I just have to ask, did your name influence your choice of profession?"

"In a way." Iris hefted the last container onto

the shelf. "My parents owned a florist shop. They named all their children after flowers."

"How many siblings do you have?"

"Three. Hyacinth, Daisy, and Rose." Iris waited for Skye to walk out of the refrigerator, then followed her. After locking the door behind them, she asked, "Is this the only key?"

"Yes."

"That's not good." Iris tucked a lock of straight black hair behind her ear. "I tend to lose stuff like keys."

"Is that why I keep finding the cabin you're using for storage unlocked?"

"Uh-huh."

"What do you do at home?" Skye couldn't understand how someone so successful and seemingly organized in every other way couldn't keep track of a small thing like a key.

"My assistant, aka husband, takes care of those issues."

"And he isn't arriving until Friday?" Skye confirmed, remembering the floral designer had mentioned the date yesterday.

"Yes, he's stopping in Chicago to pick up the crew I hired and should be here by mid-morning."

"Good." Skye smiled. "Have you ever tried wearing the key around your neck? You could put the keys to your cabin, the storage cabin, and the refrigerator all on the same chain."

"That's a great idea." Iris brightened. "But I don't have a chain that's sturdy enough."

This was like dealing with a first grader. "I'll find something that will work."

"Here, you hold on to the key." Iris thrust the tiny piece of metal into Skye's hand.

"I'll be right back." Skye ran toward the cottage where Justin and Frannie were working to get a length of the narrow favor ribbon for the keys. As she entered she heard the teens arguing.

"You tell her. She likes you better." Justin's voice cracked.

"I'm not telling her. I told her about the misspelling on the menus and programs. It's your turn." Frannie's tone was stubborn. "And she does not like me better."

Skye cleared her throat and the teens looked in her direction.

"Uh, hi, Ms. D." Frannie shoved her boyfriend forward. "Justin has something to tell you."

"I do not." Justin backed up. "You figured it out; you tell her."

Skye glanced at her watch. It was past ten o'clock. "Somebody tell me already. I'm late leaving for the country club as it is."

Frannie shot Justin an evil look, then swallowed and said, "There aren't enough pink boxes. We're fifty short."

"Crap!" Skye felt like hitting something. Preferably her cousin, the picky bride.

"I called the company listed on the packing order," Frannie volunteered. "They can't get us the rest of them until Monday at the earliest."

"Which is useless," Skye finished Frannie's thought.

"I checked online, Ms. D.," Justin offered. "But no one has the exact same ones in stock, and even with overnight shipping we wouldn't get the boxes until Thursday or Friday."

"Terrific." Skye closed her eyes. "You know what that means, don't you?"

Justin shook his head, but Frannie squealed, "A shopping trip!"

"And you know the only place around here that might have something like that?" Skye's expression didn't match the teenage girl's.

"Wal-Mart!" Frannie jumped up and down and clapped her hands. "We're going to Wal-Mart!"

Skye rolled her eyes. Just what she needed. A Wal-Mart shopping extravaganza.

CHAPTER 17

Bang for Your Buck

The Wal-Mart in Laurel was surrounded by a parking lot the size of Rhode Island. And, as usual, it was full. To most of the inhabitants of Stanley County, shopping there wasn't a quick in-and-out trip; it was a day's entertainment. It wasn't just a store; it was an amusement park.

Which was exactly what Skye was worried about. Justin had agreed to remain behind to continue assembling the favors, but Frannie had begged to go with Skye. The teen had prevailed when she pointed out that they could take separate cars, and she could bring the boxes back to Scumble River while Skye went directly to the country club. Now all Skye had to do was keep Frannie from getting distracted by the merchandise.

Frannie and Skye were able to park relatively close to each other, but their walk to the entrance was interrupted at least a dozen times by folks stopping them to say hello and ask what they were there to buy—a small-town social ritual that Skye had come to accept. Once Skye and Frannie were inside, they were hailed by another handful of Scumble Riverites before selecting a cart, and even more as they began their search for the party-supply section of the superstore.

Skye rarely entered the behemoth structure, but Frannie confidently steered them toward the right. They turned the corner next to a rack of Father's Day cards, zigzagged past the wrapping paper and bows, and entered the party-goods aisle.

Oh, my gosh! For a moment Skye was stunned, overwhelmed by the countless displays of Hello Kitty paper plates, Spider-Man napkins, My Pretty Pony tablecloths, and tiny toys of every description. Was anything here *not* designed to lure parents into overspending for little Susie's or Billy's birthday extravaganza?

Shaking off her amazement, Skye hoisted her purse more securely on her shoulder and scanned the shelves. "Do you see any items without logos, Frannie?"

The teen started to shake her head, then pointed to the far end. "Maybe down there."

Skye squinted. "Where?"

Frannie took off at a jog, tossing an "I'll go check" over her shoulder.

As Skye walked in the direction Frannie had indicated, she attempted to keep an eye on both sides of the aisle. She was in midstride when she glimpsed a patch of unadorned pink and skidded to a halt.

A nanosecond later a shopping cart rammed into the back of her knees, and a whiny female voice screamed, "Get the hell out of my way."

Flailing her arms in an effort not to fall, Skye did an awkward pirouette and found herself staring into Glenda Doozier's rabbitlike eyes. Skye's heart sank. Of all the people she didn't want to run into when she was in a hurry, Glenda and her husband, Earl, topped the list.

Skye likened the Dooziers to a pack of wild hyenas, intensely loyal to their own group but lacking the ability or desire to care about anyone else. They weren't known for being the brightest flashlights in the woods, but they did have a talent for stumbling on, and taking advantage of, those whose bulbs were even dimmer. In a town like Scumble River, which was surrounded by railroad tracks, it was impossible to say someone lived on the wrong side of them, but the Dooziers came mighty close.

Earl was skinny, except for the small potbelly that hung over the elastic waist of his shorts, and a head shorter than his statuesque wife. His greasy brown hair formed a horseshoe around a cereal bowl–size bald spot on top of his head.

He was the patriarch and unofficial ruler of a Scumble River clan the locals called the Red Raggers—a derogatory term for kinfolk who lived in shacks by the river and led a different sort of life from the majority of Scumble Riverites. For the most part the Red Raggers kept to themselves —except when they were running some kind of con on the out-of-towners.

The problem wasn't that the Red Raggers were poor, although they were, and it wasn't that they dwelled in squalor, although they did; it was more that they seemed to enjoy living that way. As Skye had once tried to explain, the Red Raggers were the original out-of-the-box thinkers—as long as the box was a case of beer.

"Miz Skye." Earl peeked out from behind his wife's shoulder. "I ain't seen you in a coon's age."

"Earl, Glenda." Skye nodded to the couple. She

had established a good relationship with Earl from working with his many children, sisters, brothers, nieces, and nephews in her job as a school psychologist, but she and Glenda had started off on the wrong foot when Skye first moved back to town, and they'd never quite gotten into sync. "It has been a while. Last Halloween, right?"

"Yep." Earl's toothless smile widened. "At the haunted house when I saved you from them-there spooks."

"Yeah, you sure saved her. If nearly gettin' shot in the ass amounts to savin' someone." Glenda snorted and hitched up her Daisy Duke cutoffs. From her grimy feet shod in red plastic stiletto sandals to her dyed blond hair with its two-inch black roots, she was the embodiment of an ideal Red Ragger woman.

"Uh, sorry to rush off, but I'm in a big hurry," Skye said. Not wanting to get involved in the inevitable squabble between the pair, she looked around for Frannie. "I've got to run."

Before Skye could move, Earl darted in front of her, his cowboy-boot-encased feet moving remarkably fast. "Whatcha doin' here anyway?" he asked. "I heard you was puttin' on that fancy weddin' for that snooty cuzzin a yours now that the other lady got herself kilt."

"That's right."

"I sure hope people don't start yellin' at you like they did her."

"I hope not, too." Skye stepped backward, trying to escape. "I'm here to pick up a few things we need for the big day." She made a show of peering at her watch. "Gee, look at the time. I better scoot."

"You know"—Earl blocked her getaway—"I was thinkin' of maybe stoppin' on by and seein' how y'all put on a shindig like that, but it turns out we got our own hitchin' to throw. Ours is on Friday, and your'n is on Saturday, but I'll prolly be too hungover to get outta bed until Sunday."

"Well, we certainly understand." Skye blew out a relieved breath. Earl may have been several inches short of a ruler, but he'd always been a good friend to her, and she would have hated to see what Riley would do to him if he crashed her wedding. "Who's getting married?"

She crossed her fingers that it wasn't Earl's younger sister Elvira, who had just graduated high school in May. Elvira was a bright girl, and Skye had hopes that she might do something more with her life than popping out a kid each year and getting drunk every Saturday night.

"Elvis." Earl's bony chest swelled underneath his tank top. "Everyone said he didn't have it in him, but the boy went and knocked up Mavis Beckman."

Elvis was Elvira's twin, but where she had gotten the brains, he hadn't even gotten the brawn. He had dropped out of school at sixteen and worked odd jobs ever since. *Odd* being the operant word.

"Okay, then." Skye wasn't sure what to say. Congratulations just didn't seem appropriate, and she had no idea who Mavis Beckman was.

"Wooee! Mavis's pa is madder'n a wet hen."

"But your family is happy about the wedding?" Skye sought clarification, something she often had to do when dealing with the Dooziers.

"Well, now, it is a durn shame she's not the purtiest pup in the litter." Earl tried to hide it but couldn't quite disguise the avaricious twinkle in his muddy brown eyes. "But Mavis's pa did promise he'd give her and whoever she ended up marryin' twenty acres and a tractor."

"I see." Skye edged backward. "Well, I really do have to go." She turned to make her escape but was blocked by a burly man holding two scrawny teenagers—his meaty hands wrapped entirely around their upper arms.

He shoved past Skye and marched up to Glenda and Earl. "Are these brats yours?"

Skye recognized the boys as the Dooziers' son Junior, who had just turned thirteen, and their fifteen-year-old nephew, Cletus.

"What's it to ya?" Glenda reached inside the too-tight purple tube top she barely wore and adjusted her breasts. "You got a problem with 'em?"

"I sure as hell do." The man's head was shaved, and he was built like a weight lifter. "These little turds have been wreaking havoc all over the store."

Skye tensed. She guessed he was security, and

239

he had no idea what a shallow gene pool he'd just entered.

"What'd they do?" Glenda narrowed her eyes, which were heavily framed in black eyeliner and false lashes. "I'm sure they were just havin' a little fun."

"Having a little fun?" the security guard sputtered. "First they took a bottle of Mountain Dew and used it to make a path leading to the restrooms."

Earl bleated, "Ya mean they wasted Dew?" He turned to Skye. "You know I raised 'em better than that. They shoulda knowed to drink it first, then use what the good Lord gave 'em for free to mark their trail."

"Shut up, Earl." Glenda flicked her spouse a poisonous glance. To the security guard she said, "That don't sound too bad."

"Next, they went into electronics, tuned all the clock radios to a polka station, turned the volume to ten, and set the alarms to go off simultaneously."

"You don't like polka music?" Earl screwed up his face. "That's just not right."

The security guard ignored Earl and continued, "I finally caught up to them when they set up a valet parking sign by the store's entrance."

"What's wrong with that?" Earl asked. "Cletus has his driving permit, and it's a long way to the back of the lot for some of the old people who shop here. They was just doin' a public service."

"Public service, my ass!" The guard's complexion turned maroon. "Either you all leave right now or I'm calling the police."

Skye cringed. Everyone in Scumble River knew you didn't accuse a Doozier of wrongdoing, at least not to his face and without backup, but this guy wasn't from town.

The guard lifted the boys off their feet, and Junior started crying, "He's hurtin' me, Ma. Real bad."

Skye noticed Glenda slipping a switchblade from her purse, and Earl was fingering a suspicious bulge in the pocket of his saggy knit shorts.

Damn! She so didn't want to get involved, but blood was about to be shed, and it might be her own. She'd seen enough movies to know that the innocent bystanders were always the first to get hurt.

Using her most soothing psychologist voice, she asked the guard, "Uh, sir, was there any actual monetary damage done by the boys?"

"They paid for the pop," the guard snarled. "But stealing a car is grand theft."

Four pair of eyes swung to the two teens. The redhead froze.

"Junior Doozier." His mother yanked him out of the guard's grasp. "You explain yourself right this minute!"

"Ma." He tried to wiggle away, but Glenda's grip tightened. "Shucks, Cletus and me was just messin' around."

"Messin' how?" Glenda shook him slightly.

"Well, we just took a couple of the cars for a little ride." Junior finally squirmed free and ducked behind Skye. "We didn't take 'em outta the parkin' lot or nothin'."

"Tell them what you did with the cars when you finished your joyride," the guard demanded.

"What did you do?" Skye stared Junior in the eye. He was younger than his cousin but, in her experience with the pair, always the ringleader.

He scuffed the floor with the toe of his tennis shoe. "Cletus and me didn't crash 'em or nothin'." He glared at the guard. "They're fine. We parked 'em in front of the store so their owners could find 'em easy-like."

"In the loading zone, with their keys in the ignition and their motors running," the guard added.

"Were they okay?" Skye asked. "No damage done and the owners got them back?"

"Yeah." The guard reluctantly nodded.

Before he could say anything more, an announcement blared from the PA. "Code Red in sporting goods. All personnel report immediately."

"Son of a bitch!" The guard froze, then blurted out, "That means someone's stolen a gun." He started to run, saying over his shoulder, "You all better be gone by the time I get back here."

As the guard dashed out of sight, Earl snickered. "I bet that's Elvis. He said he had to pick up a present for his betrothed, and he mustta run outta quarters for the claw machine."

Despite the guard's threats, the Dooziers seemed to be in no hurry to leave the store. Earl ordered Cletus and Junior to wait in the car—their own car—then held a whispered conversation with Glenda, who stomped away with a scowl on her face.

Earl sauntered back to where Skye was searching for the pink boxes, and said, "I hopes you can stop by our weddin'. It's gonna be the most fun shindig ever."

"Well . . ." Skye inspected a box but saw that there was a tiara printed on one side and reluctantly returned it to the shelf. "I'll be pretty busy with my cousin's rehearsal that day."

"But, Miz Skye, we got us the best theme."

"What's that?" she asked absently.

"Beer." Earl jumped from foot to foot like a Chihuahua about to pee. "We made this here arch outta hangers and decorated it with beer bottles, and we got big ol' beer cans that we cut in half and stuck fake flowers in for the centerpieces."

"Wow." Skye attempted to picture what Earl was describing but gave up.

Earl patted his bowling ball–size stomach. "And it was my job to empty all the bottles and cans."

"I bet that was a lot of work." Skye tried to keep the sarcasm out of her voice.

"Yep. But somebody had to do it. And he's my

only brother." Earl thumped Skye on the back. "Least ways the only one we knows about."

"Uh-huh." Skye was rapidly running out of patience.

"We even gots a mechanical bull for the reception, and you can have the first ride." Earl frowned. "After the bride and groom, a'course."

"Of course."

"Ya know, we tried to have the reception here."

"At Wal-Mart?" Skye asked. "Why?"

"Makes it easier to return the gifts."

"Good thinking."

"Thanky." Earl beamed. "But in his infantile wisdom the manager turned us down."

"That's a shame." Skye wondered if Earl really thought the man was a baby. "Where did you move the reception to?"

"Uncle Slim's big toe says it ain't gonna rain, so we're havin' it in the backyard."

"Happy is the bride who has a sun—"

"Yep." Earl interrupted. "Who has a son that doesn't arrive afore the hitchin'."

"Right."

"Anyhoo, the ceremony's at four. You really should come. The reception's right after and'll go on 'til everyone passes out."

"I'll see what I can do." Skye figured they'd be too drunk to know if she showed up or not, so there was no harm letting them think she might.

"We even got stuff to give the guests. Some

real nice-smellin' rose perfume for the ladies and a can a Copenhagen for the men." Earl scratched his head. "What I don't understand is why we gots to give people somethin' just for comin'. We're already givin' 'em food and beer, and Uncle Slim's jug band is playin'. Isn't that enough?"

Skye had stopped listening somewhere after the mention of chewing tobacco. Just as her eyes were glazing over, she saw them. There, in front of her, was just what she was looking for—plain pink boxes.

There were twenty-four to a pack and a trio of packages swung enticingly from the peg. She snatched all three of them off the hook and hugged them to her chest, then reverently stowed them in her cart. Now all she had to do was find Frannie and get the heck out of Dodge before the next Doozier disaster blew up in her face.

CHAPTER 18

A Class Act

Skye checked on the progress at the country club and arrived back in Scumble River at two forty-five. After inspecting Frannie and Justin's work, she let them go and immediately started telephoning vendors to confirm the details for the next three days.

Two hours later, Skye said good-bye to the

caterer and hung up the phone. Her ear hurt and her throat was raw, but she had managed to contact four of the major participants. She still had nearly a dozen vendors on her list, but she was meeting Wally at five thirty, so they'd have to wait until tomorrow.

As soon as she got home, she jumped into the shower. With no time for her usual makeup routine, she smoothed her curls into a French twist, dusted her face with bronzer, and brushed on a coat of mascara. After putting on a lime green and black cotton skirt and matching silk T-shirt, she dashed out the door, nearly tripping on a package with a large gold bow on top.

Skye snatched it up and opened it once she was in her car. Inside the box were several travel brochures and two airline tickets. The card read, *I think our second chance should start in Bermuda. Love, Simon.*

Sighing, she tucked everything under the passenger seat and resolved to think about both the gift and the man after the wedding was over. Five minutes later she was walking into the Feed Bag.

Wally waved to her from his seat in the booth nearest the door. The restaurant had been redecorated in 1984, with lots of mauve, brass, and plants. Twenty-one years later, time was catching up with the interior. Rips in the vinyl seats had been repaired with duct tape, smudges on the walls had been dabbed with a color that didn't quite match the original paint, and the ferns had long since withered and been replaced with plastic greenery.

After a quick kiss, she slid in across from Wally, and he asked, "How was the rest of your day?"

"I had to go over to Laurel to get something from Wal-Mart and ran into the Dooziers." Skye glanced at the menu to check out the daily special, then put it aside. She knew the rest of the choices by heart. "Did you know Elvis is getting married?"

"Yeah." Wally's eyes glinted with amusement. "I heard it was a case of wife or death."

Skye snickered. "Earl is all pumped up about the wedding. He was bragging to me about his ideas for the décor and entertainment."

"That's Earl, all right." Wally winked. "A real self-made-up man."

"Too true." Skye giggled. "He must have gotten hold of an etiquette book or something, because they're even having party favors."

"You've got to be kidding." Wally gave her a startled look. "What on earth does a Doozier give as a party favor? A possum and a six-pack?"

Before Skye could enlighten him, the waitress approached to take their order. Skye ordered a Diet Coke with lime and the fried chicken, which came with a baked potato, soup, and salad. Wally asked for coffee and the meatloaf plate.

Once the waitress had filled his coffee cup and left, Skye wrinkled her nose. "It's a good thing I skipped lunch. If I eat everything I just ordered, I won't be able to fit into my bridesmaid's dress."

"I'm sure you'll be beautiful." Wally captured her hand, caressing her palm with his thumb. "I can't wait to watch you walk down the aisle."

"Thanks." Skye flashed on a vision of herself in the Pepto-Bismol pink gown and shuddered. "But you'd better reserve judgment until you see me." *Beautiful* wasn't the adjective that came to her mind.

Wisely, Wally changed the subject. "Will the bridal party be in town tomorrow? Every time I try to find one of them, they're off on some excursion."

"They'll be at the bowling alley for the bachelor/ bachelorette party in the evening. During the day they're going to Arlington Park to watch the horse races and do a little gambling."

"Where were they today?"

"In Chicago picking up the dresses and tuxes."

"I'm surprised your cousin didn't make you go along," Wally teased.

"Believe me, it was a close call. I had to promise on my mother's life that mine would fit in order to be excused. Afterward they went to a Cubs game." Skye made a scornful noise. "Riley seems to think they need constant entertainment."

"And do they?"

"I have no idea." Skye paused, considering. "The one good thing about agreeing to take over for

Belle is that I've been able to avoid participating in all the outings. But I haven't gotten to know any of the bridal party very well."

"Good thing?" Wally questioned. "You don't think the activities would have been fun?"

"In different circumstances." Skye toyed with her silverware. "But . . . I don't know how to explain it. I guess it just seems like a forced good time to me. Everyone is so rich and so successful, but no one seems really happy.

"Look at Belle and her hunger to be famous. Who knows what she did to achieve that ambition." Skye's lip curled in disgust. "Then there's the fact that even though she was already wealthy, it wasn't enough for her; she had to scam the vendors for more money. The sheer greed is appalling."

"But hardly surprising," Wally commented. "Look at the CEOs who take huge bonuses even when their companies are going bankrupt." His expression was unfathomable. "My Dad's friends are like that. They have everything, and it's still not enough for them."

"Yes. If one of them has something, it seems the others don't rest until they have the same thing, only better."

"My mom used to say envy slays the simple."

"That's a valuable thought to keep in mind." Skye's face was sober. "It's so easy to slip into the quicksand of jealousy and greed."

They were silent; then Wally said, "I finally got hold of Belle's parents this morning."

"Did they have any excuse for apparently not caring enough about their daughter to interrupt their vacation and respond to your messages?"

"No. Her father was extremely unresponsive, even after I broke the news of her death."

"Did they tell you anything helpful?" Skye asked.

Wally started to answer her, but an angry voice near the restaurant's entrance interrupted him. "What do you mean you can't take a hundred-dollar bill?"

A man in his early thirties was arguing with the Feed Bag's owner, Tomi Jackson. She was a tiny woman; in fact, when she was working the cash register, all you could see of her was her platinum-blond beehive. Tomi, like her restaurant, was a fixture in Scumble River and appeared ageless, although she had to be at least in her sixties.

"Sorry." Tomi's voice was firm. "We don't take anything bigger than a twenty."

"Fine. Put it on my American Express." The man shoved the plastic rectangle at the restaurant owner.

"Sorry." Tomi shook her head. "We don't take credit cards either."

"That's ridiculous!" The irate diner's voice rose. "What, am I in Mayberry or something?" His suit was expensive, as were his shoes and watch.

His appearance, as well as his attitude, made it clear he wasn't from the area.

As Skye watched, the man leaned over the counter until he was nearly nose to nose with Tomi. When he poked her in the arm with his index finger, Wally slid swiftly out of the booth.

The infuriated customer was close to Wally's six-foot-plus height, and the two men together were an interesting contrast. While Wally got his physique from hard work and his bronze skin from being outdoors, the other man clearly used a gym and a tanning booth.

Wally spoke to him in a low, soothing tone, but Skye couldn't make out his words.

She did, however, hear the man's strident reply: "I am not wasting my time trying to find an ATM machine or an open bank. If she won't take my credit card or the hundred, then the meal is on her."

Wally looked at Tomi, who said, "I can't believe he doesn't have anything smaller. His bill is only twelve bucks. I'd have to give him eighty eight in change, and I don't have that much. We deposited the day's receipts an hour ago, just before the bank closed."

"Then I'm leaving." The man started for the door. "Thanks for the free dinner."

In a move too fast for Skye to see, Wally had the stranger's hands cuffed behind his back and was marching him outside.

Once the two men were gone, Tomi strolled

over to Skye and said, "Smart-looking guy like that, I would have sworn he was brighter than to try to pull that kind of crap."

"Light travels faster than sound," Skye explained. "That's why people often appear intelligent until you hear them speak."

"You got that right," Tomi agreed, and returned to the register.

Several minutes went by, and Skye was about to see if Wally needed backup when he strolled back into the Feed Bag. He stopped to hand the restaurant owner something, waved away the woman's thanks, then rejoined Skye.

As he sat down, she asked, "What happened?"

"He miraculously found a twenty in his wallet."

"You're kidding!"

"I told him I'd throw his sorry ass in jail and forget where I put the key if he tried to stiff Tomi." Wally chuckled. "After that, he folded like a lawn chair."

"Why didn't he just pay up to begin with? He certainly didn't look poor."

"It's that sense of entitlement we were just talk-ing about—like with my father's friends and your cousin's bridal party. He wanted to use the hundred, and when he couldn't he threw a tantrum."

"I guess that could be it." Skye pondered Wally's explanation as their food was served; then, once the waitress left, she said, "But why did he have such a hissy fit when he had the twenty all the time?"

"Because he's a jackass." Wally crossed his arms. "Guys like that hate to back down."

"I wonder who he was." Skye wrinkled her brow. Something didn't add up. "He sure wasn't from around here."

"Probably off the interstate."

"Maybe."

As they were finishing their meal, an idea popped into Skye's head and she leaned forward. "Maybe he wanted to use the hundred because it was counterfeit. Isn't that how they do it—make a small purchase with the phony bills, and get real money as change?"

"Hmm." Wally stood up. "You could be on to something. And just in case you are, I think I'd better drop a word of warning to the business owners around here."

"Won't the Secret Service agents be upset?" Skye stood, too. "Didn't they want the whole counterfeit thing kept quiet?"

"Yeah, but I'm not letting my people get hurt." Wally paid their bill and walked Skye to her car. "Besides, I'm sure by now Bunny has let the cat out of the bag."

"True." Skye slid in behind the wheel. "She's not known for her discretion."

"Have a good time at the shower." Wally kissed Skye lightly on the lips, then shut the door of the Bel Air and strode toward his car.

She rolled down the window and shouted at his retreating back, "Obviously, you've never been to one of my family's bridal showers. It's like having a root canal. Without Novocain. By a really bad dentist."

Skye drove straight to her mother's. As she kept her eyes peeled for a stray cow, raccoon, or deer, she tried to figure out why the shower was being held at May's.

Her mother had explained, but Skye was still fuzzy about the details. It had something to do with Anita's and Dora's homes being too small, but Skye was confused because her parents' place wasn't that much bigger. However, as Skye pulled into the already car-packed driveway, she got the picture. The party wasn't being held in May's house; it was being held in her garage.

At the same moment she understood the reason for the location, she realized her cousin was probably unaware of the arrangements. Riley had not wanted a shower, but her mother and grandmother had insisted. It was one of the few times during the whole wedding process that the bride had not gotten her own way.

Now Skye wondered what Riley would do when she found out her fancy friends would have to spend an evening in someone's garage—even if it was cleaner and nicer than many homes.

Skye mentally shrugged, picked up her cousin's present from the passenger seat, and got out of the Bel Air. This was one aspect of the wedding for which she wasn't responsible.

Huge trees surrounded her parents' redbrick ranch, and the acre of lawn was in putting-green condition. Sometimes she speculated that her dad used manicure scissors instead of a mower to cut the grass. The scene looked like a picture from *Country Living* magazine. The only jarring note was May's concrete goose, which she had dressed in a bridal gown. May tended to clothe the fake fowl according to her moods, and Skye was relieved that this time the poultry's attire fit the occasion and didn't contain an underlying message aimed at her.

Skye's gaze swept the open garage, which had been strung with pink crepe paper streamers and decorated with bunches of pink and white balloons. Mismatched tables and chairs were arranged around a long table covered with a white plastic tablecloth and sporting a centerpiece of pink carnations and baby's breath in a milk-glass vase.

The scene was set, but all the chairs were empty. At least a half dozen cars were parked in the driveway, so where was everyone?

Before Skye could figure out the mystery of the disappearing shower guests, she heard someone holler, "What are you standing around outside for? Come in and give us a hand." The salt-and-pepper-haired bundle of aggravation that had given birth to Skye stood in the open back door of the house with her hands on her hips.

"Hello to you too, Mom," Skye muttered as she grudgingly headed inside.

She put her purse and the gift on top of the dryer in the utility room, took a deep breath, and readied herself to face both her relatives and a no-doubt-unhappy bride, then followed May through the swinging louvered doors.

The large green-and-white-striped kitchen-dinette was bisected by a peninsula. Usually stools edged the counter, but today a group of women aged forty to eighty was standing by it, talking nonstop as their fingers flew at their tasks. They all looked up as Skye entered and, after waving their hellos, went back to their conversations. Noticeably missing were Riley, Anita, and Dora.

Skye's grandmother greeted her from the dinette table. "Sweetie, come give Grandma a hug." When she had Skye enfolded in her arms, Cora said, "Thank you for taking over as Riley's wedding planner. I was real worried when Miss Canfield passed away that they'd move the whole shebang to California."

"You're welcome." Skye kissed her grandmother's cheek. "I'm sure considering how wealthy Nick is, he would have found somebody to keep Riley happy."

"Money may buy you a fine dog, but only kindness will make him wag his tail."

Skye snickered. "Shh!" Trust her grandmother to neatly sum up what everyone else was thinking.

She was still hugging Cora when May ordered, "Grab an apron from the drawer, and start filling the relish platters."

Skye released her grandmother, but before she straightened, Cora whispered, "I'm happy you're helping Riley, but you be careful. You may not know this because you weren't around when Riley was a teenager, but she had a mind of her own, and she got real mean when she was thwarted."

"Good thing I'm not going to thwart her."

"That's what her high school boyfriend and some other folks thought, too." Cora wrinkled her brow. "Don't underestimate her like they did."

Pondering her grandmother's words, Skye grabbed jars of pickles and beets, plastic bags of carrots, radishes, and celery sticks, and a can of black olives from the refrigerator. Compartmentalized crystal trays were stacked on the counter, and she set to work. Was Cora implying that Riley might be responsible for Belle's death? What had Riley done all those years ago that would make Cora warn Skye?

The women had begun to transfer the food from the house to the garage when Riley and her three bridesmaids entered the kitchen. Riley greeted everyone brightly and introduced Hallie, Tabitha, and Paige.

One of the younger women—Skye wasn't sure

who she was—rushed up to Riley and thrust a garishly wrapped gift into her hand. "Open this now."

Riley complied, then stared at the pink Kleenex corsage she held. "What am I supposed to do with it?"

"It's for you to wear, silly." The woman grabbed it from Riley's fingers and pinned it to the stunned bride-to-be's blouse. "I love giving homemade gifts."

Riley's face turned red and she scowled, but before she could respond, Ilene Denison, Skye's cousin Kevin's wife, said, "Yeah, me, too. Which one of my kids do you want?"

Everyone laughed, and May swooped in, putting her arm around Riley. "Honey, the rest of the guests will be arriving shortly. Why don't you and your friends go outside to the garage so you can welcome them?"

"Sure thing, May." Riley's smile was strained, and as she and the others turned to leave, she grabbed Skye's hand and whispered in her ear, "Come with us. I have no idea who most of these people are and Mom's not here yet."

"Where are Anita and Dora?" Skye asked. It was odd that Riley's mother and grandmother weren't helping the other women prepare for the party.

"Gram is with Mom, who's still getting ready. She was wearing some god-awful dress she's had for twenty years and I made her put on something better. Which is exactly why I wouldn't let her or Gram help organize the wedding. I love them to death, but their taste is disgustingly middle-class." Riley shook her head. "They want nice; I want ferocious."

"Oh." As Skye herded her cousin and the others toward the door, she tried to imagine forcing May to change her clothes, but she couldn't picture it. "I'll be out in a couple of minutes." She had no intention of spending any one-on-one time with Riley. With her luck, the bride would think of something else she wanted Skye to do for the wedding.

With the guest of honor out of the way, the final stages of the refreshment assembly began. This was serious business, but everyone still took time to impart some advice to Skye or question her about the wedding preparations.

As Ilene and Skye were covering the chicken-salad-filled cream puffs with Saran Wrap before bringing them outside, Ilene asked, "Riley's theme is Pink Fairy Tale, right?"

"Yes." Skye nodded cautiously.

"Well, Kevin says to tell you he isn't wearing tights. No matter how much Riley carries on."

"Tights? Has Riley asked people to come in costume?" Skye crushed the piece of cellophane she had just torn from the cardboard cylinder. No way would the men in the family dress up as Prince Charmings.

May chose that moment to pop up. "You girls." She tsked. "We ask you to do one simple thing, and you do it slower than sows rolling in mud."

Ilene stomped off in a huff, muttering something about not coming here to be called a pig.

Skye closed her eyes and counted to ten, twice. Now she'd have to track down Ilene later and find out if Riley had changed the wedding into a costume party without telling her. God knows she didn't want to bring the subject up with another guest and add grist to the gossip mill, although maybe she could ask Kevin's mother. She'd also better check what other rumors were flying around about the exotic event.

The garage had been scrubbed to within an inch of becoming an operating room. Jed's workbench and cabinets were covered in white sheets, and his model tractor collection, which was displayed on a long, narrow shelf circling three of the four walls, had been polished until the Farmall red, Caterpillar yellow, and John Deere green glowed like the lights of a traffic signal.

The food was set up buffet style, and, as the guest of honor, Riley headed the line, followed by her grandmother, mother, and the bridesmaids. The other guests arranged themselves roughly according to age, oldest first. Skye had been assigned to pour the iced tea, milk, and coffee, so she was one of the last to fill her plate—which was fine with her, since she was still full from dinner.

When her aunt Kitty passed by her, Skye asked, "Have you heard anything about coming in costume to the wedding?"

"No." Kitty, married to Skye's uncle Wiley, was Kevin's mother. "Can't say as I have."

"Good." Kevin must have just been teasing Ilene. "Because it's not true." He'd probably been trying to get out of attending the extremely formal event altogether.

When everyone had been served, Skye took her place at the head table between Riley and Tabitha. Paige was on the bride's right side, and Hallie next to her.

"Hi," Skye said, determined to keep things light. "Everyone having a good time?"

"No." Riley sulked. "This day has been one big bore."

"You didn't enjoy the baseball game?"

"It sucked," Riley answered. "How long has it been since the Cubs won a World Series?"

"I have no idea." Skye shrugged. "But I do know you'd better keep your opinion to yourself. Most of the family are rabid Cubs fans, especially my mother, and you do not want to get May started."

Riley opened her mouth to reply, but Skye cut her off with, "I've been meaning to ask, do any of you know the names of Belle's most recent boyfriend or any of her exes? Maybe someone who was ticked off when she dropped them?"

The bride and bridesmaids all shook their

heads, and Riley answered for them all, "None of us were really friends with her, and from what I gathered, she went through guys like emery boards, throwing them out after nailing them a few times."

Tabitha nodded, then changed the subject. "The food is wonderful. It reminds me of my family's get-togethers. Different flavors, but that same homemade taste."

"The women on both sides of my family are good cooks." Skye patted her stomach. "Maybe too much so."

"In my culture, that's impossible." Tabitha grinned. "In fact, my mama nags me to eat more."

"Mine does, too." Skye's smile was rueful. "But then she also tells me I need to lose weight."

Tabitha tsked. "We have a saying in my country, 'Fisherman don't smell he own basket.'"

"In other words," Skye said, "a person can see the flaws of others but not their own."

"Right." Tabitha smiled. "That's why mothers are so hard to please."

"Not for me," Riley chimed in. "I don't try to please anyone but myself. And if someone gets hurt, too bad."

Skye frowned. Was Riley joking? She hoped so but couldn't be sure. And the thought made her wonder: Was her own cousin so narcissistic that she was capable of murder?

CHAPTER 19

Hair Today, Gone Tomorrow

No way!" Skye's brother, Vince, shook his head. "Sorry, but I cannot cancel my Saturday regulars and do the wedding for you." He owned the Great Expectations hair salon and was the best stylist within a hundred miles.

It was ten o'clock Thursday morning, and Skye had stopped by the salon after speaking to the hairdresser, who was supposed to be flying in from California on Friday. The woman had told her that if Belle was no longer the wedding consultant, she wasn't coming, and Skye hadn't been able to persuade her to change her mind.

"Please, please, please," Skye begged her brother. "I'll pay you twice what you'd make keeping the salon open that day, and I won't need you until nine thirty, so you can still fit in any regulars who insist on having their hair done."

"There's not enough money in the world to make me get involved with our crazy cousin's wedding." Vince's butterscotch blond locks brushed the collar of his bright blue polo shirt as he shook his head. "Loretta told me about the fit Riley threw at her shower last night. Which, by the way, I was surprised Loretta was invited to."

"Mom likes her." Loretta Steiner was Skye's

sorority sister, occasional attorney, and possibly her future sister-in-law. Until a few months ago Skye would have said the chances of the latter were slim to none, since Vince had a love-'em-and-leave-'em reputation, but he seemed to have changed. Now it wouldn't surprise her if Vince and Loretta announced their engagement by the end of the summer.

"Riley was a little distraught," Skye explained. "She didn't want the shower to begin with; then she was unhappy when it turned out to be in Mom and Dad's garage. When she realized the gifts weren't from her registry, she sort of lost it. She especially hated the macramé plant holder shaped like an owl and the traffic-cone orange plastic bowls." Skye patted his arm. "But I'm sure she wouldn't be a problem for you. Women are putty in your hands."

"No."

"I'll pay you three times what you'd make that day at the salon." As Vince started to shake his head, Skye added, "And I'll run interference with Mom the next time you're in trouble with her."

"No matter what the reason?" Vince's green eyes held a calculating expression.

"No matter what." Skye hoped he didn't have something awful in mind.

"Pinky swear?" He held out his hand.

Skye crooked her little finger through his and agreed, "Pinky swear."

As she left her brother's shop and headed downtown, Skye hummed a few bars of "Bad Boys and Blondes," the bossa nova tune she'd heard at the dance lesson. With Vince onboard, the good ship Riley's Wedding was back on an even keel. Skye only hoped the rest of the day went as well.

After meeting Frannie and Justin at the bowling alley and getting them started decorating for the bachelor/bachelorette party that night, Skye took off for Plainfield to pick up the newly engraved menus and programs.

During the hour drive, she considered what they had discovered so far about Belle—which, except for the fact that she was extremely demanding, extorted commissions from the vendors, and passed counterfeit money, wasn't much.

Skye hadn't spoken to Wally since their dinner the night before, but unless Belle's parents had told him something that suggested a new lead, or he'd learned more about the obnoxious customer who had tried to walk out on his bill at the Feed Bag, the case was at a standstill.

Just as Justin's MapQuest directions had promised, Skye found the engravers on Route 59, a little north of Plainfield's main street. The menus and programs were ready and looked perfect, and she was back in her car in less than fifteen minutes. Before she started the engine, she called Wally for an update.

"Any news on the guy from the Feed Bag?"

"Yes." Wally's amused tone held a tinge of irri-tation. "Unfortunately."

"He's the leader of the counterfeiting ring?" Skye guessed.

"No. He's Belle's father's attorney."

"You're kidding me." Skye was floored. She would have never guessed. "How did he get to Scumble River so fast?"

"Mickey Canfield sent him on the Canfield's private plane as soon as he hung up from talking to me yesterday morning," Wally explained. "A better question is: Why did he come?"

"You mean why the attorney and not the parents?"

"That, and why anyone came at all."

"And the reason is . . . ?"

"The explanation the attorney gave me is that Mr. and Mrs. Canfield are too broken up to travel." Wally paused. "Which could be true, but we're not even ready to release the body, so there was really no need for anyone to make the trip yet. It's not as if a corporate attorney would know any-thing about a criminal investigation or be able to help find Belle's killer. He admits he only met her once or twice at formal dinners."

"So you think there's something he's not telling you," Skye guessed. "Like he's here to make sure nothing we find out makes the Canfield family or corporation look bad."

"Bingo." Wally's voice was rueful. "Considering

our first meeting, the lawyer isn't exactly my biggest fan. On the other hand, he did agree to meet me at the bank to have the hundred-dollar bill he tried to pass examined, and it was legit."

"Hmm." Skye tapped her fingers on the steering wheel. "Maybe one of the bridesmaids will have an idea about what the Canfields want to keep quiet. I'll try to talk to them about it tonight at the bachelorette party. They should all be in good moods."

"In other words, you'll use truth serum on them."

"Huh?" Skye had no idea what Wally was talking about.

"Alcohol plus estrogen equals truth serum."

"That is so sexist." Skye pretended to be exasperated. "I can't believe you said that."

"Hang on," Wally backpedaled. "The alternate formula substitutes testosterone and works equally well."

"That's better." Skye chuckled. "As long as it goes both ways, you're forgiven."

"One other piece of news." Wally was serious again. "They were able to trace that threatening call of yours to Madame Olga's dress shop, and she's now in custody."

"Really? For threatening me?"

"No. The Chicago police raided her shop last night and confiscated over three hundred thousand dollars' worth of designer dress knockoffs."

"Wow!" Skye was just thankful that Riley and

her party had picked up their gowns yesterday afternoon. "Did Madame Olga admit to making the threatening call?"

"Yes. She let it slip when they arrested her."

"Good." Skye smiled. "One less loose thread to worry about."

"Unfortunately, she has an alibi for the time of the murder. She was in New York on a buying trip and didn't get home until Sunday night."

"Nuts."

After she said good-bye, Skye asked herself whether she should have told Wally what Cora had said about Riley getting nasty when she didn't get her way. Skye thought it over and decided that since Belle hadn't gotten in Riley's way, that information wasn't relevant.

Still, when she had a minute, Skye intended to locate Riley's high school boyfriend and find out what her cousin had done to him. Maybe she'd come up with a way to ask Riley who he was tonight at the party.

As a last resort, Skye would ask her grand-mother, but she didn't want her family to have any hint that she was investigating Riley. Even though Cora had warned her to be careful around her cousin, she would be upset if she thought Skye was trying to prove Riley was a murderer.

Skye drove back to Scumble River by way of the country club. The lights were being installed there today, and she wanted to make sure things were going as planned. The hairstylist had already thrown one monkey wrench into the works, and Skye didn't want to be surprised by another tool showing up.

The lighting guy was standing on the scaffolding in the ballroom when Skye arrived. He was singing an out-of-tune version of "Like a Virgin" as he wired a chandelier to the ceiling in the center of the room. Another man, apparently his assistant, silently held the huge fixture in place.

Skye stood by the door until they were finished and noticed her, then said, "I'm Skye, the new wedding planner. Do you have a minute?"

The young man nodded, told his helper to take five, climbed down, and joined Skye. "The name's Cosmo. What do you need?"

"Just wanted to see how you're coming along." Skye gestured to the dozens of sconces already lining the walls. "It looks like you've got a lot done already."

"We have two more chandcliers to hang in here." Cosmo took out a red handkerchief and wiped the sweat from his brow. "Then we'll move on to the patio and the tent."

"How long will that take?"

"We'll probably get the patio done today and finish the tent tomorrow." Cosmo refastened his ponytail. "Don't worry, dude. Brian will chew my ass out if we don't keep on his schedule."

"Is he like that for all the events you do?" Skye

asked, wondering if there was more to Brian than she had picked up on when she'd questioned him.

"Nah." Cosmo smiled widely, revealing perfect teeth. "Usually he's pretty laid-back, as long as stuff gets done on time in the end."

"But not with this job?"

"Right." Cosmo took out a pocketknife and cleaned some dirt out from under his thumbnail. "He's been freaking out about this one."

"Oh? Why is that?"

"Probably because the other planner was such a bitch." He shot Skye a quick glance. "No offense. Hope she wasn't your BFF or nothing."

"None taken," she assured him. "I know Belle could be a bit much. I was her assistant before she . . . er . . . left, and she was hard to please."

"Is there anything else?" Cosmo looked at his watch. "I really need to get back to work."

She thought a moment and said, "I thought Brian said he was the only one who dealt with Belle. How do you know she was . . . uh . . . how she was?"

"The thing is . . ." Cosmo studied his work boots. "Miss Canfield contacted me a while back."

"What did she want?"

"The first time she called, she wanted to know if I'd work for her directly and cut Brian out of the loop." Cosmo shifted from foot to foot."

"The first time . . . ?" Skye trailed off, hoping Cosmo would feel obligated to fill in the blanks.

"Yeah." He hesitated. "I told her I couldn't go behind his back like that, but she called again, a couple of times."

"What did she want?"

"She was fishing for information on Brian." Cosmo's expression hardened. "Said she was just checking to make sure he could handle such a big event."

"Did you tell her anything?" Skye asked. "Was there anything to tell?"

"No." Cosmo shrugged. "This is our biggest order ever, but Brian's cool. He had it covered."

"Did you tell him she was calling you?"

"Nah." Cosmo shook his head. "She told me not to, and it would have just freaked him out more. You should have seen him sweating Saturday while she was grilling him about the details."

Interesting. Belle was even sneakier than Skye had thought. Were there other secrets they still hadn't discovered about the wedding planner? And did one of them get her killed?

A moment later Skye realized the significance of what Cosmo had said. "You came with Brian here, to the country club, on Saturday?" Why hadn't the crew leader mentioned that when Wally questioned him?

"Not exactly." Cosmo edged toward the scaffolding. "I came here with the other workers. Brian drove by himself."

"Did he leave when you guys did?"

"Uh-uh. He was still talking to Ms. Canfield."

"Did you see him after that?" Skye asked.

"Nope. He was supposed to meet with me back at the store to tell me if the lighting designs were approved, but he never showed."

So, Brian *was* the big guy with tattoos who had been with Belle Saturday night at the Brown Bag. Why had he denied it?

CHAPTER 20

Let the Poker Chips Fall Where They May

The instant Skye reached her car, she phoned Wally to fill him in on what Cosmo had told her about Brian. After hearing her report, Wally said he was heading immediately to LaGrange to pick up the crew leader for more questioning. Brian had just edged out Iris as their chief suspect.

Skye spent the rest of the afternoon calling vendors, then hurried home to dress for the evening's activities. Although the bachelor/bachelorette parties were scheduled for seven p.m., she arrived at the bowling alley at six to check out the arrangements.

When Simon had purchased the business a few years ago, he had changed the name from the Gold Strike to Bunny Lanes. Skye had been touched by his choice. Simon hadn't always had the best relationship with his mother, and naming the alley after her had been a strong indication that he was capable of forgiving and moving on.

He had also transformed the nineteen-sixties brown and orange interior to a sleek palette of blues with touches of silver. At the time of the remodeling, he had explained that his goal was to modernize the place enough to attract new people, but not so much that he lost the old regulars. Skye hadn't been sure he could achieve the correct balance—Scumble Riverites did not like change—but he had, and the makeover was a huge success.

Having both the bachelor and bachelorette parties in the same venue was tricky, but Riley had insisted her groom be near enough that she could keep an eye on him. She had specified no porn and no strippers. In theory, Skye agreed with her cousin, but she wasn't sure that Nick's best man was on the same page. She could only do so much to prevent Zach from breaking Riley's rules.

With that concern in mind, Skye's first stop was the bar, where the men would hold their party. Previously a single long counter located next to the grill, the bar had been enclosed and expanded during the renovations and now included etched glass doors, a small stage, and a dance floor.

Frannie and Justin had decorated the bar with red and black balloons, and Skye had rented a pool table, two antique pinball machines, and a big-screen TV equipped with electronic games and a DVD player—all of which had been delivered that afternoon. Hamburgers, hot dogs, and pizza would be available from the grill, served by three attractive waitresses wearing cheerleaders' uniforms.

As Skye entered, Bunny minced over on four-inch heels and embraced her, asking, "How many guys are you expecting?"

Skye was momentarily distracted by the older woman's appearance. Bunny had plainly been ordering from the Victoria's Secret catalog again. Tonight, she was decked out in hip-hugging, see-through, black chiffon pants and a sheer white camisole that was split down the front and held together with a single red ribbon.

"Let's see," Skye finally managed to choke out. "The groom and groomsmen make five. Riley's uncles and cousins add another four, and Nick's father brings the total to ten. But I wouldn't be surprised if there are a few more. Nick and Riley have a tendency to add to the guest list. I think it goes along with their philosophy that if one is good, two is better, and a lot is best."

"That shouldn't be a problem." Bunny tucked an errant red curl into the cascade of ringlets on top of her head. "I always say the more men, the merrier."

Skye hurriedly changed the subject before Bunny could expand on her views about the opposite sex. "I really like these new chairs. This blue Ultrasuede fabric is holding up extremely well." It was a big change from the old Formica tables and torn vinyl booths.

"I'm pleased as punch how good things are going with the alley." Bunny shot Skye a quick glance. "Thanks for not telling Sonny Boy about me taking that bribe and it turning out to be funny money and all."

"You really should tell him yourself," Skye warned. "There is no such thing as a secret in Scumble River, and Wally had to warn the other business owners about the counterfeit bills, so the story is bound to get out."

"I'll cross that bridge when it starts burning." Bunny waved her hand. "Let me show you what we have for the girls' party."

"Great." Skye gave up. Bunny would do what Bunny would do. And since Skye was no longer dating Simon, his mother-son issues were no longer her problem. Another reason not to even consider his plea for a second chance.

Bunny dragged Skye through a set of swinging doors at the rear of the bar, which led to the grill. "The girls can hang out here or by the lanes."

The grill had also received a recent face-lift. The countertops were now blue faux marble, and the stools were upholstered in a denim fabric with silver studs. Justin and Frannie had decorated this area to look like a nineteen-fifties soda shop, with posters of Elvis Presley, Frankie Avalon, and

Bobby Darin. To add to the sock-hop atmosphere, Skye had rented a jukebox filled with hits of the era.

"The girls can choose from these." Bunny handed Skye a menu that included a variety of soda-shop food, including milk shakes and banana splits. "How many are we expecting?"

"I really have no idea who's coming. Besides the wedding party, Riley invited my mom, Aunt Kitty, Kevin's wife, Ilene, and some high school friends."

"Oh, well." Bunny shrugged. "I'm sure we'll have enough of everything. I doubled the original number Miss Canfield gave me." She tugged on Skye's hand. "Come on. Wait until you see the rest."

Skye allowed herself to be pulled to the back of the alley, marveling at how fast the redhead could walk in sandals that consisted of nothing more than thin soles and a single strap attached to stiletto heels.

When they arrived, Bunny swept her arm in an expansive gesture. "What do you think?"

Here, the usual tables and straight chairs had been replaced with sofas, overstuffed armchairs, and low cocktail tables. The overhead lights were turned off, and lamps equipped with pink bulbs created a rosy glow. The menu in this newly created lounge area consisted of hors d'oeuvres, flavored martinis, and chocolates, all served by a trio of buff young guys wearing tight black pants and formfitting tuxedo shirts.

"You did a great job." Skye hugged the older woman. "It's magnificent."

"You bet your butt it is." Bunny beamed. "You didn't think I could do it, did you?"

"Not at all." Skye crossed her fingers. "I had complete confidence in you."

"Sure." Bunny glanced at her watch and her expression turned serious. "It's already six thirty, and you know all the Scumble River people will be here early. I've got to make sure the bartender has the setups ready, and finish putting the snacks on the tables in the bar." She turned to leave, saying over her shoulder, "Wait until you get that bill tomorrow. I bet we make a fortune on drinks tonight."

Skye opened her mouth to respond, but the words died on her lips when Simon appeared at the lounge's entrance and said to his mother with a stern look, "Remember, you need to stop serving anyone who has had too much alcohol. No exceptions."

"Sure, Sonny Boy." Bunny walked off, not at all fazed by her son's admonishments. "Gotcha."

Watching Bunny totter off, Simon half smiled. "She always has a scheme." He turned his attention to Skye and shook his head. "But she's worked really hard to make the alley a success."

"Are you here checking up on her?" Skye asked.

"Nope." He closed the distance between them and took her hand. "I just wanted to see you."

"Oh." The tantalizing scent of his aftershave teased Skye's nose, and it took her a second to pull her fingers from his grasp. "You agreed to wait until Sunday for my decision."

"And I will." There was a faint trace of humor in the way he held his mouth. "But that doesn't mean I can't try and sway your verdict."

"Yes, it does." Skye felt guilty. She should tell Simon no and be done with it. "I'm too busy to think right now, and you're making it worse."

"Did you get my gift?" He stroked a finger down her cheek.

"Yes, and I can't accept it. I'm giving it back to you as soon as I have a minute." Skye stepped out of his reach. "Now please leave so I can do my job."

"Okay. I'll go." Simon turned but looked back over his shoulder, his gold-flecked eyes smoldering. "The trip is yours. Either we go together or you take it with Boyd—which would be the biggest mistake of your life."

She watched Simon walk away, then took a deep breath and forced his words from her mind. She had a party to put on, and she wasn't getting paid to think about her love life.

Skye's parents, along with her aunt Kitty and uncle Wiley, were the first to arrive. She hurried over to them, kissed everyone's cheeks, and said, "Hi. You all ready for some food and fun?"

"Men in there?" Jed, not one for small talk, jerked a thumb to his left.

"Yes," Skye answered. "The bar's reserved for the bachelor party."

"Good." He dipped his chin at May, said, "Later," and walked away with his brother trailing behind him.

Watching them go, Kitty said, "I sure hope that pair doesn't have too many beers."

"You got the car keys, right?" May asked. "I don't want to have to wrestle them from Wiley after he's loaded."

"Yes." Kitty nodded. "I took them from him in the parking lot."

"Good." May smirked at her sister-in-law. "I'm sure glad you don't drink, because I plan on having a margarita or two." She looked at Skye. "That's a pretty skirt."

"Thank you, Mom."

"But the top's too tight. It shows all your rolls."

Skye restrained herself from tugging on the antique tan stretch-lace blouse; instead, she looked her mother in the eye and said pleasantly, "I don't have rolls; I have curves." May had surprised her again. Skye had thought her mother would object to her skirt, to either its metallic bronze color or the filmy silk chiffon material.

"I only tell you things like that because I love you and want you to look as good as possible." May exhaled a put-upon sigh, and when Skye didn't react, she gave a brittle laugh. "Well, we're here to have a good time, so let's get to it. Where's the girls' party?"

Skye directed her mother and aunt to the lounge, then greeted Riley, the next to arrive.

Riley's first words were, "Did your bridesmaid's dress fit?" Riley had given it to Skye at the shower the night before.

"Perfectly," Skye assured her cousin, thinking, *As perfectly as a hideous dress with too little front and no back can.*

After inspecting the place, Riley pulled Skye aside and said, "Try to keep the older women in the grill so the rest of us can have a good time."

"Oookay." Skye drew out the word. What did her cousin want her to do, put up an electric fence?

"And keep an eye on the guys," Riley continued. "Zach's been acting odd, and I think he's up to something. Make sure he doesn't get Nick into trouble."

Before Skye could respond, Yves Galois, the photographer, arrived. Riley grabbed his arm and started reeling off orders as if she were a waitress and he were a short-order cook.

Yves rolled his eyes at Skye, then slithered out of the bride's grasp with the excuse that he needed to fetch some equipment from his car.

The rest of the guests began trickling in, and Riley greeted them with hugs and kisses, her Frankenbride face completely hidden. To see her sweet expression as she spoke to her older relatives, you would never know that a few minutes earlier she had been ordering Skye to keep them isolated from the real party.

As Skye directed people to the proper areas and made sure both events were running smoothly, she thought about her cousin's behavior over the past few days. Had Riley always been so self-centered and egotistical? Had her sense of right and wrong always been so skewed? Was Cora right about her, or was it just the wedding making Riley crazy? Skye didn't know her well enough anymore to decide.

After one last sweep of the bar and grill, Skye joined the women gathered in the lounge. Everyone had arrived, with the exception of Natasha and Jay Jordan. Nick didn't seem upset by his father's absence, and, for once, Riley was thrilled by Natasha's failure to appear.

Skye had just taken a seat when Riley raised her glass. "I want to thank everyone for their part in making my wedding the one I always dreamed of having."

Several of the woman commented on how adorable and charming Riley was, and Skye bit her lip. Dr. Jekyll and Mr. Hyde had nothing on her cousin.

Everyone drank; then Ilene piped up. "This sure is different from the normal nuptials in our family. Usually the weddings are just like the funerals, 'cept for one less drunk."

Skye agreed with her cousin-in-law's assessment, but seeing the storm clouds chasing their way across Riley's face, she quickly declared she had to check on the other guests and fled the room.

Two hours later, Skye looked around the lounge. All the guests seemed to be having a good time. Several of the women were lolling on the sofas and chairs eating chocolates, drinking martinis, and talking, and she could hear the others singing along to the jukebox in the grill.

Skye took a seat, tucking her legs under her, and relaxed for the first time that night. She had just taken a sip of her pomegranate martini when a commotion by the bar entrance drew her attention. She put her glass down, slid her feet back into her shoes, and hurried over. What in the world was going on?

As she neared the bar, she saw the waiters jockeying for position in front of the glass doors and groaned. This couldn't be good.

Skye pushed her way through the young men and looked inside. *Geez!* Nick and his buddies were worse than the teenagers she dealt with at the high school. The last time she'd checked on them they were all behaving themselves. Now half a dozen of the men—though, thank goodness, not her father or uncle—were gathered around the pool table playing cards. This wouldn't have been a problem except for three things: The waitresses had joined them; the game was strip poker; and the women were losing.

Skye frantically sought the door handle. She had to get those ladies dressed and on their feet before Riley found out about this and killed them all—starting with Nick and finishing up with Skye.

As she burst into the bar, Zach grabbed a topless waitress and pulled her onto his lap. When she squealed in protest, Liam leaped up and tried to pull her upright, causing Zach to hold on tighter and threaten his fellow groomsman.

Skye cringed. The situation was turning ugly fast. The waiters had crowded into the bar behind her, and with her luck, the photographer would be next.

Both Zach and Liam were standing, shoving and pushing each other. The other men formed a ring around them, egging them on, chanting, "Fight. Fight."

In a few seconds a punch would connect, or one of them would grab a beer bottle, and that would be it. If someone got hurt, no way Skye could cover it up.

She kept her eyes on the combatants as she felt along the wall. Vaguely she remembered a workshop she'd attended on how to break up brawls. It was meant for adolescents duking it out in the hallway, but she hoped the same principle applied to drunken men. The instructor had warned them never to step between the aggressors. Instead he had suggested using the element of surprise.

Without warning she flipped the toggle down

and all the lights went out. In an instant, the raucous party noise fell away to complete silence; then Skye turned the lights back on and said, "Ladies, I suggest you put on your clothes and assume the duties I'm paying you for. Gentlemen, I suggest you sober up before your wives and girlfriends see you like this, or before Mr. Galois arrives with his camera."

The waitresses leaped up, grabbed pieces of their discarded uniforms, and hurried away.

"No need to get prissy." Zach glared at her. "We were just having some fun."

Several voices chimed in, agreeing, and Skye was sure she was about to lose the battle when a voice behind her said, "What's the problem here?" It was Bunny, and she sounded seriously ticked off.

Liam, seemingly the only sober man present, said, "We were just having a friendly game of poker."

Bunny looked at the crowd that had gathered. "So, what's everyone staring at?"

One of the waiters snickered. "It was an extremely friendly game, all right."

"Shoo." Skye waved the waiters away. "I'm sure the women in the lounge need some drinks or something." Once they left, she asked the men, "Should I explain to Bunny, or are we all ready to act like mature adults?"

The men muttered but dispersed, wandering over to the pinball machines and the TV. Within seconds, it was as if there had never been a problem.

After giving a stern word to the waitresses, Skye and Bunny walked out of the bar. The redhead shook her head. "Boobs are to guys what teething rings are to babies. They feel good, especially when put in the mouth, but inevitably someone ends up crying."

Skye stifled a giggle, then headed back to the lounge. She had barely taken three steps when Riley pounced, demanding, "Where were you?"

"Uh." Skye knew that Riley would eventually hear about the strip poker game; she just didn't want to be the one to tell her. "Checking on the men. Why?"

Riley gestured with her thumb to the hallway that ran between the grill and the lounge. "You need to break that up."

"Break what up?" Skye couldn't see anything.

"Just go and do it." Riley took Skye's arm. "And don't let her know I know."

As Skye entered the hall, she stumbled to a stop. There, in one of the waiter's arms, was Paige, and she was kissing him as if he were a two-inch-thick steak and she was a recently lapsed vegetarian. Skye was going to kill her cousin.

Skye tactfully cleared her throat. When that got no reaction, she moved closer, tapped the waiter on the shoulder, and said, "You need to get back to work."

His eyes fluttered open, and when he saw Skye, he jerked away from Paige, and said, "Uh, sorry."

After he hurried off, Paige said, "I suppose you're going to run and tell Zach."

"Tell him what?" Skye turned to go, hoping she and Paige could pretend nothing had happened.

But the matron of honor persisted. "Hey, I'm a flirt. I love to flirt. It's what I do."

"Look. It's none of my business." Skye kept edging backward.

"Zach's not so innocent either." Paige's expression was inscrutable. "I've tried to change him, but it's just no use."

"Well, like my grandma Leofanti used to say, that cake is baked. If you didn't like the flavor, you should have picked a different slice."

Paige snarled, "I don't want your down-home advice."

"Fine." Skye hurried toward the lobby, in serious need of a breath of fresh air.

Ten minutes later Riley was waiting for Skye as she reentered the building. She stood with her arms crossed and demanded, "What were you doing outside?"

"I needed a break." Skye looked her cousin in the eye. "I've been running around working on *your* wedding since eight this morning."

Riley ignored Skye's irritated tone. "Did you get Paige and that guy to stop?"

Before Skye could answer, the outer door burst open and a woman in a police uniform walked in. She stood with her hands on her hips and said, "I'm here to arrest Nick Jordan."

CHAPTER 21

The Price of Beauty

Skye woke up early Friday, sure she was forgetting something. As she showered and dressed, she ticked off the day's tasks in her mind, starting with meeting Wally for a quick breakfast. Next, a brief stop at the country club to oversee the preparations there, then the bridesmaids' trip to the spa, and ending with the rehearsal that evening.

In forty-eight hours Skye would be free of responsibilities—except, of course, for the decisions she had promised Simon and Wally regarding her love life.

She refused to contemplate that dilemma now, and as she drove to meet Wally, she realized she'd much rather begin her day with him talking about the previous night's events than brood over her future.

She pulled into the McDonald's parking lot a little after eight and found Wally waiting inside his squad car. She liked that he never seemed upset if she was a few minutes late, unlike Simon, who didn't bother to hide his displeasure.

After a quick kiss, they went inside. The restaurant was busy, and it took a while to get to the front of the line, then a little longer to order because the girl behind the counter was one of Skye's students and wanted to tell her about her new beau.

Skye smiled and nodded, happy the teen wanted to confide in her. Once the girl finished extolling the boy's virtues, Skye and Wally got their food, grabbed napkins, and headed toward their favorite back-corner booth.

As soon as they were seated, Skye asked, "What happened with Brian Cowden? Did he admit to being at the Brown Bag with Belle?"

"Eventually."

"Did he give you a hard time?"

"He tried." Wally took a healthy swallow of coffee, then winced as the hot liquid burned his tongue. "He's a big guy, and he uses his size and appearance to intimidate people."

"Are you okay? I mean, I can see you're all right, but . . . He didn't attack or anything, did he?"

"I'm fine. I contacted the LaGrange police for backup before I went to pick him up, and Mr. Cowden became much more docile once he looked out the window and saw that I wasn't alone."

"Thank goodness." Skye tore open two packs of Sweet'n Low and stirred the contents into her tea. "So, what happened?"

"I took advantage of the LaGrange police department's offer of their interrogation room. It took a while to convince Mr. Cowden to cooperate, but he eventually told me the whole story."

"Which is?" Skye took a bite of her Egg McMuffin.

"Turns out he and Belle did go for a few drinks after their meeting at the country club.

"And?" Skye glared. She hated it when Wally teased her like this, trickling out information and making her beg for each tidbit.

"And that led to a quickie in her motel room." Wally crunched into his McGriddle.

"Then afterward something happened." Skye wiped her mouth with her napkin. "And he killed her."

"Not according to him." Wally leaned forward and lowered his voice. "He claims that he left her alive and well at eleven, and we know that she was still breathing at one o'clock when Hallie heard her."

"Do you believe him?"

"Well, one of the reasons Cowden didn't want to admit to being with Belle at the Brown Bag is that he's married."

"Good reason."

"His wife swore he was home before midnight." Wally drained his coffee cup. "And when you consider I had just told her he'd been screwing around on her, I kind of doubt she'd provide him with a false alibi."

"So he's off your list of suspects?"

"Let's just say he's been moved to the bottom of the page." Wally crumpled up the wrappers from their food and put them on the tray. "I finally got Belle's financial records. She was depositing two thousand dollars a week into her account like clockwork for the past six months. With her kind of business, there really shouldn't be any regular income."

"Hmm. What could it be?" Skye paused, then snapped her fingers. "I know. It's probably an allowance from her parents or income from a trust fund."

"That would make sense." Wally nodded. "I'll check with the Canfields' attorney." He took the pad from his pocket and made a note. "How were the bachelor/bachelorette parties?"

"Wild. In fact, I was so busy putting out fires, I didn't get a chance to ask the bridal party if they knew anything that Belle's family might want to keep out of the media. So I'll talk to them about it this afternoon when I see them at the spa."

"So what happened that was so wild?"

Skye told Wally about the strip poker game ending with the waitresses half-naked, and the matron of honor and the waiter making out in the hallway. She ended with, "Then a policewoman showed up to arrest Nick."

"Martinez arrested Nick?" Wally reached for his radio. "For what?"

"Being a bad boy." Skye smirked; it was her turn to dole out info in dribs and drabs.

"What?" Wally's eyebrows disappeared into his hairline. "If we arrested men for that, we'd have half the guys in town in jail, and the other half on probation."

"The policewoman wasn't Martinez. She turned out to be a stripper." Skye snickered. "I thought Riley would kill the poor woman before I got her out the door."

Wally hooted. "Who hired her?"

"The best man, of course." Skye ran her fingers through her curls. "I swear he has a death wish. First the half-naked waitresses, then the stripper. If Riley doesn't kill Zach, his wife will."

Skye breathed a sigh of relief when she pulled into the club's parking lot at ten and saw the tent-and-rental company's truck backed up to the rear of the building. She had been afraid that Wally's questioning of Brian Cowden would cause the crew leader to be a no-show. Next to Cowden's truck was the floral designer's leased van and the linen consultant's Corvette. All the key players had arrived.

Skye assigned Justin to help Iris and her team, who would be assembling the dragonwood branch trees and placing them around the patio, as well as positioning the floral hedges along the aisle in the ballroom.

Frannie was given the floor plan for the dinner and told to make sure the tables and chairs were set up accordingly, then the favors and place cards put in their designated spots.

Both teens would assist the linen consultant with the tablecloths, overlays, napkins and napkin treatments, and chair covers, sashes, and clips.

Once Skye had assured herself that everything was going according to schedule, she headed back to Scumble River. The afternoon's bridesmaid activity was one that Riley had insisted Skye couldn't miss. They were all going to the Scumble River spa to be made beautiful for the wedding. Skye wasn't sure what all that entailed, but she knew she probably wouldn't like it.

The groom and his men had opted out of the spa experience and were going golfing. Skye knew nothing about the game, but she dearly wished she could join the guys. After the horrible events at the spa eighteen months ago, during which a woman was murdered, she had vowed never to return. When would she learn—never say never?

The bridal party was scheduled for noon, and Skye was the first to arrive, so she got out her cell phone and started punching buttons. According to Belle's binder, all vendors needed a check-in call the day before the wedding.

Skye had completed three-quarters of her phone calls by the time Riley and her bridesmaids appeared—this was one event to which Anita,

Dora, and Nick's stepmother had not been invited.

The bride and her attendants were immediately shown into a large treatment room containing four stations—two chairs with foot basins positioned side by side, and two chairs with small glass tables in front of them. One entire wall was covered with shelving that contained nail polish of every imaginable color, from chalk white to coal black.

The group paused just inside the door, waiting for instructions.

One of the three aestheticians stepped forward and said, "Hi, I'm Didi, and I'll be doing the manicures." She pointed to two women who looked enough like her to be her sisters. "This is Mimi, who will be doing the pedicures. And this is Fifi, who will handle waxing. Who wants to do what first?"

Riley turned to Skye. "Why don't you go for the waxing?"

Crapola! "No." Skye's tone brooked no arguments. "Our dresses are floor-length, and no one is seeing anything that might need waxing on me. I'll pass."

Riley opened her mouth to protest, but Hallie stepped forward. "I'll go first."

"Terrific." Skye smiled gratefully at the girl. "Let's get started."

Hallie walked away with Fifi, and Paige and Tabitha sat at the manicure table, leaving the pedicure stations for Skye and Riley.

Once they climbed carefully into the slightly elevated seat and eased their feet into the hot, soapy water, Riley swished her blond ponytail and said with an exaggerated huff, "We have a problem."

"Only one?" Skye grinned, refusing to let her cousin ruin what was supposed to be a relaxing experience.

"If you can smile when things go wrong"—Riley tilted her head—"you must have someone in mind to blame."

Skye ignored her cousin. "Ah, this feels heavenly." She flexed her toes.

Mimi pulled up a low stool directly in front of Skye, dipped her hand into a jar, and worked coconut sea salt cleanser into her feet.

"Pay attention," Riley whined. "My mother and aunts are trying to ruin my wedding."

"I doubt it." Skye tuned out the bride and said to the aesthetician, "That smells delicious. It makes me want a piña colada."

"Skye!" Riley stamped her foot, causing a small tidal wave in her basin. "You're not listening to me."

"Uh-huh." Skye closed her eyes as Mimi removed a pair of terry-cloth booties from a steam cabinet and slipped them on Skye's feet.

"They want to make sweets for my wedding. I told them we're having it catered, and any additions would throw the menu off balance." Riley leaned over and poked Skye's biceps with her finger. "But they say it's tradition."

Beneath her lashes, Skye saw Mimi wheel her stool over to Riley and take the bride's feet from the bath. She quickly dried them and put them on a rolled towel, then got up to empty the container of water.

"Is it really that important?" Skye soothed. "Chill." She hoped a foot massage would relax her cousin.

"If you can stay calm about this, you don't have all the facts," Riley wailed.

"Come on. They're really good cooks."

"I don't care." Riley stuck out her lip. "Their stuff won't look professional."

"And you want me to tell them not to bake?" Skye wasn't prepared to insult the female half of her father's family over a cupcake. "I don't think so."

Riley narrowed her eyes. Silent and brooding, she pushed her bottom lip in and out. Clearly she had not finished with the discussion.

Taking advantage of the lull in conversation, Mimi pointed to the wall of nail polish and asked, "Have either of you decided on a color, or did you want a French manicure?"

"Ballet Pink," Riley answered before Skye could make a choice.

Mimi looked at Skye, who said, "Whatever she wants. She's the bride, and I know everyone will be checking to see if our toes match."

Skye watched as Mimi expertly painted Riley's

toenails, then jumped slightly when her cousin suddenly said, "Well, if you won't tell the aunts and cousins not to bake, then you'll just have to make sure whatever they bring doesn't get put out or served."

"No way." Skye shook her head. "I can't do that. You'll be gone on Sunday. I, on the other hand, live here, and have to face these women after you leave."

"Then I'll take care of it myself." Riley's expression was unreadable. "No way is anyone screwing up my dream wedding."

"Do what you have to do." Skye was relieved to let the subject drop and hoped Riley would forget her plan in all the wedding-day excitement.

After the manicures and pedicures were finished, and everyone but Skye was waxed, the women moved on to the tanning station, located in a screened-off area by the pool. The group was given paper bras and panties and terry robes and told they could relax on lounge chairs while they waited their turns.

While Riley and Tabitha were being sprayed, Hallie excused herself to make a call, leaving Skye alone with Paige. She felt a little awkward after having caught the matron of honor with her tongue down the waiter's throat, so she searched her mind for a safe topic. "Did you enjoy the races yesterday?"

"They were okay." Paige shrugged. "Not as cool as Del Mar, of course."

"Of course," Skye agreed, having no idea what made one racetrack better than another.

Before she could think of more small talk, Paige said, "About last night—"

"No need to explain." Skye cut her off. "I'm trying to make a decision about my own love life, and what you said made me think."

"Great." Paige smiled weakly. "I'm always willing to make the mistakes if someone else is willing to learn from them."

Skye nodded; then, to keep the conversation going, she said, "I'll bet you'll be glad to get home on Sunday."

"I guess." Paige didn't sound too sure. "This whole week has seemed like a dream."

"More like a nightmare to me," Skye joked. "I sure had no idea how hard being a wedding coordinator could be." Turning serious, she said, "I wonder why Belle did it. I mean, if my father was a multimillionaire, I sure as heck wouldn't be working for persnickety brides."

"You would if he cut off your trust fund and canceled your credit cards," Paige replied.

Skye was shocked. "Why did her dad do that?" How hard it must have been for a pampered socialite suddenly to have to earn a living. . . .

"Well." Paige's expression held a spark of malice. "Although it was quickly squashed by the Canfield Corporation and never became public knowledge, Daddy Canfield got a tad upset when his baby's sex video hit the Internet."

A sex video—yikes! "I can see how that might make a parent angry." Skye didn't even want to picture what her own father's reaction would be in those circumstances.

"Especially if your family's resort chain is promoting an image of wholesomeness and respectability," Paige added with an air of disdainful amusement. "Think how Walt Disney would have reacted if Snow White and Prince Charming made a porno film."

"Yep." Skye nodded. "That would be a problem. But even I know that once something's on the Internet you can't get it off every site. Since the damage was done, why would the Canfields care about keeping secret the fact that they'd taken away Belle's trust fund because of the video?"

"Because the Canfields maintained that it wasn't Belle on the video. The official statement was that one of their business competitors made the video using an actress who looked like Belle in order to embarrass the Canfield Corporation. And since you couldn't see the man's face, there was no way to find him and verify whether the woman was Belle or not."

"Ah." Now Skye understood. "So if word got around that they had cut off her trust fund, it would strengthen the case that it really had been Belle on the video and not some double."

"Right. The only reason I heard about the whole

thing was because it happened while Belle was planning my wedding." Paige inspected her fingernails. "Up until then, her bridal-consulting business had been more of a hobby and a way to get publicity. But the night of my bachelorette party she got wasted and told me about her dad cutting her off. She kept sobbing that she couldn't live without her trust fund."

Skye pursed her lips. This cleared up why the family's attorney had shown up so quickly. He was there to put a positive spin on any information released about Belle, and make sure her death didn't cause a scandal.

Skye settled back in her chair and considered Paige's revelation. Remembering the phone conversation she had overheard the day before the murder, Skye realized that GiGi was a common nickname for a grandmother. Belle's plea for another chance might have been in reference to her father, not a boyfriend.

And the wedding planner's lack of funds explained why she'd been blackmailing the vendors. Also, if she was desperate for cash, that could explain the counterfeit money. But did it help to reveal who might have killed her?

Before Skye could decide, a scream ripped through the air and Riley burst from the tanning stall, her skin a bright shade of orange.

CHAPTER 22

All That Glitters

It had taken a while to calm down Riley. Skye had tried to assure her that the spray tan didn't really look that bad. In truth, it was all Skye could do not to call her cousin Sunkist. Finally, the aesthetician slathered Riley with some "magic" lotion, then resprayed her. Only after the bride resembled a nutmeg rather than a tangerine did she allow Skye and the others to leave the spa.

In spite of Riley's tanning emergency, it was only three in the afternoon, and Skye had already called Wally to fill him in on what Paige had told her about Belle and confirmed that everything was set up at the country club for the rehearsal. She rechecked her schedule. Yep, everything that could be done today had been done. At last, she had a few hours to herself. Time to go home, make a cup of tea, and think about the murder.

Sitting in her sunroom with Bingo on her lap, Skye mulled over the past six days. There was nothing like a purring cat and a sip of Earl Grey to get her mind working. She was convinced that somewhere she'd missed a clue to Belle's death. But what?

They had found out that Brian Cowden was the mystery man at the Brown Bag, but he had an alibi.

Hallie had heard Belle arguing with someone, but she hadn't been able to identify whom. They'd found the weapon that had been used to bludgeon Belle into unconsciousness, but it hadn't provided any evidence as to who had wielded it.

What had Skye failed to notice? Someone had said something that had stuck in the back of her mind, but she hadn't followed up. She mentally went through the last few days. It hadn't been Monday, when she and Wally interviewed the vendors, or Tuesday, when she'd been at the dance lessons. The flowers had arrived on Wednesday morning; then there had been the pink box crisis . . .

Shoot! Now she remembered. When she ran into the Dooziers at Wal-Mart, Earl had bragged about having favors for Elvis's reception. Rose perfume. Just like the perfume Skye had banished to the trash can. And Frannie had mentioned hearing an animal rummaging around in the motor court's garbage. Could the Dooziers be outfitting their wedding with Belle's castoffs?

Earl had also said something about people yelling at the bridal consultant. Had he seen or heard something as he was Dumpster diving that might lead the police to the murder? There was only one way to find out.

It was three forty-five and the Doozier wedding started at four. Grabbing a gift from her emergency supply, Skye wrapped it hastily in white tissue paper, then ran out to her car. She sure hoped the couple needed a toaster.

She hadn't had time to change out of her khaki slacks and white T-shirt, but in view of who was hosting the affair, she would most likely still be the best-dressed person there. And that included the bride, the groom, and the entire wedding party.

As Skye drove north on Kinsman, she saw cardboard arrows with the word WEDDING pointing the way to the Dooziers'. It was odd seeing placards leading to their house, since their usual practice was to take *down* the street signs so people couldn't find them. Which, considering what they reportedly did to outsiders, was probably for the best.

The Dooziers' property was almost as difficult to describe as its owners. Dried-up weeds lined the cracked sidewalk, and dead grass poked between the rusty carcasses of junked cars and old appliances that littered the yard. A strange collection of garden gnomes, which hadn't been there the last time Skye had visited, was arranged among the overgrown scrubs in family groupings. While she wondered where they had come from, she doubted she'd want to hear the answer.

The house itself was an indeterminate color, somewhere between watery oatmeal and putrid oyster. It might have been white at one time, but now the siding looked like the corrugated sections of a rain-soaked cardboard box. Long years of neglect made the structure seem ready to collapse with the first strong wind or heavy snow.

The dirt driveway was full of pickups, motor-cycles, and even a couple of riding lawn mowers when Skye pulled in. It appeared that she was among the last to arrive for the festivities.

She had barely gotten out of the Bel Air when Earl rushed out of the house, letting the front door slam shut in his haste. He was wearing new jeans that were so stiff he had trouble bending his legs, a camouflage T-shirt, and a NASCAR ball cap. Although it was a pleasant seventy-two degrees, his face was shiny with sweat.

Earl loped toward her, smiling widely. "I knowed you would come. Glenda said you wouldn't, that you was too snooty. But I knowed you'd wouldn't never miss Elvis gettin' hitched."

"Of course not." Skye allowed herself to be hugged, briefly, then handed Earl her gift. "Sorry I'm late." She removed herself from the little man's embrace and said, "I wouldn't miss this wedding for the world."

Out of sight, a dog was barking, but the canine's recent visit to the front lawn was evident from the pungent odor lingering in the air. Skye felt her nose twitch and hastily reached in her pocket for a Kleenex.

As she raised the tissue toward her face, Earl said, "No need to cry, Miz Skye. It's time the boy settled down." Elvis was all of eighteen, but the

Red Raggers married young, and Skye wondered whether his twin sister was now considered an old maid. For that matter, what did the Dooziers think of *her,* still single at thirty-five?

"Has the ceremony started yet?" She needed to ask Earl about Belle but knew it was best not to question a Doozier directly. You had to mosey into the discussion, then sidestep the subject into the conversation, pretending you weren't all that interested.

"Nope." Earl pointed to a Harley skidding into the driveway. "That-there's the preacher now."

Skye tried not to stare as the tall, gaunt man, dressed from head to toe in black leather and sporting a ZZ Top beard, dismounted and walked toward them. His nearly waist-length gray hair floated around him like a cloak, and the hand that held the Bible was missing two fingers.

Earl introduced the minister to Skye, then took them both around back. Mismatched picnic tables were arranged facing a beer-bottle arch erected over a child's swimming pool that had been filled with concrete to form a dais. Sitting on the tables' benches and scattered lawn chairs were the cream of Red Ragger society.

Skye could barely keep her mouth from hanging open. There were more piercings and cleavage, and fewer teeth, than she'd ever seen gathered in one place before. Multiple earrings were stuck in every visible orifice, and probably those that weren't visible, too. Low-cut tank tops strained to cover the breasts of the female guests, and some of the more well-endowed male guests, as well.

As Earl pushed Skye into an empty seat, a cartoonlike voice screeched, "Earl Doozier, get your ass in this house right now. Your brother's locked hisself in the can and won't come out."

Earl whirled around, smashing his knee into the edge of the picnic table's bench. As the Doozier hopped around, using scatological terms Skye barely recognized, she watched an older man wearing overalls and carrying a shotgun stride toward them. Accompanying him was Earl's wife, Glenda.

"I knowed the Dooziers weren't honorable." The gun-toting man pointed at Earl. "You'd better get your no-account brother out here pronto. Unless, a'course, your word don't mean nothin'."

"Y'all hang on your britches." Earl leaned down and whispered to Skye, "As a rule, I'd beat the sumbitch up for sayin' that, but since it's Elvis's weddin' day, I'm tryin' not to stink to old man Beckman's level."

"Good for you, Earl," Skye encouraged. "You know what they say, if you lie down with dogs—"

"You'll smell bad the next mornin'," Earl finished, grinning proudly.

"Uh, right." She had to quit trying to quote proverbs to this man.

Earl punched Skye lightly in the arm, then

rushed into the house, pausing at the screen door to say to the crowd, "We'll be startin' shortly."

Skye smiled at her tablemates and willed herself to relax. Nothing to do with the Dooziers ever went smoothly. She had plenty of time, and she had a good feeling that Earl's information was the break in the case they needed.

Still, when twenty minutes went by and no bridegroom had appeared, she started to get antsy. What was taking so long? Had Elvis run away and jilted his bride-to-be?

At last, a woman slipped in beside Skye and said to the couple sitting across the picnic table, "They'll be out directly. We finally found my daughter's teeth and got her into her dress." The mother of the bride chugged a beer, then continued, "I warned Mavis not to order it over the Internet. They sent a size eight instead of an eighteen. No way would the zipper close. We had to duct tape that sucker shut."

A few seconds later Earl and Elvis emerged from the house. Earl had a death grip on his brother's arm as they took their places under the beer-bottle archway. Then the music started and the crowd stood. Skye had never heard the wedding march played on the banjo before—at least she assumed it was the wedding march; to her it sounded a little like the tune from *Deliverance*.

When the bride started down the aisle, Skye blinked. The girl's right eyebrow held three silver rings and her left had been shaved off, her fingernail polish was camouflage brown and green, and her dead-black hair was styled in a way that would look good only on supermodels and poodles. She was a scary combination of redneck and Goth.

Skye spent the next ten minutes marveling over the bride's appearance, missing most of the ceremony, but she tuned in when the minister indicated that the groom should recite his vows.

He began, "I, Elvis Aaron Presley Doozier, takes you, Mavis Charmin Beckman, to be my lawfully bedded wife because you're hotter than a Hot Pocket."

Mavis answered, "Our relationship is like a dirt road, because sometimes it's bumpy, but it's sure fun when it's muddy."

The minister pronounced them married, and as the couple kissed, Cletus and Junior threw chickens off the roof of the tool shed—nothing as tame as a dove release for the Dooziers. Skye held her breath until she saw that the poultry could actually fly. She'd been worried that they might hurtle to their doom. Then again, maybe that had been the plan, and now there wouldn't be a main course for the reception.

Once the bride and groom do-si-doed down the aisle, Earl announced, "The hog is in the smoker and the beer is in the washtubs. Y'all have a good time."

The guests quickly dispersed, seeking food and refreshments, and Skye headed for Earl.

He met her halfway. "Miz Skye, what'd ya think? Wasn't that the bestest weddin' you ever seed?"

"It was certainly the most unique," Skye assured him.

"I knows you don't drink beer, but we gots wine if you want some." Skye was about to accept when he added, "It's the good stuff. It came in a pink box."

"Really?"

"Uh-huh." Earl's expression was earnest. "And the box comes in real handy, too."

"For what?"

"Once you drunk all the wine, you can barf in the carton."

Skye decided it was time to change the subject. "Did you say you had a whole hog?"

"Sure." Earl took her arm. "Come on. I'll show you. It's out back."

"That must have cost you a fortune." Skye was well aware of how expensive feeding a lot of people could be from arranging Riley's reception.

"Nah." Earl led her across the backyard, past the dog pen, and into a small metal outbuilding. "We didn't pay for it; we hunted it."

"But there are no wild pigs around here." Skye knew that for a fact, or her own relatives would have been out shooting them.

Earl's innocent expression wavered.

"Wait a minute. Please tell me you didn't go to the Pickett farm?"

"Hell, yeah." Earl guided her inside the shed. "They got lots and won't miss one . . . or two."

"Two?" Skye squeaked.

"We needed one for the greased-pig chase." Earl patted her arm. "But don't worry, Miz Skye. We'll put that one back after the weddin'. It's too small to eat, and we don't wanna have to feed it."

She let the matter of their swine crime drop. As a school psychologist, Skye had learned to pick her battles, and today her mission was to find out if the Dooziers knew anything that would help catch Belle's murderer, not to convince Earl that stealing was wrong.

After Earl had showed her the pig in the smoker, Skye said, "When I saw you at Wal-Mart, you mentioned that you had favors for your guests."

"Yep, real purty-smellin' perfume." Earl frowned. "Buts I'm sorry, Miz Skye, we run out before you got here."

"That's okay," Skye reassured him. "I just wondered where you got it. I was, uh, thinking of getting some for my cousin's wedding."

"No, you weren't." A crafty look appeared in Earl's brown eyes. "You done throwed it away."

"Oh, so it is the bottles we got rid of," Skye said carefully. "Were you able to use any of the other stuff Belle threw away earlier?"

"Yessirreebob." Earl puffed out his chest. "Once we seed what that city slicker was wastin', we checked the Dumpster every day."

Skye opened her mouth to ask if he'd seen anything, but Glenda flung open the shed's metal door and shrieked at her, "We ain't done nothin' illegal."

"I never said you had," Skye quickly appeased the volatile woman. Dealing with Glenda was like handling wet TNT; one wrong move and *kapow!*

"If it's in the garbage, it's free for the takin'." Glenda glared at Skye.

"It sure is," Skye agreed. "I'm glad you could get some use from it. The thing is . . ." She paused. She had to be careful how she phrased her question. "I was just wondering, because Earl mentioned that people were yelling at Belle, if you'd seen her fighting with someone when you were, uh, helping her recycle."

"You bet your ass we did." Earl's noggin moved up and down like a bobblehead doll. "Saturday afternoon, some guy was screamin' at her about money or some such thing like she'd cut off his balls or somethin'."

"So, nothing early Sunday morning, like around one a.m.?" Skye questioned.

"Don't be an ijit," Glenda snapped. "Why would we go back after we already checked once that day?"

310

Skye's shoulder sagged. Another dead end.

Glenda left, warning Earl that he needed to tap the keg because they were already out of cans of beer and the crowd was getting ugly.

Not wanting to witness an ugly Red Ragger crowd, since they already seemed fairly unattractive, Skye made her excuses, assuring Earl before she left that she didn't want a ride on the mechanical bull. He insisted on showing her the wedding cake—Ding Dongs, Ho Hos, and Zingers formed into three layers of snack-food delight—then escorted her back to her car.

As they got to the driveway, he said, "That guy yellin' at that weddin' gal was sure mad."

"Oh." Skye felt a flare of hope. "Did you see him or just hear him?"

"I seed him all right. I didn't knows him. He wasn't from around here. But I seed him."

"What did he look like?" Skye asked. Earl was silent for so long, Skye prodded, "Earl?"

"Sorry, Miz Skye. I stopped to think and forgot to start again. What was the question?"

"What did the guy arguing with Belle look like?"

"Well. He was a lot like me—in his forties, you know, the prime of life, missin' some hair, and not real tall." Earl wrinkled his brow. "But he wasn't like me, too."

"In what way?"

"His clothes and such was real fancy."

"Do you think you could identify him from a

picture?" Skye asked. Earl had described both the groom and the best man.

"Nah." Earl shook his head. "I never seed his face. His back was to me the whole time."

Skye thanked him, then got into her car. As she drove home to get ready for the rehearsal, she thought about what Earl had told her. If the man fighting with Belle was yelling at her about money, it would more likely be Nick. After all, he, not Zach, was the one paying her to put on a million-dollar wedding.

CHAPTER 23

Ready, Set, Rehearse

The rehearsal and dinner afterward were being held at the Thistle Creek Country Club. Riley had originally wanted to go to Everest in Chicago, but Skye had pointed out that the three-hour round-trip into the city would result in an extremely late night for the wedding party. After a short deliberation, the bride had decided she didn't want red-eyed attendants who might be too tired to follow directions and would thus screw up her big day.

Skye's detour through Doozierland had put her behind schedule, and by the time she changed clothes and drove to the club, she had only ten minutes to check out the arrangements for the rehearsal before everyone else was supposed to arrive.

With the clock ticking down, Skye dashed up the front steps, flung open the door, and rushed inside the building. The lobby's lights blazed, but there was no sign of Allison Waggoner. In fact, as Skye hurried down the hall, the whole clubhouse had an eerily empty air. *Shoot!* Where was the event coordinator, not to mention the rest of the staff?

The first thing Skye noticed when she entered the darkened ballroom was a faint musty odor. Once she found the light switches and flicked them on, she pulled a small memo pad from her purse and using the attached pen made a note: *Febreze before ceremony.*

Other than the smell, everything seemed in order as she continued her inspection and moved on to the dining room. It was brightly lit, with large windows that overlooked the golf course, moss green walls decorated with wildlife paintings, and a large natural stone fireplace.

The tables were arranged in a horseshoe shape and set with crisp linens, sparkling crystal, and shiny silver. As Skye admired the scene, she heard faint sounds coming from behind an exit in the rear. She crossed the polished wood floor and stepped through the swinging doors into the kitchen.

"Hi, everyone." Several employees were busily preparing for the dinner, and Skye was relieved to see the event coordinator among them. "The dining room looks wonderful."

The staff nodded and continued working, but Allison separated herself from the others. "I think we're all ready for you, but let me know if you need anything else."

"Thanks." Skye tilted her head. "It sounds as if my group is here, so I'd better go get the show on the road."

The bride and groom were the first to enter, and Skye squirmed when she saw what Riley was wearing. Skye had chosen a simple black dress with an empire waist and hanky hem. Riley had on a slinky, pale pink sheath with matching Manolo Blahnik sandals and Escada croc clutch. In comparison, Skye felt underdressed and dowdy, the very picture of a country cousin.

The rest of the bridal party's arrival distracted Skye from her discomfiture, and she quickly assembled everyone in the ballroom, then checked her list. Bride, groom, best man, three groomsmen, maid and matron of honor, two bridesmaids, mother and grandmother of the bride, and photographer. They were missing Nick's father, stepmother, and half brother. And— *crapola!*—the officiant.

Skye ran her finger down the page, looking for the name and contact information of the person performing the ceremony. Nothing. *Holy moly!* The bride would have a heart attack or, more likely, a cousin attack if the person officiating was AWOL.

Skye spotted Nick in a corner on his cell phone and went up to him. Surely, he wouldn't get as upset as Riley would if there was a problem.

Nick finished his conversation. "Tell the driver to turn south on Thrasher Road, Dad. No, road, not street." Irritation roughened his voice. "The country club is a couple of miles down on the left." He hung up, muttering, "Just what I need, a chauffeur who can't read a fricking map. The limo company is going to hear about this."

Skye cringed but tried to look on the bright side. At least the groom's family was on the way. After Nick tucked the phone in his pocket, she asked, "Do you know who is supposed to perform the ceremony?"

"Don't you?"

"Well, not exactly."

"Isn't that what we're paying you for?" He glared at her. "To *exactly* know everything?"

Skye felt her cheeks burn. "Well, uh, the thing is, I assumed that Belle had booked someone."

"You screw up," he raised his voice, "and blame the dead girl?"

"I'm not blaming anyone. I'm explaining." Skye refused to back down. "I've only been the wedding coordinator for five days."

"I didn't get where I am by allowing people who work for me to make excuses." Nick's bland face was getting redder by the second. "Stop whining and find someone."

"But . . ." Skye trailed off, not sure how to respond. She hadn't seen this side of the groom before. In their past encounters, she'd been puzzled by his docile acceptance of Riley's demands and wondered why someone as powerful as Nick would put up with his fiancée's nagging. Now that she saw his true colors, she realized Gus had been right. Nick must enjoy indulging his wife-to-be, but he didn't cut anyone else any slack.

He turned his back on her and grumbled, "If idiots grew on trees, this place would be an orchard."

Why had she thought Nick would be more reasonable than Riley? "I'm not—" Skye attempted to defend herself but bit off her words when Nick whirled around, grabbed her arm, and pulled her close. She felt a moment's panic. Was this the guy who the Dooziers had witnessed yelling at Belle? Had Nick killed Belle in a homicidal rage when she messed something up?

While Skye was trying to find her voice, a hand clamped down on Nick's shoulder and jerked him backward. "Let her go." Wally's tone was low, but the threat was loud and clear.

Nick started to protest, but one look at Wally's furious expression and he shut his mouth.

Skye hadn't noticed Wally's arrival, but she was thankful to see him. She moved to his side and whispered, "I need to talk to you alone."

Once she had Wally in the hallway, Skye said, "Thanks for the rescue."

"My white horse is always at your service, darlin'." Wally hugged her. "Not to mention my pistol."

"I'll keep that in mind, cowboy." Skye grinned. "Now, let me make your day." She filled him in on the Dooziers' information, ending with, "So Earl saw either Zach or Nick arguing with Belle."

"Shoot. Earl Doozier's not exactly a reliable witness." Wally ran his fingers through his hair. "But I'll snap a picture of both guys' backs tonight and show them to Earl tomorrow morning. There's no use attempting to get an identification from him now. By this point in the festivities, he'll be too drunk to see straight."

Skye nodded. "At least we know neither Zach nor Nick is going anywhere for the next twenty-four hours." She bit her lip. "Unless I can't find someone to perform the ceremony, that is." She explained about the lack of an officiant.

Wally pulled out his cell. "Want me to try and get a county judge?"

"Do you think one of them will do it?"

"Probably," Wally drawled. "They all owe me a favor or two."

Skye kissed him. "You're the best."

"I'll remind you of that on Sunday," Wally teased, then turned serious. "I checked with the Canfield attorney, and he claims the two-thousand-

317

dollar weekly deposits into Belle's account did not come from her parents. And Belle did call her grandmother GiGi, so it probably was her father she was referring to when she asked for a second chance."

"Something isn't adding up here."

"You're right," Wally agreed. "I have a feeling that if we could find the missing piece, we'd solve the murder."

Nick's family finally arrived at that moment, and Skye turned her attention back to her wedding-planner duties. After explaining that Wally would fill in for the officiant tonight, but a judge would be there tomorrow for the actual ceremony, she rounded everyone up and proceeded with the rehearsal.

The run-through was going smoothly until Skye handed her cousin the mock bouquet.

Riley's brow furrowed, and she hissed, "What's this piece of crap?"

"We always attach the bows from the shower gifts to a paper plate for the bride to use at the rehearsal," Skye answered. "It's considered good luck." Which her cousin would need if her groom turned out to be Belle's killer. "I know you've been gone from Scumble River a long time, but really . . ."

Natasha, Nick's stepmother, had been standing to the side with her son, Luca Jay, the ring bearer. At Skye's words she taunted Riley, "Come now, darling. Since you insist on having wedding in flyover country, surely you are willing to abide by quaint customs."

Earlier, Skye had found Natasha's slight Eastern European accent charming, but she was beginning to reconsider.

Riley glared at her future stepmother-in-law. "You haven't come to one single event before this. And now you appear wearing that . . . that hideous outfit. You have no room to talk, so just shut the hell up."

Skye had to agree with her cousin; Natasha's attire did seem more like a costume than a dress. It looked as if a red silk and gold lace tablecloth had been wrapped from her chest to her knees. Then a tutu skirt of tulle fluttered from her shins to her feet. Circling her brow were three gold chains with a huge ruby brooch in the center.

"You will not speak to me that way." Natasha shook her head, sending her long curls rippling down her back. "This gown is Alexander McQueen original and cost over ten thousand dollars." The shapely blonde sneered. "I am Russian royalty and you are country bumpkin."

"Royalty, my ass!" Riley screeched. "More like a mail-order bride from Siberia who married some rich old geezer to stay in the United States."

Natasha took a deep breath that nearly had her breasts escaping the confines of her dress's bandeau top. "Last person who talk to me that way no longer alive."

Skye took a hasty step between the two women, wondering whether Natasha and Belle had ever crossed paths. "Ladies." She glanced down and saw that Luca Jay's baby blue eyes were rounded and his rosebud mouth puckered, as if he were about to cry. "Not everyone knows you're kidding."

Natasha and Riley followed Skye's gaze and moved apart, but the women continued to glower at each other.

Finally, Riley turned her back on the older woman and said to Skye, "Let's get this over with." She grabbed the paper plate bouquet, then ran a slim hand down the pale pink charmeuse of her strapless sheath. "How do I look?"

"Truth aside," Natasha sniggered, "you look fabulous."

Riley stiffened, then almost as if in slow motion, she swung around and smashed her mock bouquet over Natasha's head, causing the paper plate to disintegrate into confetti. Who knew such an ethereal-looking bride could pack such a wallop?

In the next instant, Natasha lunged and fastened her hands around Riley's throat. Instinctively, Skye wrapped her arms around the older woman's waist and pulled with all her not inconsiderable weight. Natasha's grip loosened, and she and Skye staggered backward, falling into an ungraceful heap on the floor.

Everyone had been staring, frozen, but when Skye and Natasha hit the ground, their menfolk ran toward them. As Wally helped Skye to her feet, she watched Jay Jordan lead his son and wife away while picking ribbon and bows out of Natasha's hair.

Once the Russian woman was gone, the rehearsal went smoothly. And when they entered the dining room, Skye was relieved to see that Nick's stepmother was seated at the far end of the horseshoe, and Riley was at the center.

After popping into the kitchen to let Allison know they were ready to eat, Skye slipped into her chair. Wally was on her right and Paige on her left. The food was delicious, and a different wine was served with each course. Skye was careful to take only a sip of each, but Paige drained every glass.

As they waited for the dessert, Paige got unsteadily to her feet and marched toward the door, announcing that she needed to use the little girls' room. Skye observed her wobbly gait and hastily decided to join the tipsy woman, discreetly steadying the redhead as her stilettos skidded on the slick hardwood floor.

When Paige emerged from the bathroom stall, Skye was applying a coat of red amber to her lips. She dropped the lipstick tube into her purse and said, "Well, only one day to go."

"Right." Paige washed and dried her hands. "And once Riley has her perfect wedding, we can all relax for a while." She ran a comb through her hair; it fell in a flawlessly straight curtain nearly to her waist. "Things certainly would have been different for her if she'd married her high school sweetheart and never moved to California."

Skye couldn't believe her luck. She had almost forgotten that she wanted to know what had happened with Riley's hometown beau. "You know, I wasn't in Scumble River when Riley was in high school. Who was her boyfriend, and why didn't she end up marrying him?"

"I don't remember his name. Riley told me about it our freshman year of college, so it's been a while," Paige explained. "But they broke up briefly the middle of their senior year."

"Briefly?" Skye asked. "I'm confused. Did they get back together?"

"Yeah, a month or so later they made up. But it was too late."

"Too late?" Skye couldn't contain herself. "What do you mean? What happened?"

"He had already asked another girl to the senior prom and refused to renege, which meant Riley didn't have an escort, and by that point, all the decent-looking guys were taken." Paige frowned. "I think that may be another reason she decided to have the wedding in Scumble River. She wanted to show the town that she was no longer the girl without a date to her senior prom. Now she's a princess."

"You're probably right," Skye agreed, then asked, "So they broke up again. This time for good."

"Yes." Paige tsked. "But the worst part was that the night of the prom the brakes failed on his car, and he and his date were in an awful accident. The girl was scarred for life, and he never walked again."

"Oh, my. How awful. Riley must have felt terrible."

"Not so you'd notice." Paige shrugged her tanned shoulders. "When she told me about it, she almost seemed to be gloating."

"I'm sure that's not the case." Skye scrambled for something to say, wondering how far Riley would go if Belle had somehow disappointed or upset her.

"And now that Riley has found her true love, I'll bet she's really sorry about what happened the night of the prom."

"I wouldn't call Nick Riley's true love, but he has all the characteristics that make her happy."

"Oh?"

"Yeah." Paige pushed open the restroom door and said over her shoulder, "She and I both like our men the same way we like our chocolate bars: rich with big nuts."

CHAPTER 24

Final Touches

"Vince, this is Paige Hathaway, Tabitha Urick, and Hallie Jordan." It was the day of the wedding and they were all gathered in the dressing room at the country club. "Ladies, this is my brother, Vince Denison." Skye finished the introductions, then asked, "Who do you want to work on first?"

"I usually start with the bride, but you said she was running late." Vince plugged in a set of hot rollers and a curling iron.

"She just phoned and is on her way, but it'll probably be at least thirty minutes."

Skye frowned, thinking of the call. Riley had been hysterical because she couldn't locate her grandmother's silver cake server. When Skye reminded her that Dora had brought it to the club last night and it was lying on the cake table ready to be used, her cousin had slammed the phone down, but not before Skye heard her screaming at her mother.

While Vince and the makeup artist, who had arrived late yesterday from California, got started on the bridesmaids, Skye went to check on the groomsmen, who were assembled in the country club's bar. Since Nick had rented the entire clubhouse for the day, they had the whole place to themselves. Skye found them sprawled on sofas and chairs, drinking Bloody Marys and watching ESPN.

She examined their tuxes and saw that they were all in order. Jay and Natasha had promised to bring Luca Jay already dressed at one p.m., just in time for the pictures to be taken before the ceremony. Everyone agreed the little ring bearer would be bored waiting around the country club with the rest of the bridal party, which provided Skye with a good excuse to keep Natasha and Riley apart for as long as possible.

As Skye walked back through the lobby, Frannie and Justin arrived, along with Iris Yee, her husband, and the crew she'd hired from Chicago. It would take several hours to set up the flower arrangements, even with the teenagers' help, and the floral designer waved but didn't stop to speak.

Next to walk in was Yves Galois. After escorting the photographer to the bridesmaids' dressing room, Skye inspected the ballroom, patio/pool area, and tent.

Finding everything in order, Skye crossed her fingers. If all the vendors showed up on time, and with the goods they had promised, Riley would have the dream wedding she wanted. That is, of course, depending on what Wally found out when he interrogated Earl Doozier.

Wally was giving the Red Ragger until noon to

sober up, then would show him the pictures of Zach's and Nick's backs. Skye refused to think of what it would mean if Earl identified either man. Could she talk Wally into waiting until after the wedding to question whichever guy had been fighting with Belle? But if it was Nick, shouldn't Riley know that before she married him?

Pushing that conundrum aside, Skye checked her watch. The bride should be arriving any minute. As Skye approached the lobby, she saw Riley, Anita, and Dora swarm through the entrance. A few steps later they converged on her like a cloud of killer bees, demanding to see the venue before getting their hair and makeup done.

While the three women inspected the tent, Skye thought about Belle's killer. They'd eliminated several of their prime suspects, although Iris and the other vendors the wedding planner had been shaking down continued to be possibilities. But Skye wasn't convinced any of them had a strong enough motive to kill Belle. Could the bride obsessed with perfection be the murderer?

What had she and Wally learned so far? One, Belle had expensive tastes and no longer had a trust fund to support them, but she was still making two-thousand-dollar weekly deposits into her bank account.

Two, Belle had given Bunny a large sum of counterfeit cash, and the money hadn't come from the vendor kickbacks she'd demanded because she wouldn't get her cut until they received their final payment.

Three, she'd been overheard arguing twice. Was it with the same person both times?

And four—

"Skye! Pay attention!" Riley poked her shoulder. "The material at the sweetheart table is supposed to be swagged and it's not."

"Since the linen consultant isn't here today, I'll ask Iris if she has something to fasten it with." Skye pulled out her memo pad and made a note. "I can pin it up while you all are getting your hair done."

Riley nodded, and they walked back to the clubhouse and into the ballroom. Skye sniffed discreetly. Yep. The Febreze she'd sprayed as soon as she'd arrived at the country club that morning had worked.

"Skye!" Riley poked her again. "Did you get rid of the stuff my relatives insisted on baking?"

"No." *Shoot.* Skye had been hoping Riley would forget about the homemade goodies. "I told you I wasn't going to get in the middle of that issue."

"Honey," Anita pleaded with her daughter, "can't you just put it on a side table?"

"But, Mom," Riley whined, "it'll look tacky."

"Sweetie pie." Dora patted her granddaughter's hand. "Please, for me."

"Okay, Grandma," Riley sighed. "But it's not going to be served on the living buffet." The older women nodded their agreement, and Riley turned to Skye. "Is Nick here?"

"Yes . . ." Skye answered cautiously, hoping that was what her cousin wanted to hear.

"Good." Riley turned. "I thought of something last night that needs to be done before the pictures."

Skye shuddered but followed Riley, Anita, and Dora as they marched down the hall. What did Riley want now?

When they entered the bar, Riley strode up to Nick and said, "Hale needs to shave off his facial hair and remove all his earrings."

"Okay." Nick's attention was on the TV, but he absently patted his fiancée, then said, "Take care of it, Son."

"No way, Dad!" Hale howled.

"Just do it."

"Why should I?" Hale griped. "She's not the boss of me."

"But I am." Nick tore his gaze from the screen. "Unless you don't need me to pay for the rest of your college education."

"Dad . . . ," Hale whined.

"The money or the beard?" Nick stared at his son. "Your choice."

"I don't have a razor," Hale said, his expression smug. "Do you?"

Nick shook his head, and Skye said, "I've got one in my emergency kit." She hid her grin. Hale never should have called her fat at the dance lesson.

"Thanks." Hale shot Skye a dirty look. "For nothing."

Skye ignored the petulant young man and added, "I also have a sewing kit, Buttoneer, stain-removal stick, and first-aid supplies, so come find me if you need anything."

After leading Riley, Anita, and Dora to the dressing room, Skye borrowed some fasteners from Iris, then returned to the tent. As Skye gathered up the fabric, she noticed a label. It read MADE BY WILMA SNOW, CHICAGO, IL. *Hmm.* The lace was supposed to be imported from France.

She finished swagging the material on the head table, then phoned the linen consultant. Skye assured Angela that as long as her bill was corrected to reflect the lower price for the domestic lace, Skye didn't care where the material was made, since it was gorgeous. She also reminded the woman that on the day of the wedding no planner in her right mind would be willing to upset the bride about something as petty as the source of a tablecloth.

Having been reassured, Angela admitted she had been waiting for Wilma Snow's husband, Al, to deliver the overlays the day Skye and Wally talked to her. She was afraid Al would arrive while they were there, and Skye would find out about the lace being local versus imported. And no, Belle had not known about the substitution.

With that mystery solved, Skye mentally crossed Angela off her suspect list.

Two hours later, the bridal party's makeup was done and Vince had just finished Skye's hair when Allison poked her head around the door and said, "Cake's here."

Skye excused herself and, still wearing shorts and a T-shirt, went to greet the pastry chef from Deliciously Different, the Chicago bakery Belle had hired. The shop specialized in one-of-a-kind creations, and the groom's cake was in the shape of Nick's yacht.

Skye escorted the talented woman and her helper to the tent and showed her the specially lit tables where the cakes were to be displayed. The five-tiered wedding cake was covered in pleated pink fondant with hand-detailed piping, and had fifty pushpins of Swarovski crystal, two hundred handmade pink icing flowers, and dozens of blown-sugar bubbles more delicate than glass.

Due to the complicated structure, and the price tag—the groom's cake cost nine hundred dollars and the wedding cake four thousand—the pastry chef had agreed to stay with her creations until they were cut after the dinner.

Walking through the lobby, Skye glanced out the front doors and noticed a line of limo-buses disgorging the California guests who had been flown in by private jet. They all wore expensive designer formalwear and bored expressions.

As soon as Skye got back to the dressing room, she was immediately shoved into her brides-maid's gown, and Yves led the group outside to where the formal pictures would be shot. This was Skye's first glimpse of Natasha, and she held her breath. Riley had been right. Nick's step-mother had definitely chosen her dress to outshine the bride. It was nearly as outlandish as last night's creation, and very, very purple. Thousands of tiny appliquéd violets made up the short skirt, and the bodice looked like it was constructed entirely of pavé diamonds.

Skye braced herself for Riley's explosion, but the bride merely whispered to her, "Remember you promised to seat her in a dark corner."

Swearing that Natasha's table was in the back and partially obscured by a floral screen, Skye whispered a silent prayer of thanks that Riley hadn't remembered her original plan to pour a drink on her future stepmother-in-law.

It was quarter to three when the photo session ended, time to get everyone inside and in place for the ceremony. Skye ushered the bride and her attendants back into their dressing room and herded the groom and his men toward the ball-room.

She arranged the guys along the raised platform, checked that the string ensemble was in place, and shooed guests into their chairs.

Once everyone was settled, Skye hurried to the

dressing rooms. On her way, she noticed Yves huddled in an alcove, speaking on his cell.

As she passed, she heard, "No! I must have that green card right away. I'm too vulnerable without it."

Skye slowed down and listened to the photographer.

"Word has gotten around among the wedding planners that I'm in this country illegally, and now they're all blackmailing me into doing their events."

Ah. So that's how Belle had persuaded Yves to photograph Riley's wedding, even though he hadn't wanted to leave the city. But if all the wedding planners knew his secret, he had no reason to murder Belle. There went another suspect out of the pool.

Skye sighed, then hurried away to fetch the rest of the wedding party. After they were all assembled, she lined everyone up along the hallway, starting with Dora and Anita, then Hallie, Tabitha, herself, and Paige. Last, just before the bride—who had chosen to walk down the aisle unescorted—was the ring bearer.

Luca Jay's blue eyes sparked with excitement, and he was loudly telling everyone what he had learned in his Bible class. "St. Paul cavorted to Christianity. He preached holy acrimony, which is another name for marriage."

Skye laughed along with the others, then got out

of line and knelt down next to him. Putting a finger to her lips, she said in a low voice, "Shh. We need to be quiet now."

Luca Jay's forehead wrinkled. "Why do we have to be quiet?"

"Well . . ." Skye searched her mind for a reason a six-year-old would understand. "This is sort of like church."

"Oh." He nodded. "I remember Mommy telling me you have to be quiet in church." Skye patted his shoulder just before he said loudly, "That's because people are trying to sleep."

Once everyone stopped giggling, Skye stepped up to her cousin for one last inspection. Reciting the old rhyme, she checked out the bride—something new was more than taken care of, something borrowed was Dora's lace handkerchief, something blue was the bow on the garter. She frowned and asked Riley, "What's your something old?"

Tabitha answered for the bride, "It's the antique bouquet holder Paige and I found for her."

"What bouquet holder?" Riley objected. "You guys never gave me any antique holder."

Tabitha turned to Paige. "Where is it?"

"Oops!" Page widened her eyes. "I forgot all about it. It must still be at home."

"Oh, that's a shame," Skye quickly interjected, not wanting a bridal meltdown. "But your grandma's hanky is old, so you're covered."

Before Riley could react, Skye signaled to Allison to throw open the ballroom doors. The string ensemble began playing Pachelbel's Canon and the wedding officially began.

CHAPTER 25

Icing on the Cake

As Skye walked down the aisle, she grinned at her beaming grandmother, but her thoughts were on what Tabitha and Paige had just said about the murder weapon. Paige claimed she'd forgotten the antique bouquet holder at home, but wouldn't she have told Tabitha that earlier or even had someone send it by overnight mail to Scumble River? Was Paige the murderer? An antique bouquet holder *was* the weapon used to bash in Belle's skull. How many of those things could be floating around this wedding? Still, what could the matron of honor's motive possibly be?

Skye needed to talk to Wally ASAP, but she couldn't exactly whip out her cell phone to make a call now. With the consoling thought that Paige wasn't going anywhere until the ceremony was over, Skye turned her attention back to the proceedings at hand. A moment later, the music swelled and everyone stood to watch the bride's entrance.

Catching her breath, Skye stared in awe. Riley

truly was a fairy-tale princess. Her silver-blond hair, gathered in a waterfall of curls, was luminous under the gold-embroidered veil, and she appeared ethereal in her pearl silk wedding gown. Looking straight ahead, a secret smile on her shimmery pink lips, she seemed to float toward her groom.

As Skye glanced over at Nick, who was gazing at his bride with an expression of both pride and triumph, she finally understood why such a rich and powerful man put up with her demanding cousin. May had mentioned that Nick collected art; clearly Riley was his ultimate acquisition.

After the ceremony, the bridal party and the guests moved to the patio. Skye excused herself, pausing only long enough to hear the trumpeters and watch the butterflies being released; then she confirmed that the mixologist was on duty behind the monogrammed ice bar that was carved to look like Riley's veil, and the actors dressed as fairy-tale characters were all present.

Assured that the cocktail party was all set to begin, Skye tried Wally's cell, but the call went directly to voice mail. She left a message for him to contact her immediately, then went to check on the rest of the vendors. The caterer was busy sending trays of crab claws and beggar's purses out to the hungry crowd, and Skye snatched one of the tiny caviar and cream dumplings as she moved to the reception tent.

The photo booth, cigar roller, candy bar, ice

sculpture, and martini luge were all in place. The DJ and band were setting up, and the "living buffet" had just walked in the door. Skye greeted the woman who would be dressed in a Cinderella gown—the skirt of which would be a round table filled with desserts. The performer would move among the guests once dinner was over.

Satisfied that all was in order, Skye tried calling Wally again but still was sent to his voice mail. He hadn't attended the ceremony, and she wondered whether he'd gotten hung up interrogating Earl Doozier. Perhaps, since neither the groom nor the best man had been taken into the police station for questioning, the Red Ragger had been unable to identify the man who'd been arguing with Belle.

Back at the cocktail party, Skye divided her time between watching Riley bask in the limelight and avoiding all the relatives who thought this was the opportune moment to question Skye about when *she* was going to get married.

The two family members Skye couldn't dodge were her mother and grandmother. May and Cora found her behind a dragonwood branch tree and dragged her out into the middle of the party.

Cora hugged her, then announced to the guests milling around them, "My granddaughter planned this whole wedding."

"Not really, Grandma." Skye blushed. "I just carried out the plans that were already in place."

"I'm so proud of you." May put her arms around

336

Skye. "And you were the prettiest bridesmaid, too!"

Wow! "Thanks, Mom." Skye couldn't remember the last time her mother had called her pretty or said she was proud of her. Maybe all the agony of this past month had been worth it.

Skye had just asked Allison to begin directing the crowd into the reception tent when Wally finally stepped onto the patio. Leaving the event coordinator in charge, Skye hurried over and led him back into the clubhouse.

Once they were in the dressing room with the door closed, she said, "Did you get my messages? Why are you so late?"

"Sorry." He kissed her cheek and said, "Earl went and drank himself into a near coma. I've been waiting for him to come to."

"Is he okay?"

"He's fine, but he wasn't coherent until about an hour ago." Wally shook his head. "And his information was only marginally helpful."

"How so?"

"The good news is he was sure your new cousin-in-law wasn't the man he saw arguing with Belle."

"And the bad news?" Skye was relieved Nick was in the clear.

"He couldn't say for sure it was Hathaway."

"So Zach is still a suspect." Skye tried to think what motive the best man could have to kill Belle.

"What's going on here? Your messages sounded urgent."

"I found out something involving Paige just before we walked down the aisle."

"What?" Wally asked.

"She and Tabitha bought an antique bouquet holder for Riley to have as her 'something old,' but Paige claims she forgot it at home."

"So the weapon wielded by the killer was last in the possession of the matron of honor," Wally murmured. "And if she didn't know it was used in the murder, why claim she left it in California?"

"That's right." Skye froze; the notion that had been bothering her all day suddenly crystallized. "Oh, my gosh! It wasn't Zach; it was Paige."

"Explain." Wally pulled a notebook from his suit jacket pocket.

"Okay." Skye gathered her thoughts. "We know that Belle had no qualms about seducing men that most women would think were off-limits. Brian was married; Hale was much too naive for her. She even seduced the bride's father on one of her previous weddings. So why not boink one of the grooms?"

Wally raised an eyebrow.

"And we know she gave Bunny the counterfeit money—not many people carry that much cash, except maybe someone who has just received a blackmail payment to keep from telling a wife about an affair with her husband. Which could be what Earl heard Belle and Zach arguing about."

"That's a big leap of logic to make."

"Except . . ." Skye slapped her forehead. "I just remembered something. At the attendants' party Saturday night, I heard a couple arguing. The woman said something like, 'How could you?' And the guy said he was sorry. Then the woman said, 'But all that money.' And now that I think about it, the voices sounded a lot like Paige and Zach."

"But why were the bills counterfeit, and why would Belle use her own funds for a wedding-related expense?" Wally asked.

"I don't have an answer to the first question, but the second is easy. Bunny wouldn't take a check, and Belle could just reimburse herself."

"Anything else?" Wally's expression was skeptical. "Most of what you've said is conjecture."

"Yes." Skye's voice grew more confident. "Think about it. The two-thousand-dollar weekly deposits into Belle's bank account. We know it's not from her family, and it exactly matches the amount Belle gave Bunny."

"Okay." Wally was beginning to look convinced. "Let's see how this would have worked. Early afternoon Saturday, Zach argues with Belle but pays her to keep quiet about their affair. Later Belle uses the money, which turns out to be counterfeit, to bribe Bunny. That evening Paige and Zach argue, and when they get home from the party, Paige goes to tell Belle she knows about her screwing Zach. Belle and Paige fight, which

Hallie overhears, and then Paige smacks Belle in the head with the antique bouquet holder. Paige stuffs the unconscious vic into the floral refrigerator, where you find her Sunday morning."

"Yes." Skye ran the scenario through her head. "What do you think?"

"I think you could be right. One or two of these points might be circumstantial, but you've come up with quite a list, and juries have found people guilty on much less than this." Wally sighed. "Still, I wish we had hard evidence."

"Maybe we do." Skye smiled. "Remember the abrasions on Belle's face? Paige was wearing a green dress with zippers running up both sleeves and down the front. I'll bet that when she hit Belle those zippers scratched her face. And the reason no incriminating fingerprints were found was because Paige had on lace gloves that night."

"We need to take her and Zach in for questioning." Wally took out his cell. "I'll call for backup and get a warrant to search the Hathaways' cottage for that dress. If Belle's DNA is caught in the zippers, that'll convict Paige."

Skye glanced at her watch. "It's nearly time for the guests to go into the tent for dinner. I need to line up the bridal party for their grand entrance. Is that okay?"

"Sure." Wally held the door open for her. "I can keep an eye on the Hathaways until Martinez and Quirk get here."

The last of the guests were entering the tent when Skye walked onto the patio, and Riley hurried over to her. "We have a problem." For a moment Skye wondered how the bride had found out that her matron of honor and best man were about to be arrested, but Riley continued, "Even though the invitations clearly said adults only, some of my dumb-ass relatives showed up with their squalling brats, so we don't have enough tables and chairs."

Skye thought fast. "I'll find Allison and ask if they have any extra tables; we can take the chairs from the ballroom."

"I'm not going in until everyone's seated." Riley thrust out her bottom lip. "I don't want people watching the tables being set up instead of me."

"Fine." Skye turned, saying over her shoulder to Wally, "Help Riley line up the wedding party. I'll be right back."

It took nearly half an hour, but tables were found, chairs were moved, and all the guests were finally seated. Skye cued the DJ, then got in line. As Hale and Hallie's entrance was announced, Quirk and Martinez appeared on the patio.

From her position in front of the matron of honor, Skye observed her out of the corner of her eye as Wally talked to the two uniformed officers. Paige's normally creamy skin had turned the color of sour milk, beads of sweat clung to her upper lip, and the pulse in her throat was visible.

When Quirk glanced at her, Paige's breathing quickened and she edged backward.

Was she looking for an escape route? Skye tried silently to convey to Wally to get the show on the road, before Paige bolted. But instead of immediately taking her into custody, Martinez pointed to Paige.

Damn! The inexperienced officer had made a rookie mistake by telegraphing her intention to the suspect. It was clear that now Paige was on red alert. She held herself stiffly, and her gaze darted around the patio.

A moment later, Martinez started toward Paige, and Skye watched in alarm as the maid of honor kicked off her shoes, gathered up her huge bouffant skirt, slipped a derringer from the holster strapped to her leg, and took off running.

Even wearing the cumbersome bridesmaid's dress, Paige was fast, but Martinez was only a few steps behind her. While Quirk secured Zach, Wally ran after the two women. Skye followed, but she was nowhere near as quick—her dyed-pink silk high heels slowed her down considerably.

Paige had entered the reception tent at the rear and was darting among the seated guests. At first the crowd thought she was a part of the entertainment, but as Paige careened off a table and a centerpiece smashed to the floor, a wave of hysteria swept the crowd. Screams ripped through the air, and people tipped over tables, scrambling to get away from the crazed woman. Riley's beautiful reception was turning into a scene from the *Titanic*.

Martinez zipped around a tuxedo-clad waiter, then closed in on the runaway matron of honor as Paige neared the front of the tent. At the same time, Wally, who had taken a different path, came at her from the side.

With his gun drawn, Wally shouted to Paige, "Put your weapon down."

Paige jerked toward Wally and shot. For a long second, the scene seemed frozen, but an instant later Wally sprang into action, tackling her and knocking the gun from her hand. Both teetered for a moment, then, almost in slow motion, toppled backward. With a giant splat, Paige landed dead center in the wedding cake, followed by Wally, who took out the remaining layers.

Skye cringed as she simultaneously heard the blown-sugar ornaments shatter and saw the Swarovski crystals fly into the air like beads being thrown from a Mardi Gras float.

A nanosecond later, Wally grabbed Paige and hauled her upward. "You have the right to remain silent." As he finished reading her rights, he handcuffed her and marched her out of the tent, pink frosting blooms dropping off them like a flower girl's trail of rose petals.

Skye stared in horror at the destroyed wedding cake, then buried her head in her hands. They had caught the murderer, but Riley was going to kill her.

EPILOGUE

Happily Ever After
(or Not)

Skye smiled at the sounds of hammering and men clomping overhead in her master bathroom. Tomorrow would be exactly two weeks since the Erickson-Jordan wedding to end all weddings, and the construction crew had begun the renovations on her second floor. The local animal shelter had already received the check Skye had promised herself she would send.

To Skye's surprise, Riley had not blamed her for the ruined cake or the arrest of the matron of honor. In fact, once the mess had been cleaned up, Skye had been astonished when her cousin had gone on with the reception as if she wasn't at all bothered by what had happened.

After that, Riley had actually loosened up, becoming the lovable girl Skye remembered. Furthermore, in the end, before riding off into the sunset with her fairy-tale prince, Riley had handed Skye a check for the full amount she was owed and assured her that Nick would buy her wedding dress as promised. No mention of the event's imperfections had been made.

Over the remodeling noise, Skye heard her telephone ringing. She grabbed the handset from the kitchen and went out the back door. The land-scaping team had finished their work the day before, so outdoors was the only place that was quiet.

"Hi, sugar." Wally's smooth baritone flowed from the receiver, reminding her of another shocker—his suggestion that she postpone her answer to his marriage proposal until after the case against Paige had been wrapped up. "It's done. I'll pick you up at five thirty."

"Great." He'd told her last night that the case would be delivered to the district attorney for prosecution today.

"We have reservations at seven at Tru. I hope you have your answer ready."

"I do," Skye promised him. "Do you have time to tell me how it all ended up?"

"Definitely." His tone was teasing. "I know your curiosity is killing you, and I don't want to dis-cuss it tonight."

"Hey, I figured out who the murderer was; I deserve to know the rest of the story."

"You're right." Wally's voice grew serious. "The DNA evidence came through, and it was Belle's tissue caught in the sleeve zippers on Paige's dress."

"Phew." Skye sat on her back step.

"When Zach and Paige heard the news, they both accepted plea bargains."

"I suppose that's for the best. It will sure save the

taxpayers a lot of money." Skye was disappointed that the Hathaways wouldn't be punished to the full extent of the law, but she knew that neither she nor Wally had any say in the matter. "Now, tell me all the details."

"Zach admitted that he was being blackmailed by Belle over a fling they'd had while she was working as the bridal consultant for his wedding."

"Right."

"Because his wife was getting suspicious about the money missing from their account, he paid her off in counterfeit hundreds he'd purchased for pennies on the dollar through some underworld connection he had via his construction firm."

"Sure. After nearly six months, two thousand a week is hard to cover up." Skye tapped her foot. "What happened then?"

"Paige Hathaway saw her husband give Belle the bogus bills and confronted him. They fought during the attendants' party and he admitted to the affair."

"Was that when Paige decided to kill Belle?" Skye asked.

"No. It was when he told her he'd paid Belle off in funny money. Paige, being smarter than her husband, recognized that passing counterfeit currency was not a good idea." Wally sounded amused. "Adultery she could overlook, but committing a federal offense was another matter. Money was her main motivator."

"Geez Louise." Skye rolled her eyes.

"And as luck would have it, because Paige was smashed when she and Zach got back to the motor court after the party, she decided she not only had to confront Belle right that minute; she also had to give Iris the antique bouquet holder she'd bought for Riley's flowers."

Skye shook her head. "Drunks." Their actions rarely made any sense.

"She found Belle alone in the storage cottage," Wally said, then added, "We have no idea what Belle was doing there at one in the morning."

"I do," Skye piped up. "She used to brag about needing only four hours of sleep a night."

"That answers that question," Wally said. "Anyway, Paige tried to get Belle to give the cash back."

"And Belle refused," Skye guessed.

"Yep. She told Paige she'd already spent it. So in a fit of anger, Paige whacked Belle on the head and knocked her out, which is when the zippers on her dress left abrasions on Belle's face."

"Why did Paige put Belle in the floral refrigerator?" Skye asked.

"She claims she thought the cool air would bring Belle back to consciousness, and she locked the door so Belle would be out of the way while she searched for the counterfeit money. She says she didn't believe Belle could spend the cash so fast."

"I think she meant to kill her."

"Probably," Wally agreed. "There was no indication that Belle's cabin was searched."

"I wonder why Paige ran when Martinez approached her." Skye shook her head. "It just made her look guiltier."

"Turns out she has really good hearing. She heard parts of what I was telling my officers about the zippers on her dress matching the abrasions on Belle's face." Wally's tone was rueful. "Then, when Martinez pointed at her, she knew something was up."

"What *I* don't understand is why Paige was packing heat." Skye checked her watch. She still had a few minutes to spare. "I mean, a gun in her garter—come on. It's like something out of the Wild West."

"Paige claims that having grown up on a ranch and living in L.A., she always carries the derringer for protection."

"Protection from what?" Skye asked. "From what I gathered, they don't exactly live on the bad side of town, and the most dangerous thing in Beverly Hills is a Rolls-Royce salesman."

"Well, that's her story, and now that she's agreed to a plea bargain we won't be getting any more answers."

"Okay." Skye got up and went back into the house. "I've got to go. See you at five thirty. Bye."

She had just enough time to get ready for her

next visitor. Last night after Wally had told her he'd be finished with the investigation today, she had phoned Simon and told him she'd give him her answer that afternoon. She'd wanted to tell both Simon and Wally her decision on the same day, before either heard anything through the grapevine.

Skye was putting a tray with a pitcher of lemonade and two glasses on the porch's wicker table when Simon pulled into her driveway. He got out of the Lexus, waved at her, and ran up the stairs.

He tried to hug her, but she sidestepped him and sat down. "Take a seat." She indicated the chair next to hers. "I wanted to talk to you before I give Wally my answer to his proposal tonight."

"Oh?" Simon's expression was a combination of hope and apprehension.

"Yes." Skye chose her words carefully. "I've thought long and hard about what you said to me at dinner that night, and it's not that I don't still have feelings for you—"

"Wait," Simon interrupted her. "I know giving me another chance is a risk, but happiness is the ultimate risk."

"That's just it, Simon." Skye's smile was sad. "When I look back at when we were together, I don't remember a lot of happy times."

"How can you say that?"

Skye winced at the raw hurt in his voice but

knew she couldn't soften the truth. "When I was with you, I constantly felt as if what I did wasn't quite good enough. That my actions disappointed you. That you wanted to mold me and improve me."

"That isn't true. I just wanted you to be the best you could be."

Skye noticed that new lines were etched around his mouth and eyes. "I was always waiting for you to get over being mad at me." She took a deep breath, hating that she was hurting him. "I discovered something when I was with Wally. Life doesn't have to be about waiting for the storm clouds to pass. It can be about embracing the rain showers and laughing while you splash through the puddles."

"I'm so sorry." Simon's handsome face crumpled. "I never meant to hurt you."

"I know." Skye's tone was kind. "In a way, it was good for me. I learned that being broken makes you stronger. Strength comes from the courage to heal and go on."

Simon leaned toward her and caressed her cheek with his thumb. "I truly am different now."

His hazel eyes were mesmerizing, sending a ripple of awareness through her, but Skye forced herself to stand and move out of his reach. "For your sake, I hope that's true."

"It is." Simon followed her and took her by the shoulders. "Please, just give me the time to prove it to you before you accept Boyd's proposal."

"I can't," Skye said. "It's too late."

"It can't be too late." Simon bent his head and touched his mouth to hers.

The feel of his lips caused a swirl of pleasure in the pit of her stomach; for a moment Skye responded, but a second later she pushed him away. "I've made up my mind. I'm going to marry Wally."

"No, you aren't." Simon swept her into his arms and kissed her with a savage intensity before letting her go. "I'm not giving up until I see a wedding band on your finger." As he walked away, he said over his shoulder, "And maybe not even then."

Center Point Publishing
600 Brooks Road ● PO Box 1
Thorndike ME 04986-0001 USA

(207) 568-3717

US & Canada:
1 800 929-9108
www.centerpointlargeprint.com